THE WORLD IS SIX FEET SQUARE

This is an escape book, and a prison book. There is not a dull page in it. Alan Caillou has humour, a sense of the dramatic, and the ability to make the reader share intensely the privations, emotions, hair-breadth escapes and hopes and fears which fell to his lot, and over which in the end he triumphed.

'Something very much out of the ordinary run.'
—TIMES LITERARY SUPPLEMENT

'An intelligent and unusual book, full of good reading.'
—PUNCH

toExcel
San Jose New York Lincoln Shanghai

The World is Six Feet Square

Published by toExcel
an imprint of iUniverse.com, Inc.

For information address:
iUniverse.com, Inc.
620 North 48th Street
Suite 201
Lincoln, NE 68504-3467
www.iuniverse.com

ISBN: 0-595-09147-4

Printed in the United States of America

Chapter One

THE rain was making little rivulets in the red sand when we set out, drumming a monotone of *pit-pit-pits* about our feet, and the cold wind was driving it hard into our faces, fresh and wet-smelling, running in trickles down our necks to join the sticky sweat beneath our uniforms and cloaks. The hills we had to cross seemed a long way off, purple and blue in the distance beyond the wet brown sand of the desert, barely visible through the driving, steady rain, in the light of the vivid thunderstorm.

I was thinking of the task ahead of us, excited as always at the outset. It was not an easy job, though simple enough on paper. The hills ahead were the dividing line between the Allied Forces and the Germans. Farther beyond, pushing up from Tripoli, the Eighth Army was on the move again. The Germans and the Italians were compressed into a strip of land along the coast from Tunis to Sousse, from Sousse to Sfax, on to Gabes and a few miles beyond to the Mareth Line. On the western flank lay the desert, as always thinly held; on the east lay the sea. Well inland, away from the road, the greenery and the water, a vast yellow no-man's-land stretched out in soft dunes, hard sandstone and salt lake; a desert as empty and still and silent as only a desert can be, with nothing but coarse grey thorn and dry grey camel-shrub pathetically struggling for survival. Its silence, its stillness, its vastness were broken by nothing natural; neither gazelle nor lizard lived here; there were no birds. Across this huge and empty motionless space the desert boys sometimes moved, tiny insignificant columns, heavily armed, labouring slowly against the sand, man-handling their trucks up the giant dunes, speeding like dust-tailed insects across the gigantic flats—British, German, French, Italian, Polish, Hungarian, Czech, the desert knew them all; sometimes its fine dust covered their bones. It was a vast chess-board and the squares were the oases, the rare and precious water-holes.

But—here there was no line to cross, no fortification to break through, no minefields, barbed wire or tank traps. With luck, a little knowledge and a lot of water one could move about, freely, and for us it was the quickest way, and

5

the overall plan, the basic idea, was simple. Cairo wanted to know what was going on in the tight compressed German sandwich between the Eighth Army and the First. We went in to find out. Nothing spectacular, just three of us with a little food, a little money, radio. batteries, and whatever we thought we'd need and knew we could carry on our backs once the camels had been turned loose. We were to collect information from the Arabs, watch the roads, report on Divisional signs—those somewhat unnecessary signboards, shoulder-badges and so forth which gave away so much to a skilled collater in H.Q. We had to move lightly, ready to slip from hide-out to hide-out under cover of night, lying up in the day in *wadis*, scrub-patches, caves, dried-up wells, or whatever cover we could find. It was a hard life, but the job, well done, was worth it.

A study of the map had shown us, back in Cairo, which was the best way in. We flew to Algiers, took a truck through Constantine to the Oasis of Gafsa, where the American para-troopers were waiting for reinforcements, with a youthful, energetic Colonel in charge with his "anti-tank bayonet" welded on to his carbine, and now we were on the last stage of our journey. Gafsa's fort, fringed with palms and castel-lated like a movie-set, was behind us. The lorry that brought us was on its way back to Algiers, winding its empty way between the trees and the rocks of the coastal road. Our French friend, Guidot, had watched us set out in the early black of the night, frowning thoughtfully. Guidot knew the Arabs, knew them well. I said,

"We've done this often enough before. *mon cher*, there's nothing to worry about."

But he was unhappy.

He said, "Well, I wish you luck. But if this were my party, I would not allow you to go. Perhaps it is possible in the Senussi country; I do not know. I know only that it is not possible here. The Arabs of Tunisia are not like the Senussi. You cannot trust them. You must not run the risk of trusting them. *Méfiez-vous des Arabes.*"

He was a striking figure in his bright orange cloak over his tight *Mehariste* uniform. His face was sharp-featured and erudite, his hands were delicate, expressive, competent. He knew the Arabs and he said it couldn't be done. He was in the Deuxième Bureau and knew what he was talking about. But I remembered also the scoffers in Cairo who first said, a

6

long time ago, *it cannot be done*. And yet, during the Battle of Alamein, we lived in the hills around Benghazi, eight hundred miles behind the lines, where we made friends with the Arabs and lived among them. We gave them tea, sugar, money; we even gave them medical treatment of a sort. We carried a letter from their exiled leader, Said Idriss, stamped with his holy seal. The Senussi, traditional enemies of the Italians, were on our side and they gave us splendid support. Of course, there were the bad hats as well. Sometimes the odd renegade reported us (there was a heavy price on our heads) and we had to pack up and run, or cower in the remotest broken corner of a disused cistern, hidden in the dark and friendly blackness while the Italians hopefully threw grenades at every shadow. Sometimes they just pretended we had been sold out, and they brought us false warnings for the sake of our financial gratitude, and we were often caught like this in the petty jealousies of rival sheikh-doms. But on the whole they served us well. They ran heavy risks to do this. And most important, they brought us the information. Not a convoy stirred, not a ship arrived, not a gun was moved, without our knowledge. Others had done it before us; others had done it since. The Long Range Desert Group took us out, and they brought us back for rest a few months later. We sent our messages to Cairo by radio twice a day. Every movement was reported to H.Q. within a few hours. It was a good system, and it worked.

" But," said Guidot, "*méfiez-vous des Arabes*."

Well, I had been one of the scoffers myself once, till I found out how easy it was.

The three of us were well on the way now, on the last lap, pushing heavily forward in the resisting rain, our uniforms covered with the Arab *burnous*, the heavy goat-hair cloak, to hide us from inquisitive eyes, keeping clear of everybody, trusting no one, keeping always out of close sight. In the flat, stony country, we could see the Arabs long before we came upon them, and could change our course so as to miss them; it was easy. But the driving rain was a nuisance. It made our cloaks heavy and burdensome. It worried the camels and made them mutinous, strung behind us in a groaning, complaining line of misery. They slipped on the greasy soil. They stumbled and threw their loads, so that we had to catch them, force them to their knees and struggle with the baggage-ropes

7

while one of us, armed with a stick against the vicious teeth, stood on a bent foreleg to hold the animal down. When we tried to reload, they tried to rise; when the load was ready, they refused to get up. They wanted to stop and wait for better weather. So did we, but we had to push on, leaning into the driving rain.

This is the desert, I thought; *it is supposed to be sand and burning sun.* We ate as we went, munching chocolate while it lasted, and dates and almonds, wiping our hands on our wet cloaks. We had left the lorry and changed to the camels in the first hours of a moonless night, and it was raining. We slithered in the mud while we loaded the angry animals, and it was raining. We reached the foothills, where the green corn-shoots were sprouting, by the following evening, and it was still raining.

I said to Frank, our radio operator, "Another hundred and fifty miles of this."

He replied in his peculiar, precise English, careful to avoid mistakes, "I do not think it will rain tonight. There is blue in the sky ahead of us. How far have we come?"

It was a long day's march.

"Thirty miles. We're not doing too badly, in spite of the rain. I wish to hell we'd brought gas capes."

"I'm bloody cold, are you not? Really, I do not like being so wet. It makes it very hard to sleep."

Sayed, the camel-man, hired for us in Gafsa by Guidot, was soon collecting *mithnan*, the flimsy desert shrub that, wet or dry, burns like petrol. The fire was going strong in a few minutes, filigree twigs of *mithnan* flaring up hot and bright, thorn roots smouldering for embers, sending up steam from the wet soil. We brewed tea syrup in the tiny metal pot, sweet and strong as the Arabs drink it, and ate biscuits and dates. Mohamed, our Sudanese interpreter (he could also work the radio), who had a weakness for jam, opened a tin and finished it off. Frank lay down and slept, his unbooted feet wrapped in a towel. Mohamed and I smoked and talked. He said, "I do not like the people here. I do not trust them. I think we shall have trouble." He spoke almost perfect English.

"Tomorrow," I said, "we shall cross the line, such as it is. If there is no trouble tomorrow we shall be over the worst part. After that it will be easy."

8

"Yes. If there is no trouble tomorrow. But I think there will be. It will be hard to make these people work for us. I saw in Gafsa how they hate the French."

Our camels in the distance were eating somebody's corn-shoots, happier than any of us. I said, "We shall have to get rid of the camels soon."

"I was thinking," Mohamed said, "perhaps we can keep them a little longer by pretending to be tea-smugglers. There is a lot of smuggling going on across the lines. All the Arabs who are not involved in it keep away from the smugglers because they are afraid of the police. If we tell what caravans we may meet that we are doing that, the word will get round and they will leave us alone. We can keep our Arab clothes on for the whole journey."

It seemed a shrewd idea. "All right," I said, "let's do that. We must get as close as possible to Gabes before hiding the supplies. That will also enable us to travel more quickly."

We spent most of the night sleeping. At dawn we went on the air, made some more tea, ate a few almonds, and set off before the sun was up. It had stopped raining at last, and the early sky was clear. The sun rose and dried our shivering flesh. It warmed our spirits too. At midday we stopped for an hour to water the camels, and Mohamed dragged a sodden copy of the *New York Times* from his pocket. "This is a splendid paper," he said; "look at the size of it!" I told him not to let bits of it fly about, and he looked at me reproachfully. It was hot now, and we were perspiring freely under our heavy cloaks.

We saw our first Italians in the evening. A lorry-load of them passed us on a near-by track. They gave us no more than cursory glances. Frank said, "Well, we're here, anyway. I wanted to say '*Va fa'n cullu*' as they passed." We saw a German armoured car a few hours later, then a truck-load of troops in the dusk. Mohamed frowned as he asked, "Surely we are not over the line yet?"

"These are only patrols," I told him. "We're just as likely to see our own people here. We shan't be in enemy territory proper until we get to the hills. That's where the trouble will begin."

We made the foothills by midday after a good night's sleep, warm in our now dry cloaks. It was hot and tiring work getting through those steaming cliffs. We knew the

9

map by heart, with the enemy positions marked covering the passes. But there was a goat-track through that Sayed knew of. It was rough and hard to climb, but we struggled up the steep slopes, belabouring the complaining camels, beating them into obedience, sweating and cursing till we reached the top. We kept in single file in case of accidents, to give those in the rear a chance to get away if the man in front ran into trouble. We saw one or two Italian posts, mostly small stuff which we watched for a while with our glasses and then left behind us.

It took us several hours to get to the top, but at last we saw the splendid blue haze of Chott Djerid, the great salt lakes, ahead and far below us in the distance, blue and copper-coloured in the evening sun; it was a magnificent sight. A few clouds of dust where transport moved on the plain told us that the roads were drying out. Our clothes were heavy with perspiration and dust, our limbs were weary, our tempers short. But there below us lay the remnants of the Afrika Korps, and we were on our own once more. It was a good feeling. In the distance, the long green strip of the Oasis of El Hamma marked the German camps. It was a quiet and peaceful scene, and quite beautiful.

We sat on the rocks and stared. Frank said, "It's a lovely sight, *hein*? What a pity it is full of Bosches. Do you think we shall reach Gabes?"

"I think so. We haven't done too badly. And thank God we've passed the hills. We shall have easier going now; no more climbing. I wish I felt happier about the Arabs."

Mohamed called out, "It's time to go on the air, almost. Is this a good spot?"

"All right. You do it. Frank and I will have a look round."

Frank said, "There are some Arabs over there"—pointing —"better be careful. We might go and talk to them."

"Wait till Mohamed's finished, then we'll see. Keep the aerial as low as you can, Mohamed."

The schedule was quickly over. Our radio was most efficient, a light-weight, compact affair that could be carried on the back with ease. The batteries, which weighed thirty-five pounds each, were another matter. The aerial was a length of wire slung over the nearest bush. We had little to tell, just a note of our position. To let them know we weren't too happy, I added a rider, "The ice is a bit thin."

The plan had been to collect information from the Arabs,

10

as we had done before, paying them well for the risks they ran. We ourselves were to hide out in caves or *wadis*, on the move the whole time, living as best we could and sending the collated information to the Eighth Army via Cairo. It was a plan that had worked well in the past. But it depended on the Arabs' good faith, and as we drew nearer to Gabes they were more and more hostile. Mohamed sounded them first. He was an Arab, and the least likely to be betrayed by them. They told him they would not work for the Allies. They hated the French and they feared the Italians. Once or twice they must have reported our presence; twice we saw a truck-load of troops drive to our hide-out of the previous day. Once a party searched the hills around us for two days and we slipped away in the night. We had to move fast all the time.

We buried our stores and turned all but one of the camels loose to fend for themselves, two heavy, slow old fellows and one little youngster, snow-white and pretty as a kitten but vicious and more trouble than the rest put together. We carried the barest necessities, just the radio and the heavy batteries, a mess-tin between us for cooking and drinking, a water-skin, the little pot with tea and sugar, and a good supply of dates and nuts. One can live on tea, if it's sweet and strong enough, Arab-style, like treacle. All the time we sent what messages we could, nothing of great importance.

A convoy of trucks loaded artillery troops moving south, twenty ten-tonners, seven medium tanks moved south, ten empty flats north on rail, no guns this position, twelve light armoured cars into Gabes this a.m., this position abandoned, convoy seventy-two trucks unloaded, four Storch under tents grounded here, direction south, direction north, red piping on shoulder, no information this matter, description divisional sign, direct hits, petrol dumps, supply points, patrol passes this point each 06.00 hours, tank crews as infantry, sailors as infantry, airmen as infantry, so it went on.

We drew still nearer to Gabes, but could do little more than a road-watch unless we called in the Arabs to help. We were not getting the stuff we wanted. Cairo at last radioed, "Suggest you pull out, position looks bad; or can you move north a little?" The B.B.C. said, "The battle for the Mareth Line has begun."

I called a conference. I said, "This is no good, we can't pull out now."

11

Frank said, rubbing his feet, "If they want us to withdraw I will ask for leave: I will take it here. Then I shall not have to walk all the way back again. I do not like walking even in good company. I prefer to sleep, really."

I said, "We've come the hell of a long way. We've crossed the line and we're right in the middle of them with a radio on our back. It doesn't make sense to pull out now."

Mohamed said, "We can get into civvies and go into Gabes if you like. You couldn't pass as an Arab at close range, but Frank and I could. You could hide out somewhere and co-ordinate the reports."

Frank said, unhappily, "All right."

I didn't agree. I said, "Neither of you could fool a local Arab for long. You could get past a German or an Italian; I can do that myself. Besides, if anything happens to Mohamed there's no one to work the radio if anything happens to Frank. If we had some ham. Besides, it will be much too slow. No, there are only two ways about it. One, we return to Cairo; two, we call in the Arabs."

Nobody spoke for a while. None of us wanted to go back with the mission half-fulfilled. Nobody wanted to trust the local Arabs. We voted on it. Everyone said, all right, call them in. After all, that's what we came here for. But for Heaven's sake let's be careful.

The next morning, Mohamed pulled his *burnous* closely about him and went to the nearest tents. He carried a bag of tea as bait. Everything was ready for instant flight. He came back in an hour and said,

"The local headman is there. I stuck to the story about smuggling tea and said we were also selling information to the British. I told him there's a lot of money in it and he wanted to come in on the deal. The Italians killed two of his camels and he doesn't like them. Shall I bring him over? What do you think?"

"Bring him over," I said.

"This," said Frank, "looks like a beginning. We'd better be careful."

"I'll get on top and keep an eye out. Let him think you're an Arab, so don't talk unless you have to. Let Mohamed do the talking. If you think we can trust him, give me a shout. Don't let him think you are French whatever you do."

When they came, Mohamed was leading the way, the old man following. He was small, slim, dignified. From the top

12

of the rocks, immobile, I watched him scramble down to our hide-out, then kept my eyes on the track behind them. Half an hour later Frank came up. He said,

"He seems friendly enough. He wants to help us. He says they all want to get rid of the Italians, who are worse than the French. He says he would hide us in his tents if it were not for the women. He says that he and his son and his brother will all work for us. Sounds all right to me."

"What does Mohamed think?"

"He thinks we can trust him."

"All right, let's go and see him. I hope to God we can start work; I've had enough of this mucking about."

When I reached the hide-out, the sheikh came to meet me and gripped my hand warmly. His wrinkled, aquiline face shone with pleasure. His eyes, like most of the Berber Arabs', were pale blue.

He said, "Why did you not come to us before? There is much we can do to help you. No trouble shall come to you while you are on my land, and all the people of my tents shall work for you. Tonight I shall take you to a safer place and we shall eat together. Then you shall tell me what you wish to know. My whole family and all loyal Arabs will work for you; you are welcome here."

Well, that was quite a speech. We had some tea together and we discussed the move that was to take place that night. When he went, I watched him carefully, and we also watched the black tents for the rest of the day, but saw nothing but goats and women casually going about their ways. In the evening he came back with a large untidy bundle. I slithered down to the hiding-place so that he should not know we had been watching his camp. He brought bread and eggs, a goat-skin of thick sour milk and a cooked chicken. We ate hungrily together in silence. This, I thought, was a good thing, for the Arabs will not readily betray a man when they have eaten food with him. We talked a while, each of us trying to sound the other, each not quite unaware of the other's distrust. When it was dark, he guided us along the face of a sharp cliff to a crevasse in the rock where there was water and whence we could see the whole of the plain below us; it was an ideal hide-out, but it had no "back door." We gave him tea and money, which he accepted with a protest. He said, "The tea we will drink together. I accept the money only for my children."

13

We chatted a little longer in the darkness. When he went, Mohamed followed unseen to the tents and watched for a while. As soon as he returned, we moved a few miles farther up the mountain to a point from which we could see the tents and the hiding-place he had shown us as well. We were determined to take no chances.

"Well," I asked, "what do you think?"

Mohamed said thoughtfully, "I think he's all right. But we shall have to be careful all the time, just in case."

Frank said, "I think we have made a start. But I agree with Mohamed, we've got to be careful."

"Tomorrow morning," I said, "when he returns, one of us will go to the edge of the escarpment and keep watch. We'd better do that for a few days until we know whether he's to be trusted or not. We must remember what Guidot said."

"Well, let's hope for the best. I hope this leads to something, really. I am tired of walking about for no reason."

"Let's also open our last tin of jam," Mohamed said. His eyes and teeth shone white in the darkness.

I suppose the conclusion for this episode was inevitable, although at the time we did not think so; we had begun to expect better results at last. But the Italians came suddenly the next day. There were three truck-loads of troops and about forty Arabs armed with rifles and they suddenly appeared on the skyline behind us and fired a burst over our heads. It came as a shock, with startling suddenness. We heard the shooting, right behind us, and I thought in the flash of time it took to realise that they were shooting at us, *Good Lord, that's close, we'd better move out for a bit.* I didn't realise at once that they were firing *at us.* Then I looked round and there they were, a whole crowd of them, shouting and running down the hill. We made off as fast as we could, thinking, *Well, that's the end of that, now we've lost our radio.* I saw Mohamed lash out with his foot at the set as we passed it, and I grabbed up the bag of papers; the codes were in my head, but there were two messages waiting to go off and a few other things I was anxious to save. Frank was also busy tearing up papers as he ran, swearing in an odd mixture of French, Italian and Arabic. Mohamed saved his breath and ran faster than either of us, but then stopped and ran back to look for something. I was ahead of Frank and saw him, panting and cursing, hard behind me.

It all happened so quickly that it frightened us more than it should have done; we felt suddenly very much on our own. The radio was our moral support, our *raison d'etre*, and without it we felt lost and foolishly vulnerable. We had done this sort of thing so often that we thought the danger had gone out of it. But it was the excitement that had gone; the danger was still there and we had forgotten it. So we were frightened, very frightened. It was not the shooting; the shooting was not near enough to worry us unduly, and we'd all been shot at on occasion before. It was not the desert, because we knew the desert well and understood it; it was on our side. It was the unexpectedness of it all, the element of surprise in its truest form.

They went on shooting at us as we ran. We ran so hard up the mountain-side that after ten minutes or so we were stumbling down to a walk, and so were the Italians behind us. It was like the picture of the dog chasing the rabbit and it's so hot they're both walking.

I thought, *If we can get over the hill we'll be all right, they'll never catch us. The sun will be down in an hour and they'll never find us in the darkness. They have timed it badly, they should have come in the morning. We can get twenty miles away before daylight and hide out somewhere. There's plenty of water about and we can manage without food. We must get to the top of the hill.*

I lost sight of Mohamed; he was behind us. I learned afterwards that he had not seen me pick up the papers and had stopped to find them. They picked him up right away. He had a bad time with them—they didn't like blacks. Sayed had been out grazing the camel and we hoped that he would get back and report what had happened. We went on running, Frank and I more or less together. Frank said, gasping out the words slowly, "If we're caught, don't let them think I'm Italian." I said, "Save your breath." It was an effort to speak at all.

They dropped behind us quite a bit in the next half-hour. The going was hard, murderously hard, and we were fitter than they were. It looked as if we might have a chance to get away with it. They kept stopping to fire, and we knew that they were stopping because the climbing was too hard for them. Their firing was more and more erratic. They only had rifles and machine-pistols, stubby Berrettas that were no good at more than two hundred yards. They had started

15

a hundred yards behind us; now we were five hundred yards and more ahead. I saw some Arabs off to the right of us, running fast and easily, with long graceful strides. They were trying to cut us off. When they were a hundred and fifty yards or so away I fired my long-barrelled Luger at them, three shots rapidly, not stopping to aim. One of them fell to his knee and I thought I had hit him; then I saw that he was only stopping to take aim with his rifle. We exchanged a few harmless shots. But they stopped running and fell back a bit, leaving it all to the troops. The Italians were well behind now, the officers even farther behind than the soldiers. It looked as if we might get away, even now, if we could only hang on till dark. But I knew we couldn't run much farther.

Frank said, "I'm done in. We'll have to hide somewhere."

It was the same thought that was beating in my head with the pounding of my heart. I was ready to drop. I said, "All right, get over the hill first."

We reached the top at a stumble. We saw they were a long way behind. The Arabs were nearer, to the left and to the right. Ahead were small, broken hillocks. We dropped down a few yards of hillside and we were alone. I said, "Hurry, they'll be over the top soon. Half an hour to darkness."

We dived into a small gully and scrambled along it. There were bushes there, thick bushes. We crawled a hundred yards or more among them and lay down. It was hard to breathe silently. I could hear Frank's heart beating, I was all in too. My mouth was sticky. It would have been physically impossible to go another hundred yards. We had reached that point where physical exhaustion overcomes all mental capacity to resist; it is not that one wants to go and can't but that one doesn't want to any more. One starts saying, *What the hell*, *anyway*, and sits down to wait for whatever is coming. I had come across this phenomenon before and knew it to be dangerous.

We lay there absolutely still. I wondered if I had destroyed all the papers in the frantic tearing as I ran. I wondered where Mohamed was. We heard two Arabs run past us, close by, stopping to peer into the bushes, then running on again in long, easy strides. I thought, *If they haven't spotted us, the Italians never will. Maybe we shall get away after all. What then? Keep moving fast, west. The Americans have lost Gafsa,*

16

but they're probably still in Tozeur. Better still, strike out in the desert, ten days or so without food won't hurt, maybe forty days, if Moses could do it I'm damn sure I can, pity we haven't got a water bottle. Then we heard the heavy feet of the Italians. Some were still running, panting. Most of them were walking, tired out. We heard their heavy breathing. Some shouted, *This way, over here, look in the bushes, get up on the hill, where the devil are the Arabs, disgraziati loro.*

I could see the white top of Frank's bald head close to the ground. Through the bushes I saw a little Italian corporal running on ahead. He was tiny and very scruffy. There were others behind him, always stumbling, always out of breath. I thought, *If they pass us now we're safe, another twenty minutes and it will be dark. They'll never find us if we hold out till dark.* The night was our friend. We had often got away in the dark. But they'd never been as close as this before. And we'd lost the radio, our kit, our water-bottles. We were more alone than we'd ever been before. Now Cairo was two thousand miles away; before it had been just a few seconds on the air.

Then the bushes behind me stirred and someone said, "Here they are, both of them."

Well, that was the end of that. A sergeant and a private stood pointing their machine-pistols at us, a few feet away. An Arab slipped in quickly and snatched the gun from my belt. It was the old sheikh, our friend. He said, "The officer told me I could have this; they said I could keep his gun." The sergeant didn't understand Arabic. I was afraid the gun would go off in his hand. I was excited myself. I thought, *Anything might happen now.*

An officer came running up, breaking into a walk as he drew near, trying to get his breath and his dignity back. They took our daggers and Frank's gun. My knife had a knuckle-duster handle and the sergeant slipped it over his own fingers. I said quickly to the officer, "Can I have some water, please?" The officer laughed and said in English, "Yes, I need some myself." He passed me a water-bottle, and I drank as much as I could, still thinking that we might perhaps get a chance to make a break later on. The officer said, "That was quite a chase, wasn't it?" He spoke carelessly accurate, beautifully modulated English. I thought, *He'll spot Frank's accent.* Some of the other officers came up and we were marched back to the plain, to a point just below our

17

hide-out. I stared at the trucks in surprise, then realised they must have brought them up afterwards.

Mohamed was there. A very angry Colonel was yelling at him, shouting, "Stand to attention!" Mohamed didn't understand Italian and the Colonel kicked him in the leg. I said, "All right, Mohamed, better stand to attention." I told the Colonel, "This man is an officer. He does not expect such treatment." The Colonel said, "Oh, you speak Italian. Well, shut up."

There were about sixty of them. There were half a dozen officers and one civilian who was, we found out later, from the Questura, among other things. It was an untidy scene. The soldiers in their grey-green uniforms and unpolished leather were crowding round searching us haphazardly. They stuffed everything of value into their own pockets, only making a pretence of a search. The sergeant stopped them in time to get my fountain-pen for himself. They took my watch, my pipes, my pouch, my soiled handkerchief. I complained at odd intervals to the English-speaking officer and got some of my stuff back. It was soon taken again, and I complained once more and so it went on. By the time they'd finished I suppose we had about half each. I lost my watch twice and regained it twice. The civilian stood to one side, pretending to be slightly bored with the whole thing.

Then at last they got the trucks going and they bundled us aboard. The trucks were British Army Chevrolets. Just as we were moving off, the civilian called the Colonel over and spoke to him. The Colonel called for the Lieutenant and finally they tied our hands together. The Lieutenant said, "I'm sorry. It is only a formality." I knew it was no use our protesting. We set off across the Chott for the Oasis.

I felt, strangely enough, an enormous sense of relief. The chase was over and there was no more responsibility. It was for someone else to decide what to do now. I was merely a passive bundle in the back of a truck. Here, there, wherever they wanted me, they could take me; it was no affair of mine any more what happened. We should have to get away some time, of course, but that could wait. There was time for that later. *Meanwhile, just lie back and relax. Everything's going to be all right. It will sort itself out somehow or other. Just relax. Everything's going to be all right.* I found I was humming. Frank said sourly, "What the hell have you got to sing about?"

For the first twenty-four hours things were not too bad. They put us for the night in a small tent with a heavy guard around it. We could see the soldiers quite clearly after the bright desert moon rose, stamping their feet in the shadows of the tall palm-trees, and we watched them through the chinks of the tent. There was an iron bedstead to sit on, and we talked most of the night, getting our story ready. We were not very happy about the fact that we had been wearing our *burnous* when they had first seen us, and there was the radio too. It was going to be hard to say that we were just an advance patrol.

Although we had been searched after a fashion we still had a lot of kit hidden away. We had money, gold coins, francs and lire, a supply of tiny compasses, silk maps, a slim hack-saw blade sheathed in thin bakelite, slim enough to hide most successfully. We shared out some of these things in case we should become separated. We discussed the chances of dashing off there and then, but frequent visits outside for a quick look—we had only to shout *"Fare acqua!"* and they took us out at once—showed us that there were too many of them to risk it.

The night passed slowly, and in the morning they brought a heavy truck along and collected us. Our hands were tied once again and we were taken to a tented office in the centre of the camp for interrogation. The English-speaking Italian did all the talking, and a German officer who was present toyed with a silver pencil. We gave our rank, name and number, and little else. They tried to draw us out, one by one, on politics. They asked if it was common belief in England that if the Allies won the war then England would be overrun with Russians. As at that time the Germans had already fairly overrun Italy, it was hard not to comment upon the fact. The Italian flushed, the German remained immobile. They started to talk about entirely unimportant things, the theatre, music and sport, and I recognised the technique at once. I stopped answering questions as soon as they tended to become more relevant. They did not insist.

In quite a short time it was all over, and we were driven off into Gabes. We exchanged glances as we entered the town; we had reached our planned objective at last. They took us to a prisoner-of-war camp, somewhat to our surprise, which lay on the southern edge of the town by the dunes.

It wasn't much of a camp. The two wire fences were a

19

mere five feet high, and the gates were only broken-down knife-rests. Two tents stood in the centre of the enclosed compound, and the quarters of the guards were outside. We thought at first that we were the only inhabitants, but finally two American airmen crawled out of the tents and greeted us. It was good to see friends again. They were nice fellows. One was a tall blond youngster from Ohio, who continually mooned about with his hands in his trouser pockets, singing quietly,

"I'm dreaming . . . of a white . . . mistress,"

and breaking into loud cheering to annoy the guards every time the bombers flew over. The other was small and dark and came from Boston. He wore bedroom slippers and pyjamas under his flying jacket because he'd been called out in a hurry. They were both Lightning pilots, and had baled out right over Gabes when their planes were set on fire. They kept talking all the time about food. The mother of the man from Boston had sent him a cake and he was rueful because he hadn't started eating it, and now all the other fellows would get it all.

We discussed the chances of escape. He said,

"Easy enough if these sonofabitches didn't sleep in the tent with us. Boy, they *smell*. If we could all get out together we ought to make it if you guys know all about the desert. We've only seen it from up there; looks awful big from up there."

"Let's wait a day or two," I said, "and see what happens. Is the food really as bad as they say?"

"Boy, it's worse. Bread and *brodo*. I'm beginning to get real hungry and I've only been here three days. Imagine spending the rest of the war in here. No, sir."

They came and took Mohamed away a few hours later. That was the last we saw of him. It disturbed us at the time because it meant they had not finished with us yet after all. Before he went we had time to pass him some more money, just in case he could make a break on his own. He seemed to have the best chance of the lot of us. If he could get out of his uniform they would never catch him again. He also had maps and a compass. I had no time to give him some of the gold coins, which were hung round my waist on a string so that the heavy bag hung low at the crutch. It was a good hiding-place during an ordinary casual search, and if touched during the running of the hands along the legs, then it caused no more than an ejaculation of admiration; if one had to strip, it could fairly easily be taken off and slipped into the searched clothing. It required only a certain sleight-of-hand and an affectation of modesty.

We could not guess what they wanted Mohamed for. We knew he would not talk, but we also knew that the Italians had no love for the Arabs. I remembered seeing the Colonel kick him the day before. Frank said, "I don't like it. I don't think they will leave us here long."

"It's more likely," I said, "that they are moving Mohamed into a camp for coloured troops. If they were going to move us, they would not have brought us here in the first place. Where do you expect them to put us, in the civil jail? We're not criminals."

"I think they will move us. I think we shall be taken to a safer place than this. I believe that civilian was a member of the Questura or the Ovra. I believe their Foreign Office is interested in us."

"Rubbish. We are just ordinary prisoners of war."

But we weren't. They came for us the same evening. The officer merely said we were being taken to another place. Frank was silent because he had been right; I was silent also because I knew that I had agreed with him and had not wanted to admit it. They tied our hands and drove out of the tiny camp with the Americans waving to us. We had already given them our names and addresses in case they got away. As we left, they were bombing the Mareth Line again, forty or fifty Fortresses flying in close formation, the sun shining on their sleek flanks. The black puffs of flack mingled with the white puffs of the clouds. The drilling, vibrant drone of the engines was heavy and insistent.

That was the last we saw of Gabes.

We drove north for an hour or two and turned left off the main road before we reached Sfax. We pulled up at a house set back from the road in the shelter of an olive-grove, and the officer with us lit a cigarette and went inside. He was gone a long time. Frank looked at the badge painted over the door and said, "This is a Carabinieri Headquarters. I do not like it. The Carabinieri are bastards."

I said, "I wish they'd untie our hands."

"I wonder if Mohamed is here. Do you think he will talk?"

21

"Less likely to than any of us. Don't forget what we decided. Stick to your story, but try for number, rank and name."

One of the guards said, "*Stai zitto!*" We sat silent on the truck. It was a long time before the officer came back. They took us inside and motioned us up the stairs. It was a big, rambling house of stone and wood, a typical Arab house. They showed us into a little office; the civilian we had seen before was sitting at a table. He was pleasant enough, and pushed chairs forward. I showed him our hands and he ordered the guards to untie them. He offered cigarettes, a light, lit one himself and stared at us for a moment. He said, "Are you wondering why I am going to interrogate you together?"

I stared. That was precisely what I had been thinking. He spoke in French. I didn't answer. He turned to Frank and said, "You at least speak French, of course?" Frank said nothing. He stared hard at us. He was an ugly man, short and stubby, too well-dressed. His nose was enormous and he had that harsh, rasping kind of voice that is sometimes associated with venereal disease. His eyes were pale, streaked with yellow, and the teeth at the side of his mouth were gone. He asked my name, still in French. I gave him my rank and number as well. He waved his hand airily and said, "No, no, I don't want all that nonsense. I want to know how you managed to get through the lines. Which way did you go? You are L.R.D.G. of course?" I told him we had nothing to tell him. He smiled.

"Don't be silly," he said. "That sort of thing is for the soldiers. I think you and I understand each other. What about your friend? Is he French? Italian, perhaps?"

"Why don't you ask him?" I said.

"Perhaps he does not speak French. Perhaps he only speaks Italian?"

I asked, "Where is the Sudanese officer who was with us?"

"I do not know. He does not interest me. I am not interested in black men. I am interested in your friend. Is he French?"

Frank said, surprisingly, "I was born in London of English parents. Why don't you speak English? Your French is terrible."

This frontal attack made him angry for a moment, then he smiled again. He was always smiling, showing his yellow

22

teeth. He said, still in French, "I think you understand French better, is it not so?"

Frank continued his attack. I could see he was angry. He said, "Well, so far we have established that we speak French and you speak English. We're not doing very well, are we?"

The smile never left his face. He insisted, "I wish to know how you crossed over into Italian territory. We found no motor-tracks where you were caught."

I thought, *Thank Heaven here's something we can legitimately be reticent about.* He went on, "Come, come, I don't want to know how many guns, how many tanks there are in Gafsa. I am not interested in that kind of nonsense. Toy soldiers. I want to know which way you came. We found your maps, of course. It was very careless of you to mark your route on them."

I said, "If you found the maps, then you know the way we came."

"No, I'm afraid not. You see, it is not possible that you followed the pencilled marks you made. You would not have got through at all that way."

I wondered where all this was leading. The pencil marks on the map were indeed the route we had taken. I wondered if he wanted me to verify it, so I kept silent. He lit another cigarette and again offered them with elaborate friendliness. He did not want to show his friendship; he wanted to say, *We are intelligent people, you and I. Let us ignore this vulgar warfare that goes on around us. Let us enjoy a cigarette together and discuss it objectively.*

"Still," he said, "I expect you were fairly safe from observation in your Arab clothes?" I was glad then that I had not answered the question about the route. Instead, I said, "What new nonsense is this?"

"Were you not dressed as Arabs?" he asked.

"Rubbish!" I tried to be as short as possible. "We had cloaks over our heads, I remember, because we were caught in the rain."

"And you had no raincoats? I thought the British Army was so well equipped. I thought only the poor Italian Army had no raincoats?"

"We brought none with us. We were travelling light."

"Then where did the cloaks come from? Did you not bring them with you from Gafsa? Remember, before you answer, that Gafsa is in our hands."

23

"We borrowed them from the Arabs. The Arabs who sold us out."

"Yes, that is a good story. Were you with Stirling?"

"Stirling?" I tried to keep the surprise from my voice. Colonel Stirling had been on his way up from the Eighth Army side when we left Gafsa. I wondered how they knew about it. He told me. He said,

"Stirling was captured, you know, a little while ago. In much the same place. He was also wearing Arab dress. You are from his party, of course?"

I said nothing. He added, thoughtfully,

"Your French friend doesn't quite look the part, somehow. You admit he is French, of course?"

I said, "This can go on indefinitely. Why do you think he's French, anyway? Some sort of complex because his French is better than yours? Well, mine is too. Most Englishmen speak French."

I thought, *If this is rank, name and number, I'm doing the hell of a lot of talking.* Then he said,

"I'm sorry you won't talk to me. I can make things very much easier for you. But I must confess, when I found out who you were, we didn't expect you to tell us much."

I said, "I wish you'd tell us what happened to the other officer. The Sudanese."

"He was your operator, wasn't he? The Arabs told us a lot about him. I thought the English believe in the colour bar?"

"He is an officer in the British Army."

"Yes? Well, I am sorry you are not more co-operative. I am sending you to a place in Sfax. I do not think a camp would suit you. But we shall be seeing quite a lot of each other. You must let me know if they do not treat you well there. Perhaps I shall be able to do something for you. Good evening, gentlemen."

They took us back to the truck. The guards were lounging about by the lorry, smoking a cigarette between them, each taking a puff and passing it on to the next. They climbed aboard with us. One of them, grinning, offered the end of a cigarette, saying, "You want? English cigarette." He threw it in the gutter; it was the fraction of an inch long. A soldier standing by walked over, picked it up and examined it carefully, then put it in his pocket. We set off for the town.

We discovered eventually that the name of this man was

24

Luzzati. We met him often, but he refused to tell us his name. Frank found this out by listening carefully at the door of the cell in the prison every time he called, to hear what the whispered conversations in the office would have to disclose. When he discovered this, I addressed him as Signor Luzzati, and had the satisfaction of seeing him go white with fury. We heard him giving the guards hell afterwards because he thought they had been talking to us about him. Perhaps it was a silly thing to do, but it gave us a bit of momentary comfort. We always listened in at the door when a visitor called, hoping we might hear something of importance. We never did, of course.

We spent the short journey into Sfax quietly telling each other we would have to escape pretty quickly. We took it for granted that it was only a matter of time. I had already studied in Cairo so many reports of escaped prisoners-of-war that it seemed quite a simple thing to do. And it occurred to me that in certain circumstances an ordinary prison might be much easier to escape from than a camp. Luzzati's remarks indicated that we had seen the last of the camp at Gabes and a civilian jail was the obvious substitute. I knew too that the Italians considered the desert as their main line of defence against escapers. It is no easy thing to cross several hundred miles of desert on foot, unless one knows the ropes; but we knew the ropes, and that made it easy. Our escape kit afforded us a lot of satisfaction. We had so many compasses concealed on us that Frank said, "My God, if I stand on one leg I shall swing round north, really."

We had benzedrine, too, and it's wonderful stuff to keep going on. All we had to do was to get away from the immediate vicinity of our captors; the rest was easy. But the interview had left us worried. We did not like to voice our fears, but we knew we should have to hurry up. There was no time to waste. They intended to be unpleasant.

Chapter Two

BUT we did not go at once to the prison. We were taken instead to a fine old farmhouse in the centre of a big orchard. I remember thinking how beautiful the blossoms were; great masses of pink and red hung down from the trees, and a single red carnation, blood-red against the grey stones, stood in a pot on the low wall of the verandah. Frank saw some awful significance in this blood-red flower, and we started bickering immediately. The shock of capture was beginning to shorten our tempers. Meanwhile the guards stood lounging about, paying us little attention, and we thought fleetingly of making an attempt at escaping there and then. The night was approaching in an hour or two, and once the darkness came the rest would have been easy. But there was a stretch of a hundred yards or more of open ground to the trees, and beyond was an unhealthy high cactus hedge. We decided to leave the idea alone, but to concentrate instead on showing ourselves to be quite harmless people, so that the word would get around, if we kept it up long enough, that we were not very difficult to cope with. They soon began, in point of fact, to regard us in this manner.

Then an officer appeared from behind the farmhouse, a surly Sicilian, a Lieutenant of Carabinieri. He was brusque to the point of offensiveness, and I took an instant dislike to him. We were told to turn our pockets out on to the table in the yard. This was the nearest thing to a joke that we'd heard since our capture, and I pointed out with heavy sarcasm that we had been "searched" before. This annoyed him intensely, but I was suddenly aware that his annoyance was with his own troops who had robbed us. We produced the few articles we had left; I had two pipes, a pouch well filled with tobacco, a comb, a cigarette lighter; Frank had a packet of cigarettes, matches, a watch (1 recovered mine once again later on), a few odds and ends. One of the odds and ends was a gold sovereign that was supposed to be hidden away; but he showed it to the Lieutenant quite frankly and said, "Old Arab brass coin; looks almost like gold, doesn't it?" The officer examined it and then gave it back to him. He then examined my lighter, which was a good one, looking for an excuse to confiscate it. It rattled ever so slightly when he shook it (it had never done so

26

before) and he said, "Ah, you won't mind if I take just one flint? One does not find them here." He opened it up, found no spare flints and started to look for the rattle. He was astonished when he found the very small compass that caused it. He examined it with admiration and then renewed his search.

He found Frank's silk map, but nothing more. My own map had already been found at the first search, and this was annoying, because we were now mapless and had a super-abundance of compasses. We each had a few under our pips, in the linings of the uniform, one in a pipe stem; two others had gone with my fountain-pens. We had plenty of the things we didn't really want. I was worried about my thin hack-saw blade, and resolved to remove it from under my medal-ribbons and hide it in a safer, if less comfortable, place. He found some tablets of benzedrine loose in my pocket, the best possible hiding-place under the circumstances, but let me keep them when I explained that it was medicine "for my heart".

At last the search was over. I pointed out that we had had no food for twenty-four hours, but he ignored me and we were pushed into an out-house for our trouble. It was a sort of kitchen where a cook was working, and we were promptly pushed out again. I managed to get hold of a turnip as we went through the door. We stood about munching it for half an hour in the cold of the twilight, shivering and cursing the guards, till the out-house door was flung open and an arrogant little private appeared and shouted, "Come here!" I turned my back on him, and he repeated the order in Italian. As we still ignored him he disappeared and the officer stuck his head out of the door and said, "Come on, the tea's getting cold." The order was addressed to us, and not to the men who were looking after us. I didn't quite understand what he had said. Frank nudged me and said, "He's made some cha, come on."

Unbelieving, I followed him inside, and there, sure enough, were half a dozen chipped coffee cups on the table filled with a cloudy, yellow liquid that was indubitably a sort of tea. I can't think to this day how they managed to make it look so horrible. The Lieutenant and the arrogant little private (who had made the tea, he proudly explained, from captured stores) stood with us and drank also. We became quite cheerful again, and I began to understand something

27

of these people. It seemed suddenly obvious that their surly detachment was nothing more than ignorance and poverty, and resulted from their abnormally low standard of living. I noticed now that the officer's hands were black with dirt, his nails filthy, his boots down at heel. He was a simple peasant doing an officer's job, and I felt sorry for him. We almost became friends.

But not for long. Tea over, we were taken to a tiny room, so small that I was about to object to the lack of breathing-space, when, to my horror, a small cupboard in the wall, close to the floor, was opened and we were motioned inside. It was a sort of box-room, two or three steps below the level of the floor, and so low that one could almost, but not quite, sit upright. It was about ten feet long and four feet wide, and ventilation was by means of a hole in the wall where a brick had been removed. Before I could protest, the door was closed behind us and we heard furniture being dragged against it. It gave one a frightful feeling of claustrophobia. It felt like being shut in a coffin, and it was here, I think, that the hopelessness of our position was really impressed upon us and we became really miserable. I had stumbled in the darkness coming down the few steps and hurt my knee; that served to shorten my temper very considerably. As our eyes grew accustomed to the light we realised that it was just the Arab equivalent of a cupboard under the stairs, meant for storing jam, or domestic utensils, or garden tools; anything, in fact, except bodies. The light was such that for the first five minutes we could see nothing at all, even had there been anything to see, and the small patch of green outside which showed through the ventilator served only to accentuate our misery.

We stayed in this tiny closet for a day and a half. All the time we had no food and were getting more and more hungry, though we were allowed to drink water when we went out to relieve the pressure caused by the last long drink. I was more lucky than Frank here, for early in the morning a "pilot" was brought in, an "American airman". He told us he'd been captured the previous evening. I wondered how he had managed to shave that morning. He spoke very fluent American, but he seemed to know the tiny room too well; he didn't stumble down the unexpected steps as we had done. He walked down them carefully. Before his eyes became used to the semi-obscurity, I signalled to Frank to be careful. And a few minutes later, I was taken outside for "exercise". I was outside for over an hour, and when I returned the "American" was gone. Frank confirmed my suspicions. In my absence he had been carefully questioned. It was a pathetic effort. In the few minutes we had all been together the "airman" had showed a singularly narrow conception of how the war was going on. He was so misinformed that he would never have fooled a child in arms. He didn't even know the population of his own home-town. But the episode was not entirely without results. I had been an hour outside with only one careless guard to watch me, and I was able to show Frank a very useful find—a rusty, broken knife-blade, some four inches long. I had an idea it might come in handy. It slipped nicely into the side of my boot.

At the close of the evening following our hungry introduction to the farmhouse, and still hungry, we were taken to the main H.Q. of the Royal Carabinieri in Sfax, a dull, cheerless building with the inevitable air of a police-station about it. Again we spent a long time hanging about. It seemed that we always arrived when everybody was off duty. It took the full working day to arrange to move us from A to B, and by the time we got to B only the duty officer was working and we had to wait again for the next day before anything else could be done. It was always like this. But this time our patience was rewarded. I had been mentally preparing a long and elaborate speech about feeding prisoners-of-war, and the duty officer happened to be a nice fellow. He listened for a while to the story about our hunger, and then produced a large bowl of macaroni and beans, and, what was more a full *fiasco* of wine. I was lucky enough to catch the order to the soldier who brought it, to the effect that we were to have as much of the wine as we wanted. It obviously meant as much of that particular bottle, but the soldier also was a nice fellow, and by the time we had finished arguing and drinking, we had three bottles between us, the orderly included. It did us a lot of good. It took away the hardness of the wooden bench we sat on.

A few odd officers appeared from time to time and stood by in little groups watching us. Some of them took offence because we were eating, and it was not until later that I discovered the awful fact that they were all permanently hungry. The British Army ration is perhaps a little uninspired, but at

29

least no one ever goes hungry. Bread is quite often thrown away, and I have seen crated hundreds of bully-beef tins sent back to stores because nobody wanted them. But in the Italian Army the ration is incredibly poor, and the pay does not permit its improvement from local supplies. So almost everybody was normally hungry. We saw here for the first time the look of silent hunger which was later to become so commonplace in Europe. It is the look a hungry dog has when it stands at the kitchen door, afraid to go in and beg.

For some hours we sat there. The office was comparatively warm, and I took the opportunity to sleep. The wine was a great help, though Frank woke me from time to time to tell me of little pieces of news he had overheard. We decided there and then to pretend that I was the only Italian-speaker in the party. Frank was to play dumb and pick up what he could when they were talking among themselves. When the time came to escape, this was a great help; we knew they would be looking for two non-Italian-speaking Englishmen, one of whom had a smattering of the language. My own Italian at this time was pretty bad, and the idea was that when we escaped, we should change roles: I would keep as quiet as possible and Frank, whose Italian was of course perfect, would do all the talking. We kept to this plan satisfactorily right up to the end. It was a great help.

We slept fairly well till past midnight. One thing disturbed us; one of the soldiers was called to run a message. "Tell the Captain," he was told, "that from tonight the prison will be functioning *for a little while*." We didn't like the sound of that "for a little while".

The hours passed slowly in that drab office with its brown woodwork walls bare of decoration save the usual posters of *il Duce* looking tough, and a few inscriptions, "*Ritorneremo* . . ." and all the other bombast. It seemed a bit out of place, somehow, above the shabby uniforms and the hungry faces. It was dawn when they started to move. A heavy lorry drew up to the door and we were ordered into the back. A heavy guard was waiting for us and for the first time our thumb-strings were changed for the Italian handcuffs, the *ferri*, thin steel links of chain bound round the wrists and padlocked. They are unpleasant things, and the Carabinieri are expert at tightening them so that they cut into the flesh. The Italian criminal, however, is equally expert at slipping them, and we soon found out how this was done. It had to be done fast, before the flesh started to swell. At the time, I was not unduly upset by them, because there was an element of humour in being trussed-up like a dangerous criminal. One felt a certain indignity, but the fact of the handcuffs themselves was so unusual as to provide a compensating interest. I spent most of the truck-ride twisting my hands about in an effort to see if they could be slipped. I did my wrists a great deal of harm, and nothing else. The main problem was that they were also chained together, which made movement difficult.

We arrived eventually at the prison, a truly terrifying place, if only from the point of view of hygiene. It was an old grey building, part of the original town wall, and built partly of rough-cut stones, partly of wood and concrete. It was unbelievably filthy, and it stank to high heaven. We climbed the steep stairs ahead of our escort, and there was a great deal of excitement from everybody before the formality of handing-over, with its attendant counting and signing, was completed. The two of us were counted so many times that I began to wonder if there were perhaps more of us than I thought. They got it right eventually, and we were taken to a cell on the first floor which was so dirty as to defy description. Let it suffice that a heap of excreta on the floor was barely noticeable in the general filth and stench. We were rapidly becoming resigned to the progressively worsening stages of our adventure, but this was too much. We flatly refused to go inside, and stood firm until some other prisoners, Arabs, were produced to wash the place out. When the smell had partly cleared we went inside and inspected our new home.

It was a long, narrow room, some fourteen feet by six, and about twelve feet high. At one end, the farthest from the door, was a small grille set high in the wall, about ten feet from the ground. I climbed on Frank's shoulders to have a dekko, and found it to be fourteen inches wide by seven deep. It was covered with iron bars, five-eighths I think they were, about five inches apart. 1 remember that Jasper Maskelyne, who ought to know, had once told me that the smallest opening a normal man could get through was fourteen inches square; it was something to do with the trap-door of a disappearing act. I wondered how we should ever be able to get through a window half that size. The door was a solid affair of heavy red-wood on iron hinges, both hinges and the bolt being on the outside only. There was no peep-

31

hole. Over the door, eight feet off the ground, was a large barred opening. We soon found that it was commonly used to give the prisoner an idea of what was going on outside the cell. If anyone called, for instance, white hands gripped the iron bars above the doors of all the cells, and with a shuffling of foot-wear against the timber, one white face after another appeared at the grille. They could be seen by the guard, of course, and were usually ordered down pretty smartly; but from time to time it served a useful purpose.

Lying on the floor in the cell was a piece of timber, part of an old door. It had been used as a sort of bed-board, but was too small to serve that purpose properly. However, I spotted a possible use for it, and when it was removed as offensively filthy, I asked to have it back again for use as a paradraught. It occurred to me that it might make a useful "step" up to the window. The floor was of cement, and the walls had once been whitewashed. There were small blood-marks on the walls; it looked as though frequent fingers had been dipped in blood and then wiped clean on the plaster. The guard saw Frank frowning at them and grinned. "Eh!" he said. "This used to be a women's prison. Dirty creatures, Arab women." I sighed. It was no use complaining. But I managed to kick over the stone jar in the corner and break it, to ensure that we might get out to use the lavatory occasionally.

When we were alone there inside, with nowhere to sit but on the cold floor, we felt incredibly depressed. Very soon after they locked the doors on us we hammered at them and demanded to see the officer in charge. The guard outside the door told us there was no officer in charge; the prison was under the command of the sergeant-major we had seen. "All right," we said, "then send for him." The guard grumbled a bit but finally marched off to find him. A moment later he appeared and let us out for a parley.

Of all the people I met in jail, I remember this fellow the best. He was the only one who showed us any real kindness. His friendly attitude started the moment we spoke to him and continued till he was transferred shortly before our first escape. There was little he could do. Not only was he bound by the prison laws, which he largely broke in our favour, but the physical necessities were lacking. Toilet kit, for instance, just did not exist. The guards themselves, when they washed, which was rarely, washed without soap and dried their faces on odd bits of rag or their shirts. They had

32

boards on the grounds as beds, without mattresses of any sort, and only two wretchedly thin blankets to cover themselves. Medical kit was unheard of, and insecticides ...

But the good fellow did his best. He brought us old cardboard boxes which we used as insulation against the cold floor. He gave us four blankets each instead of the regulation two. He allowed us to use the lavatory, such as it was, instead of having a bucket in the cell. And after the first day he allowed us to remain on the verandah outside the cell for two or three hours a day. This was a great thing. First, though there was little to see, as the balcony looked down on the centre of the prison yard, one could see the sky above it. And more important, it gave us a chance to study the guards and the lay-out of the building. The guards got to know us, too, and soon realised that we were quite harmless and had no intention of escaping. I reasoned that when we finally got down to it, it would be a lot easier if we understood the mentality of the warders a little. So we watched them carefully as they lounged about the verandah, rifle carelessly slung over the shoulder, in twos or even singly. We noticed that their rifles were never cleaned and the barrels were rusty, so we knew they would not be particularly reliable if they were needed in a hurry. Furthermore, out on the verandah, just round the corner from the office we were always near the sergeant-major, and I was most anxious to improve my Italian as rapidly as possible. I found him to be very partial to a chat and he was good company. We swopped experiences and talked at great length of the campaigns in the Western Desert. He was torn between two desires—one to get back to his wife in Italy after seven years in the Colonial Armies, and the other to get captured and put an end to seven years of being chased about Africa. He was afraid to mention his desire for captivity, but it was obvious that he thought a lot about it.

We soon got to know our way about the prison. It was quite a small building, built on two floors. First, just inside the main gates, which were of iron and rarely used because the lock was stiff, was a small courtyard, some thirty feet square, and containing a dilapidated well which in theory was used by the prisoners for washing. In practice, as there was no soap, no towels, no wash-basins, no one ever did wash. Facing on to this yard were the four cells, each containing about twenty prisoners, all Arabs. For an hour a day they were allowed out into the yard, one cell-full at a time. During this period, the cell was sometimes swept out and the stone jar was emptied.

From the yard a flight of stone stairs in a corner led to the cells upstairs. There were only two or three of them, one at each end of the balcony, and an "occasional" cell in the centre which was not generally used. Here also were the guards' quarters and the sergeant-major's room. At the entrance to these two rooms was an open square with a sky-light, and from here a stairway led down to the street, the back door, so to speak, of the prison. A sentry was stationed permanently at the head of this stairway, and the door was kept locked, though sometimes the key was lost and it remained open for a few hours till it was found. It was our special care to notice where the key was kept, as we felt we might have to use it one day.

Every morning at six they brought the breakfast, which consisted of four ounces of black unsweetened coffee, made from maize, and in bulk about the size of a decent double Scotch. We drank it out of a tin lent to us for the purpose. The next break was anywhere between eleven and three when the main meal of the day arrived. This was macaroni boiled in water, with no seasoning, and was terrible, and two small black loaves, each about the size of a man's fist. The bread was so bad as to be almost inedible for the first few days, after which we were hungry enough to eat anything that came our way. Finally, some time in the evening, the famous Italian Army *brodo* arrived. This is simply a meat soup, made by boiling meat in water. The water is served as soup, and the meat is then fished out, with the fingers, and eaten, with the fingers. The snag is that the whole animal goes in, and only the lucky ones get the edible pieces of meat. This *brodo* is given three times a week, and the other four days is substituted by boiled rice, boiled cabbage-leaves, boiled beans or anything that happens to be lying around. This is the standard ration of the Italian Army. The guards had just the same as we had.

The food came from somewhere in the town and frequently did not arrive at all. On these occasions the emergency ration was issued in the evening; this was one sardine, raw, salted, unfilleted and unwashed. On these wretched little fish we were expected to satisfy a day's hunger. But the sergeant-major always came to the rescue. He used to give

34

us a little olive oil from his own stock, so that we could eat bread and fish slightly more palatably. He also taught us how to clean and bone the sardine so that it had the spicy taste of an anchovy and wasn't too bad. Sometimes the guards produced an octopus, either bought or stolen. We used to watch them pounding it on the stone floor of the yard to soften it. After that they boiled it in a great copper urn borrowed from the neighbours, beat in a paste of pepper and oil, and presto! that was supper. Once or twice we got a share in this, and it wasn't at all bad. On the whole the food situation was wretched, but the sergeant-major, good fellow, tried his best to make it tolerable.

I remember the first time the poverty of the food really was impressed on me. While the bread was being dished out one day, a young Sicilian guard made a request that I did not understand, in dialect. He repeated it in a sort of un-couth Italian, and I caught the word *pane* repeated several times, so I handed him a loaf of bread, guessing that he was begging. At that time, the bread was still unpleasant enough to our taste to be valueless. So when we were alone I asked Frank what it had all been about, and the answer shocked me badly. The poor fellow had asked if I would keep the crusts for him as he had noticed that, since they were too hard to eat, I usually threw them to the cats.

The first thing we had to do, of course, was to devise a means of escape. It seemed at first that we should have to take the prison by storm, though this would not have been too difficult under the right conditions. There were no more than nine guards in all, including the two N.C.Os., and they were most of them young Sicilian peasants, very dull-witted and very undersized. I felt that they would not have put up much resistance if we had been able to seize a rifle from the sentry, in itself an easy feat. We used to squat on the floor of the cold verandah, or stride up and down to keep up our strength, but all the time watching them surreptitiously as they lounged about day-dreaming, their rifles often left leaning against the wall almost unattended. We toyed with the idea of knocking a sentry out quickly and quietly, then holding up the others with his rifle and locking them in our own cell.

The main difficulty was, of course, that we might succeed in merely starting a battle in which we would be hopelessly out-numbered if something unexpected happened at the outset; if, for example, a couple of soldiers turned the corner as I hit the guard over the head—only one shout would be needed to give the whole game away. So we decided to bide our time. "Wait and see" is a fine policy. It also gave us a certain pleasure to know that on one or two occasions when four or five of them had gone on the everlasting search for food, they were not much stronger than we were and that we could always put the plan into execution if it became desperately necessary. Once out of the prison, however, it would not have been so easy. We needed darkness to hide our uniforms. We tried every device we could think of to stay longer out of our cells, on the verandah, but we were always locked away inside long before it was dark. When we were let out a little later than usual, we told the sergeant-major our funniest jokes, our best yarns, in an effort to hold his interest till night fell and we could make a break for the rifle; but he never fell for it, and we were always put away for the night most carefully.

Then one day we made an important discovery. We were sitting on the verandah, by one of the square pillars that supported the roof, idly chatting about nothing in particular and fingering the masonry. Frank was in a very critical mood, and was declaiming against the Arabs, towards whom at the moment we felt very bitter. He suddenly broke off the conversation, and said scornfully, "Pah, they can't even build a house properly. Look!" And he showed me a hand-ful of sand which had trickled out of a hole in the wall which he had enlarged with his fingers, a small hole chipped in the weak cement plaster which covered the sand and stone of which the walls were built. Then suddenly the significance of his remark struck both of us together. The walls were indeed worth a closer scrutiny.

Waiting till the sentry had turned his back on us, we examined the spot carefully. The cement covering had been broken away and exposed the interior of the wall; it was almost pure sand and stone inside, the cheapest of cheap concretes. The implications of this were enormous. The window!

We had already been at work on the window of the cell. We had measured ourselves as carefully as we could, standing against the wall and squeezing ourselves into as small a space as possible, measuring with outstretched eight-

36

inch finger-spans the breadth, depth, thickness, every measurement of our bodies. The width was all right; it seemed that we could constrict our shoulders to fourteen inches; but by no effort of will or physique could we manage to squeeze our back-sides to seven inches. But now it seemed as though the restricting wall was not so solid an obstacle as it had seemed. We knew the bars could be cut—we had already half-cut them through at the top, by way of getting a little practice in with the hidden hack-saw blade. It might be hard to break away a section of the wall quickly and still silently, but we could at least try. We were anxious to get back inside; and that was the first day we stayed out till it was dark.

However, the moment the door had at last been closed behind us, I stood the bed-board on its end by the window and Frank hoisted me up on it. I stood with one foot on the board, the other on Frank's shoulder and carefully examined the window-ledge. With a rusty nail pulled from the wall I scratched the surface, and in a very few minutes our wildest hopes were realised. The coating of cement was thin and old, and underneath was rubble. I kept silent while Frank was fuming below, excited to know the results; I laboured till I had made a hole in the surface of the ledge a good two inches across, saying nothing the while. Then I levered out a huge stone and handed it down to him. His bald head was red with excitement, his eyes wrinkled up and he was about to boil over. It was hard not to laugh out loud. He handled the stone lovingly, fingering it like the breast of a woman. He said, "Really, it is a very nice stone. But the sergeant-major would be very angry if he knew we were taking the prison to pieces, really." His teeth, incredibly strong and white, gleamed brightly. "What shall I do with it?"

I said, "Don't be vulgar. Anyway, it is too big."

It was obvious that our way out was now clear. We needed only a better tool than a rusty nail. I retrieved my knife-blade from its hiding-place and cut a piece of wood with it from the bed-board. Then we pulled lengths of thread from the blankets and twisted them into strong cord. With this we bound the wood to the knife to make a crude handle. We spat on the stone floor and scraped the blade to sharpen it. Within an hour we had a fine useful tool. It was a great success. We took it in turn to clamber up on the board and work on the ledge. Within a couple of hours almost half the horizontal surface had been exposed, leaving the dusty rubble underneath. By this time our fingers were sore and bleeding, and our knife was blunted. So we called it a day and returned to our beds. There was a lot to discuss, and we talked over the new development till the sheer excitement of it all sent us to sleep. For the first time in captivity we slept like logs.

Chapter Three

BRUSQUELY, frighteningly, our composure was shattered the next morning like a glass that has had boiling water poured into it. Soon after they brought us our coffee, an officer came to the prison and there was a long whispered conversation downstairs, with Frank straining against the door to try and hear what was being said; we heard continued references to us, but no more. We never liked the appearance of officers in the jail: it always seemed to have a personal and unpleasant significance. At last we were called from our cell and taken to the "office"; the office was the sergeant-major's room, and smelled as strongly as our own. There was crude bedding on the floor, and there were onion skins in the corner. The officer, a Captain of the Carabinieri, was seated at the table. He carried a cardboard file of papers and a heavy manual. His fingernails were carefully kept. He said, speaking very slowly to make sure I understood:

"I have come to inform you that you are to be tried under section seventy-nine of the Italian Military Penal Code. Would you like me to read it to you?"

I said, "Tried? What on earth for? We have committed no offence."

"According to the law, anyone who enters Italian territory in disguise is guilty of an offence."

38

I said, "Don't be damn silly. There is no question of disguise."

"There is plenty of evidence to the effect that you did. But you will have a chance to tell your story later. I wish only to inform you of the position and ask if you require the services of a lawyer."

"I would certainly like a lawyer if your people are going to such ridiculous extremes. I would like to have a Swiss lawyer. I suppose we are entitled to the assistance of the Protecting Power?"

"I am afraid that is out of the question. We shall provide you with an Italian lawyer who will look after your interests. But I wish to read you the article of the law under which you are to be tried. Please pay attention. I am sorry I could not bring an interpreter. If you do not understand, please say so."

He opened the manual and read, "*Il Militare che travestito siasi introdotto ... sara considerato e punito comme spia ... Sara parimente considerato e punito comme spia ogni individuo dell'esercito nemico, o al servizio dal governo nemice . . .*" He looked up and said "Do you understand all that quite clearly?"

I said, "I understand, but I wish to translate for the benefit of my friend; he does not understand Italian." I said to Frank, speaking rapidly, "I don't quite know what to do about this. They're going to be very unpleasant. There's not much we can do about it."

Frank said, "My God, they are going to try us after all. Tell him there's no case to answer, for Christ's sake."

I said, "We cannot do more than protest against this abuse of International Law. But I insist that we have a representative of the Protecting Power present. Otherwise the trial will be a mere farce."

"There is no possibility of such a thing. The trial will take place tomorrow afternoon, and I will send your lawyer to you in a little while. He is already well acquainted with the important facts."

"But, God Almighty, that doesn't give us time to prepare a proper defence. I have never heard of such monstrous illegality. I demand more time. I demand a Swiss lawyer. I demand proper legal assistance."

The officer studied his nails. "I am sorry. The trial is tomorrow."

39

He signalled to the sergeant-major, and we were bustled back into the cell. It was all over.

Frank said, "My God, what's going to happen now?"

I was very angry, frightened—I said, "How the hell should I know what's going to happen?"

"I must say you didn't handle him very well."

"Handle him?" I was furious. "What the bloody hell did you expect me to do?"

"You should have protested."

"Oh, shut up, for Christ's sake."

We spent a long time without talking. There was nothing to say.

The lawyer came about an hour later. He was a thin, unpleasant-looking man of about fifty, with thin features and a sallow complexion. He looked more like the cheap shyster than the barrister, and he inspired very little confidence. He seemed to speak a certain amount of English, but he had brought along an interpreter. The interpreter was a nice fellow; he was an Italian-American from Detroit and was not so suave as his companion. He took charge of the interview and I was grateful for his friendliness.

He said, "Now don't you guys worry too much about all this. This lawyer is good, I know him. He's one of the best they have."

Frank said, bitterly, "I don't doubt it. But who pays him?"

"Who pays him? Oh, I see what you mean. No, no, he'll do his job properly, it'll be all right, you see."

"Well," I asked, "what are we supposed to do?"

"Just tell him exactly what happened. The main point is about those Arab clothes you were wearing."

"Wearing nothing. We had cloaks over our shoulders to keep dry, that is all. It was raining. The troops who captured us know that."

"Did you have a radio?"

"Of course. We were in contact with our Company."

"What arm of the service are you in?"

"Transport. R.A.S.C."

"The Arab who was with you has made a statement that you crossed the lines in disguise."

"*Coglione!* He couldn't have said that, it's too stupid for words. Let them produce him in court and see if his statement will stand up."

"They can't do that. He escaped."

40

"What! He escaped?" Frank looked up sharply and studied his face intently.

I said, "My God, is that true?"

Frank said, "Nothing is true that an Italian says. You will find that out when you know them better."

The interpreter flushed. He said, "That's all right, I know how you boys feel. But it's true. They got a statement before he escaped."

I noticed his use of the word "they". I said, "Well, I hope he made it. Better ask this chap what he intends to do for us."

He translated our conversation to the lawyer. The lawyer said, "That's a likely story. Tell them to plead guilty and ask for clemency."

I said, "I got that. Tell him we will not plead guilty. Tell him we shall tell the truth. We came out on patrol and went too far, that's all. There's nothing more to it. They got our maps and they know our route. They know we didn't have to be disguised to get through. Besides, we're in uniform now, aren't we? Do they think we went home to change?"

The lawyer said, in English, "O.K. I tell them like that. Maybe everything O.K. You be ready tomorrow. Perhaps it is O.K." He gathered his papers together.

The interpreter said, "All right boys, just don't worry about it, that's all. I know it's a bit unpleasant for you now, but it'll turn out all right."

They bundled us back in the cell and Frank said, "My God, I don't like this a bit, they are determined to harm us. Don't they know the war is practically over? Really, their ignorance is astounding."

"There's only one thing for us to do. We've got to get out quick."

"You mean try and get the sentry's rifle? There won't be time to finish the window."

"No, let's leave that till the last minute. If we fail there'd be a most unholy shindy and we shouldn't have another chance. We'll try and get the window done in time. If that doesn't work we can always try and dash for it afterwards. We need three or four more days for the window. Maybe less. Maybe we can do it in one night if we keep going."

"If we work after midnight, they'll hear us. It's much too quiet then."

"Well, we'll try. Let's get cracking."

Frank said, "My turn. Hoist me up on your shoulder. Really, this is most uncomfortable."

We took it in half-hour turns; the deeper we got the easier it was. The surface of cement was patchy in its strength, and with the home-made knife it was simple to lever out great hunks of rubble. Some of the stones were dropped outside on the wide ledge beneath the window. When their size made it likely that they would drop noisily we took them in the cell for subsequent disposal in the lavatory. There was deep earth on the shelf outside and it was covered with grass and weeds, so there was little danger. But it was tiring work. We found it was impossible to work for more than half an hour without resting. Our tools were hopelessly inadequate, and we had to go very slowly to avoid breaking the crust of the inner wall. The deeper we got, the better we realised how it was going to work out. It looked as if we could go on digging down deeper and deeper till the window-sill became like a hollow boot-box, with just the thin plaster of the wall to break at the last moment. But it was slow, cautious work; a break of that plaster camouflage, so exactly resembling solid wall from below, would have exposed the whole plan. And the dust, the particles of sand, were continually being blown into our faces, giving us considerable eye-trouble. But the approach of the trial gave us little time to waste, and we went ahead as fast as we could. Our main fear was that we might be transferred to another building, or put into separate cells. It seemed incredible that they had not already separated us.

By the evening, when they brought the *brodo* and let us out to eat on the verandah overlooking the courtyard, we had dug down to several inches, and still the sides of the "boot-box" were undamaged. It became necessary to hide our hands from the guards while we ate. There were small cuts and bruises all over them, and the tips of our fingers were badly broken and bleeding; if they had been noticed it would have given the game away at once.

Again, we were anxious to be put away early, and once again we were left out later than usual. Indeed, it looked for a moment as though we might be able to pull off the other plan and get away in the darkness. We were very undecided about this, because the main plan of getting out through the window, unseen, would give us at least six hours, perhaps eight, good start before they began to look for us, whereas

42

the secondary idea would have them hot on our trail in no time at all.

On the other hand, it looked as if the opportunity we had been waiting for, for plan "B", was being handed to us if we could only make up our minds quickly enough to act upon it. While we were discussing this, the sergeant-major caught us whispering, and hastily put us inside, thereby solving the whole problem for us. We worked hard for the rest of the night, then downed the tools when the silence became so acute that we were afraid they might hear us. We had guarded against sudden surprise by ramming pieces of matchstick into the lock from the outside, very surreptitiously, so that it always took them the devil of a time to open the door. But we did not want to arouse their suspicions and have the cell searched. We lay down on the cold cement floor, pulled our thin blankets around our shoulders and slept. I slept very badly that night, waking at frequent intervals.

They came for us very early in the morning. It was quite in keeping with their policy that when we had to move an hour's run away we had to start at least half a day before it was necessary to arrive. The coffee was cold as it always was, but there was plenty of it, which was unusual; and we ate a loaf that we had saved the previous day. They took us down the stairway at the back under a heavy escort of Carabinieri. It gave us an opportunity to see some of the roads we should have to use when we escaped. They bundled us on to the waiting lorry, then off again while they push-started it (self-starting lorries were rare in Tunisia), then on again—and off we went. We were handcuffed again. By this time I was becoming quite accustomed to the feel of *ferri*, but they were still an abomination. But every time they put them on our wrists was one more opportunity to practise slipping them off. Before long one could get them off with a certain amount of ease and a lot of discomfort, though it was always considerably harder to get them back on again.

The trial was held in a small house set apart from the town a little. There were other cases being tried when we arrived and we had to wait in the courtyard outside. They removed our irons, locked the door of the yard, and left us more or less alone with the Carabinieri, soldiers, officers, and the handful of civilians who regarded us curiously. I suppose we

43

were a museum-piece. I spotted the young English-speaking Lieutenant who was present at our capture, and also one or two of the soldiers.

I asked the officer for a cigarette as an excuse for getting him to talk. I said, in English, "I suppose you are here to give evidence against us?"

He spoke regretfully. "Well, I am afraid I am."

"They seem to think we were disguised," I said, "if you ever heard of anything so ridiculous. Surely it was obvious that we only had those damn cloaks over our shoulders to keep the rain off?"

He was a nice fellow. He said, "I am surprised, as a matter of fact, that there is to be a trial at all. I expected you would have been held in a prisoner-of-war camp. I only heard about this yesterday."

"This seems to be the work of a gentleman in your Foreign Office. You can see what happens to a soldier when civilians interfere with the conduct of a war. It looks like a serious business."

"No, surely not. Perhaps it is only a formality."

"I think not. It is all very sad and makes me most unhappy. But perhaps you know best; you are, after all, the principal witness. Perhaps it is, as you say, only a formality."

The officer looked thoughtful. He was about to say something when one of the Carabinieri interfered and broke it up. He went across to the others and started an argument, but we could not catch what was going on. Some more civilians arrived and banged impatiently at the door of the yard until the soldiers let them in. Frank was listening, straining his ears to catch what the officer was saying. He said, "Nice work. I wonder if we can get at the other ranks; they are more dangerous." The civilians stood in a solemn circle around us silent and rather pathetic. Somebody said, "They have real rubber on their boots." There were some women there, the first we had seen for a long time. One was a pretty girl of twenty or so; she had the long legs and high breasts of a *Triestina*, slim and fair. She saw me looking at the tight line of her thigh and looked away.

Then an imperious banging on the door heralded the arrival of the Foreign Office gentleman, Luzzati. He saluted us elaborately.

I said, "This is your big day, I suppose?"

He replied, "This is a very painful duty for me. Sometimes

44

we start things and have to finish them even if we do not like the way they turn out. You serve your country, I serve mine. We are at war." Then he added, curiously, "If it does not go well, I shall be really sorry. Please believe that." I did not know whether he meant it or was trying to get us rattled. If he was trying to frighten us he certainly succeeded.

I said, "There is no case against us at all. Moreover, I shall appeal against the competence of this court to try us in the absence of a representative of the Protecting Power. I cannot understand why this charge was ever brought."

Luzzati did not answer. He bowed slightly and walked away. One of the Carabinieri spoke to him, and he called the young officer over, then took him inside one of the rooms. I could not hear what was going on, but when the Lieutenant appeared again he looked very abashed and avoided us like the plague.

It must have been about seven when we arrived at the court. The trial began in the early afternoon. The Bench consisted of a Colonel, as President, and four other officers. One was in the sombre uniform of the Blackshirts, a stout, white-faced man whose uniform accentuated the pallor of his complexion. He was a Major, but the Colonel treated him with the greatest deference. I thought, *He's the one who will be most difficult*. The Colonel had the palest eyes I have ever seen, and a row of medals that was impressive. The other officers were a bit nondescript, except one who looked rather like a tired and kindly old schoolmaster; he was also a Major. The courtroom was tiny and had once been a school-room. The Bench sat at a table underneath an ivory crucifix, and we stood against the opposite wall. Our lawyer, who arrived at the last minute, and the interpreter, the same one we had had before, were at a table in the middle. The crowd and the soldiers came in untidily and milled about noisily. It was hard to concentrate on what was being done.

The President formally opened the court by glaring at everyone and shouting "*Silenzio!*" Then one of the other officers read out the charge and asked us if we pleaded guilty or not guilty. Our lawyer said "Not Guilty", and the trial started. I interrupted to say that we did not recognise the power of the court to try us and also asked for an adjournment to prepare our defence. It seemed very necessary to gain time. The President looked at me very coldly and said, "Let us get on with the proceedings."

The Major shuffled his papers and called for the first witness; it was the young Lieutenant. The Major showed him a paper and asked, "Is this the report you made yesterday?"

The Lieutenant glanced at it and said, "Yes, that is the statement I made to the Questura."

"You said that these men had Arab cloaks on their backs. That means, does it not, that they were disguised as Arabs?"

The Lieutenant hesitated before replying.

"No, I don't think so. It looked rather as though they were sheltering from the rain."

The Colonel was visibly angry. The Major produced a second sheet of paper. "This," he said, "is the statement of the sergeant who was with you. He says that everybody thought they were Arabs. Does that not indicate that they were disguised as such?"

"It was too far away to be certain. It was also raining a little, and visibility was bad."

The Colonel interrupted impatiently. "Did you recognise them as enemy troops?"

The young officer hesitated again. He said, "Well, it was hard to see. It was a long way away."

"The sergeant states that it was one hundred yards. Can you see one hundred yards?"

"Yes, sir."

"Well, then, were they, or were they not, disguised?"

The Lieutenant gave up. He said, "I don't think they were, but I suppose it could be regarded like that."

"In short, you did not recognise them as enemy troops because they were disguised as Arabs?"

"Yes, sir."

I protested vigorously. I said, "You are putting the words into the witness's mouth. He stated quite definitely that he could not see clearly."

The Colonel said quietly, "You will please keep silence."

"I will not keep silence," I shouted. "You are forcing the witness to change his own evidence." The Colonel ignored me, and asked our lawyer if he wanted to cross-examine the witness.

The lawyer said, "Were they wearing uniforms or civilian clothes?"

46

"Uniform."

"When they stood up as you started firing, could you see that they were enemy troops?"

"Yes, it was quite clear."

The Colonel said angrily, "The point has already been made clear. When they were first seen they were disguised. That they shed their disguise later is quite irrelevant."

The lawyer prudently sat down. I was about to protest again, when the Colonel said, "I am prepared to stay here all day, but I will not allow interruptions of the proceedings."

He called the sergeant as second witness. He was a small man, no more than five feet high, a Sicilian. The same performance was repeated. In his evidence he said, "It was obvious that they were disguised; we all thought they were Arabs. Besides, the Arab who gave us the information said they were dressed in Arab clothes."

I said, "What sort of evidence is that? Hearsay evidence is not acceptable in any court."

The Colonel shouted, "Be quiet!" The sergeant went on, "We thought they were Arabs and fired over their heads. Otherwise they would have been killed at the first shots."

I was not given a chance to examine him, and our lawyer had no questions to ask. They produced a statement which they said Mohamed had made. The interpreter read it out. He cleared his throat and read,

"My name is Mohamed bin Omar Hussein. I am an officer of the Sudan Defence Force." (Neither of these two statements was true.) "On the second of February at five o'clock in the evening, I was captured with two British officers between Chott Djerid and Gabes. We had come from Gafsa with a radio to send information to the Eighth Army. We were able to cross the lines because we were disguised as Arabs. We passed many Italian posts, but we were not molested as they did not recognise us. Once we were challenged, but we answered in Arabic and they left us alone."

This was preposterous. I said, "Where is the man who is alleged to have made this monstrous statement?"

The Colonel asked, "Is the witness present?"

The Major fingered his papers and said, "No, sir. When he was being taken from the Camp at Gabes where the prisoners were first sent, the lorry carrying him was machine-

47

gunned by enemy aircraft and he escaped in the confusion. I regret that he has not yet been re-captured."

I was astounded at this revelation. And it sounded possible. I asked,

"If that is true, when did he make that statement? Any way, if he is not here to support it, it cannot be accepted as evidence."

The Colonel said, "I will decide what is and what is not evidence."

"All right," I said, "but when did he make that statement if he escaped on the second day?"

The Colonel had very little patience. He raised his voice and said, "I will not have the honesty of the court questioned. The evidence is accepted as it stands."

"It is an obvious fraud," I said.

"Keep silent!" shouted the Colonel.

"I will not!" I shouted back. "It is an obvious attempt to produce false evidence. He had no time to make a statement, he is not here to support it, and the whole thing is a pack of lies."

The Colonel jumped to his feet and shouted, "Silence! I tell you to be silent! If you speak again I will hear the case in your absence."

He turned to the lawyer and said savagely, "Do *you* have anything to say?"

The lawyer rose and said drily, "No questions."

I looked at Frank. He was pale. He understood all this far better than I did, and was trying to conceal the fact.

A soldier was called and repeated the evidence of the sergeant. Then the Prosecutor started making a speech. I only understood half of it. He rumbled on for a long time and said, at the end,

"This is another example of the insidious methods used by the enemy in their conduct of the war, methods which are quite contrary to the finer chivalry of the Italian soldiers. It is not the first time these methods have been tried, and it is no less serious because it failed. We do not know what irreparable damage was done, how many of our noble sons were killed, as a direct result of their efforts before they were captured. In less civilised countries it is usual to put such people up against the wall; under the noble law of the Romans, they are given a fair trial first." I lost the trend of this speech while ruminating on the ambiguous nature of this remark, but heard him say, "In consequence, therefore, I demand the utmost penalty that the law can give, which is death."

Our legal representative rose and, after his long silence, made a brilliant speech. He did not state a case for the defence, he said, because there *was* no defence. We were ignorant of the subtleties of the Italian laws, and although this was, in itself, no excuse, it could at least be counted in mitigation; the crime was there, but not the intention. He let the words roll off his tongue splendidly, and one had the impression that he chose them rather for their euphony than for any possible relevance to the case. I interrupted once to correct an assumption he made about the statement alleged to have been made by Mohamed, which was, of course, a complete fraud, but I was ignored. I did not understand at least half of the words he used, and the speech rolled on and on. His gestures were magnificent, but I soon lost interest when I lost the trend of the argument. I noticed that the Court was absolutely silent for the first time. I watched the faces of the spectators. They were staring at the speaker, fascinated. I thought, *Maybe he is a good lawyer after all.*

The Triestina girl with the slim hips was there, in front, close beside me. She held my stare quite dispassionately, and I wondered whether she was getting a kick out of it all. I felt no enmity towards her for it. I let her see what I was thinking.

The lawyer went on and on. I tried to pick up the threads again. He was saying,

"I do not therefore plead that they are innocent of the crime for which they are here. I plead only that they are soldiers and as such entitled to the protection which their uniform allows them. The prosecution has made much of the fact that they were carrying a radio. Does not every patrol carry a radio? Are they not now, in the presence of this court, in full uniform? Can, therefore, the prosecution seriously allege that they were disguised? I state categorically that they were merely performing a routine patrol. I ask for the clemency for which the Roman law is justly renowned."

He sat down.

The Colonel said, "The court will be cleared."

Everybody pushed untidily out and broke up into speculative groups. The Carabinieri stood beside us in the court-

49

yard, and Frank said, "Let me listen to what they are saying." After a few minutes he said, "The lawyer thinks he's on a good wicket. He thinks he's won his case. He certainly made a very fine speech. Did you understand it all?"

"About half of it. It was a hell of a farce as a trial."

"Yes, I didn't like the look of the beginning. Do you think Mohamed really made that statement?"

"Of course not. I'm glad he got away."

"Yes, if it's true."

"Don't you think it is?"

"I don't know. If it is, I am very happy, really. But I think it is more likely that they have killed him. You know how they treat the Arabs."

I said nothing; the same thought was at the back of my own mind.

Frank said, "I heard somebody mention a word which means life imprisonment. So even if they find us guilty, it might not be so bad."

"No, life imprisonment would be fine, with the Eighth Army around the corner. But I should think they'll probably give us ten years. I suppose technically it is espionage; but not a very serious case."

"Are you trying to convince me, or yourself?"

I said, "Don't be cynical, Frank, this is not at all the place for cynicism. Personally, I am most unhappy about the whole thing."

"Yes, me too, really. They didn't give us much chance to defend ourselves. And I didn't like the way they asked for the death penalty."

"It was obviously prejudiced. The President knew all about the case before he started."

"If Mohamed got away, then he is very lucky." Frank sighed. "This is really very bad for my nerves. I do not like uncertainty. I like to know what is happening."

"I, on the contrary, do not like to hear unpleasant things. I would much rather the case took a year than hear an unpleasant verdict. I do not in the least mind waiting for unpleasantness; I hate it like hell when it arrives."

"That is a very fortunate disposition. I cannot feel the same way. Perhaps I am more sensitive than you. All this makes me very unhappy."

"Well, I'm with you there."

50

"If Mohamed escaped, at least Cairo will know what has happened. Not that they can do much about it. Do you think they will be angry with us?"

"These things happen all the time. It is unfortunate, that's all. They will be very sorry."

"I wish we had started on that window a little earlier. How much longer do we need?"

"It's hard to say. With luck we could be out in a couple of days. I feel very confident about that. So it really doesn't matter what the verdict is."

"Yes, if only . . ."

"If only what?"

"I am afraid they might move us. Or separate us."

"If we are separated, there is only one instruction. Get out under your own steam as fast as you can. We'll have to be on our own. It will be harder, but it will have to be done. But perhaps they will leave us where we are. I hope so. I hope to Christ they do."

They called us back into the courtroom. The crowd surged in after us. Luzzati, who had been leaning nonchalantly at the door, was gone. There seemed to be more people than there were before. I thought, *This is where they put their thumbs up or down.* Nice people. The President called for silence. There was a shuffling noise as everybody tried to get a better view. The court stood up. Everybody followed the President when he raised his hand in the Fascist salute. It felt strange now that the difference between us was so accented. We felt very much alone in that sea of hands. It seemed to make the room smaller, everybody with a raised hand, just the two of us different from the rest. It made us feel less personal; we felt like strange creatures, as though we were not people at all, really; we were odd creatures who did not raise their right hands, strange objects of academic interest . . . different . . . very much alone among the others.

The President said, keeping his hand raised, "In the name of the King and the Leader." I noticed that the King came first and was glad of it for a quickly-passed moment, and, as I wondered why, I heard snatches of what he was saying: " . . . found guilty after a fair trial . . . this court . . . to be shot . . . sentence to be carried out within twenty-four hours . . ." and then I did not hear any more till everyone said *"Viva il Duce"* and lowered their hands.

51

I heard the word *colpevole* and then *fucilati* and the interpreter, the very nice fellow from Detroit, much embarrassed, starting reading the translation. The President was gathering his papers and looking at his watch even before the interpreter started reading. He hesitated, and forgot how to say "through the breast" in English, and said instead, "through the . . . through the . . . here, here . . ." pointing at his own chest. He was very upset. Then the crowd, having seen the show, went off to their own affairs and to tell their friends all about it.

The guards pushed towards us and took hold of our handcuffs and chained us together quickly and efficiently, and pushed us out. I thought, *My God, this is it, there's not much we can do now.* I knew then that we had both known this was going to happen, and each had been afraid to say so to the other. I felt that the blood had gone from my face and there was an empty feeling inside. I wanted to say something to Frank, but couldn't think of anything. His face was pale, but he looked calm enough, calmer than I felt, though a little angry. It was harder for him because he had been under my orders and might have done differently by himself. I was responsible for the mission, and knew that he was thinking it was my fault.

We were pushed outside, and there was a double file of soldiers facing us, and I thought, *Christ, they're not going to do it now, in front of all these people?* Then I saw that they were merely an escort. The lorry was waiting for us at the gates. They put so many guards with us that there was hardly room for us all in the lorry. I looked around to see if there was any chance of making a dash for it, and then thought how stupid it would be to try it while we were chained together, that there was no hope at all. I was scared, angry. Angry with Frank because I knew that he wouldn't blame me for it as he should have done, angry with myself because I couldn't see a way out of the mess, angry with the office because they should have known there was no hope, angry because it hadn't come off this time. And I was numbed, too; the reality of it all did not strike me till later.

They took us back to the jail and pushed us up the stairs ahead of them. The sergeant-major was waiting for us, smiling. He said, "Well, it wasn't so bad after all, was it?"

I said, *"Fucilazione,"* and saw his face change. He went quite pale. I saw the blood coming back again to his face.

I heard the shuffling of feet as the occupants of the other cell pulled themselves up to the window over the door; a pale round face appeared and stared and said, *"Courage, mon brave,"* and that made things worse. Then the Carabinieri handed us over and we were locked in the cell.

I sat on the floor, looking at Frank. He dropped down on the blanket and said nothing. For a long time we just sat there, staring at nothing. I became conscious that my mouth was open, and shut it. I said, "Sorry, Frank, I suppose this is all my fault." He didn't answer, but just sat there staring. Then he said, "This is so near my home. If I had a car I could be home tonight. I cannot even write to my mother, she won't know what's happened to me." The stone wall was cold against my back. The floor was cold, cold and hard. I said, "There's not even time to get out. It will be in the morning. We need another two or three days on the window. There's no chance at all. I'm sorry, Frank."

There didn't seem to be much we could do about it. We had been so sure of getting out; now there wasn't time. The main trouble was that we now realised that we had known all along that this was going to happen. If we had not been afraid to think about it, perhaps we could have found some desperate measure to get us out. Now it was too late, and our own cowardice had betrayed us. I wondered why we both weren't more moved, more emotionally upset. I remembered a line in the anthology I carried,

"I tell you hopeless grief is passionless,"

and I said out loud, "How the hell did she know that?" and Frank said, "There's nothing we can do, nothing." I didn't know whether it was a question or a statement. Then he got up and started banging his head against the wall, and saying, *"Mon Dieu, Mon Dieu, Mon Dieu"*; it was the first time I had seen anybody do that, and I thought, *My God, now we shall start fighting, we mustn't do that, not now.*

I started looking for something to do, anything to keep things rational. I cleaned my nails with a matchstick, and then the shock of it all hit me suddenly, like a physical blow. I thought of my home, my family, everything I used to know and love. It took me very badly and is very unpleasant to remember. Frank kept saying, *"Rien a faire, rien a faire,"* and I started blaspheming as violently as I knew. Then we started arguing and abusing each other, and I thought, *Jesus, this is the end of everything, we've got to get out of it.*

A long silent time passed. At last we heard someone coming up the stairs, and I felt better and said, "Well, here they are, Frank, they're not wasting much time." Frank stood facing the door and straightening his jacket, very pale. We both waited. They unlocked the door, taking a long time over it because of the matches we had wedged in the lock to give us more time, more warning to get away from the window. When they opened up, the lawyer was there with the interpreter, and I wanted to shout at them, then thought, *Oh, what the hell anyway.* The interpreter was smiling and said,

"Boy, what a lousy trial that was."

I stared at him and he said, "Believe me, I'm sorry about all this, but I've got some news for you. It's not finished yet, not by a long way. Listen carefully, because this will cheer you up. General Messe's representative was at the trial, and is going to write a report on it for the G.O.C. He says you weren't given a chance to defend yourselves, and some of us think the President will get it in the neck. Now, there's only one thing you fellas gotta do, you gotta sign an appeal, for, how do you call it, a commutation of sentence. That has to go to the King himself. They call it in Italian *la domanda per la grazia.* It's the usual procedure, and your chances are very good."

I said, hearing myself speak rather than consciously forming the words, "That means a request for mercy. I won't do it." I felt I had to make some protest. I knew it was not a very nice thing to have to do. I knew also that I didn't care a damn about the niceties, I just didn't want to be shot, that was all. I said, "I won't do it," and waited for him to argue.

He said, "Now don't be like that, be a good fella, will you? It's only a formality. You got the same thing in England, we got it in the States, but here they just call it by a different name, that's all. It's only an appeal, that's all. You guys let me write the petition, just say you didn't get a fair trial, that's all, you don't want to make up a story. Then it will go off to Rome, to the King, and you'll get ten years instead, what do you care? Just sign the paper and I'll do the rest."

54

He sounded as though he was pleading for his own life. He said, "Go on, be a good fella, will you?"

I said to Frank, "What do you think?"

He said, "Well, what are you waiting for? Only we'd better write it ourselves."

The interpreter took a paper from his case, and said, beaming, "That's the idea, I knew you guys would be reasonable. I got it all written out ready. All you gotta do is sign it. I already wrote it for you."

It was in Italian and I read it carefully, aloud, in Italian and then in English and said to Frank in Arabic, "Is that right?" He said "Yes," and nobody knew that he had checked the translation for me. We signed it and gave it to the lawyer. The interpreter said to him, "Now don't forget it has to be in H.Q. by tomorrow morning. I'll go along and tell them you've got it." Then he turned to me and said, "That's all, boys. I want you to know I'm on your side. This country's not like England or the States, they do this all the time here. Ask any of the fellows here, they know all about it. And besides, your people will be here in a week or two, you just gotta hang on till then. But don't say I said so, see? They don't like people to talk like that. Half the witnesses in your case were caught, or gave themselves up, in El Hamma; that's right near where you were picked up. But don't say I said so, will you? And don't worry, it's gonna be all right."

Frank said, "Does that appeal go to the King or Musso?"

"The King. I don't quite know how those two guys tie up, but this has to go to the King; the law's quite clear about that."

"In Rome?"

"Yes, in Rome. Oh, I get you. Sure, that'll take one hell of a long time. You'll be all right."

I said, "If the Army pulls out, will they leave us here?"

He looked a little uneasy. "Well, I wouldn't know about that. They haven't got much transport left, and all the high-ups are already fighting each other for passages out. Say, I shouldn't talk like that, I'm liable to get me in the same sort of trouble. So long, you fellas, and don't *worry*."

When they had gone, the sergeant-major said, "You have done the right thing. Everybody makes *la domanda*."

"There was a soldier here a little while ago," said the corporal, "who threw a hand-grenade at his officer. That

55

always happens. They sentenced him to death and the *domanda* changed it to four years' suspended sentence. They said they would wipe it out if he volunteered to go to the front, so he did. They sent him to the Mareth Line." He looked thoughtful. "They say he's deserted already. They say that as soon as the troops see the Allies, they run towards them as hard as they can and surrender."

One of the faces over the door watching us, jeered. "Yes, unless it's the Australians. Then they run as hard as they can in the other direction."

The sergeant-major snatched the corporal's cap off and threw it at the face. He shouted, "Get down from there and mind your own business, you whore's abortion." He said to me, "These people are very ignorant. But sometimes they speak the truth. I think everything will be all right. I will let you stay on the verandah till this evening. You will not want to be locked inside now."

I couldn't tell him we would rather be inside. He would not have understood. I did not want him to be suspicious, so we had to wait till nightfall. The good sergeant-major gave us some bread and oil to cheer us up, and the occupants of the other cell gave us some wine they had bought. I was touched by their compassion. But we wanted to get on with the window. We didn't know how much time we had. And we didn't know how much we could believe of the things they told us. Frank said,

"Remember the lies they told us in court about Mohamed. Of course he didn't make that statement. They tell lies out of preference. So how much of all this can we believe?"

I said, "There's only one thing. We've got to get out fast. Waiting like this is worse than being certain. We've got to get to work.   With luck we can make it in about two nights' time. That's all I want now, just a few hours alone at that bloody window. I'm not worrying about what happens next. If we pass the first obstacle, they'll never see us again."

Frank said, "I hope you're right."

"Of course I'm right."

When they put us inside we went straight to work. The window was getting deeper and deeper. Still the plaster of the wall held. There was no sign of the damage from below. The way was becoming more and more clear. We went to work with great enthusiasm. The shadow over our heads was cold.

56

Chapter Four

THE following day we felt a lot better, secure in the knowledge that we had done a lot of work the previous night. And while we were sitting on the verandah eating the midday meal, cursing the kindness of the sergeant-major that kept us out when we wanted to be locked inside, we had a stroke of very good fortune.

We noticed one of the guards handling a file, an eight-inch rasp that should never have been allowed in a prison. I had a sudden inspiration; I snapped my pipe in half, and, taking it across to the sergeant-major near-by, asked if I might borrow the file to re-shape the stem. He looked at me suspiciously, somewhat naturally, but at length I managed to persuade him that I intended only to carry out a small repair job, and he agreed, telling the guard to keep an eye open. The guard watched me like a lynx, and when I had finished, half an hour later, I waited till the sergeant-major was busy talking to the sentries, then called out, "Thanks for the file, sergeant-major," and laid it very ostentatiously on the sill of his window. He watched till I was sitting down on the floor again, then went on with his orders. Quickly, I snatched the file away again and laid it in full view on the woodwork of the verandah, hardly moving to do so. The rust-coloured iron scarcely showed at all against the woodwork, and the camouflage was excellent.

We were careful not to move from the place we were occupying, and at last, when the loss was discovered, we were made to stand and submit to another search. I protested indignantly that I had been seen to lay the file down on the window-ledge; we had not moved from our places since. I made a great show of being hurt that we should be suspected of such a breach of friendship, such an abuse of their kindness. They did not search the cell because the door had been closed the whole time. They looked everywhere for it. It was under their noses the whole time.

At last they realised that we had had nothing to do with the theft and were most apologetic for having suspected us. "We have to be careful, you know," said the sergeant-major, "please do not be offended." They gave it up as a bad job. Fortunately there had been some workmen repairing the doors upstairs and they had since gone; it was obvious that

57

one of them had stolen it. Well, it didn't really matter, it was an old file anyway, quite worn out and useless.

Before they had locked us up again, I had slipped it down the side of my boot.

We found it a most useful article. The end was broken and sharp, and it made an excellent lever for digging out the stones, for breaking up the cement. We kept the level of the now-deepening boot-box of the ledge fairly smooth, so that as time went by we passed the bare minimum necessary to permit the passage of our bodies, but went on with the work so that it would be relatively more easy when the time came. We were not quite sure what the true minimum size would really be; the position of the window, up near the roof, was obviously going to make it harder to get through. And we had more work to do on the bars. We found that each cut took about two hours. It was extremely awkward to work in such a cramped position, one foot on the board, just the narrow edge of the board supporting a narrow strip of foot, the other leg dangling in mid-air or pressed down on a soft, unresisting shoulder. Moreover, the wind blew the filings into our eyes, making them very painful indeed. But slowly the work progressed, and at last the bars were cut through to our satisfaction, with just the slightest thread uncut. We camouflaged the cuts with a paste of bread, dirt and water. With the bars cut through, the hardest part was done. From our position on top of the board edge, we now had a fine boot-box of a ledge; the plaster side of the "box" was thin but undamaged, and the rubble that was the bottom of it was deep and smooth, and getting deeper every minute. It was slow work, but at the end of a few hours, the difference was very remarkable. We carried on, dropping the small stones silently on to the ledge outside the window, and putting the very big ones in the corner of the cell for subsequent disposal in the lavatory.

This lavatory needs some description. It was a most useful place for us, as it was up a few steps on the way to the roof, and through its window we could see a lot of the road we should have to use, both north and south. We could see that we were well to the south of the town. We spent a lot of time there at frequent intervals, and I once heard one of the sentries say, "They spend a lot of time up there; I think they're hoping to get to the roof and escape."

The sergeant-major replied, "Nonsense. They just want

to see outside for a bit. They're not used to this sort of thing. They don't want to escape, you can see that."

All the same, I saw him checking the door to the roof immediately afterwards. He was taking no chances; so he thought.

The following day there was almost a calamity. They decided to white-wash our cell. We had asked for this to be done in such bitter terms on the day that we arrived and saw the filth we were to live in, that there was not much we could do now to prevent them. We tried to get them to do the rest of the jail first, but not a bit of it. We tried to "help", but the sergeant-major insisted that we should have no hand in such menial employment, and brought the Arab prisoners up to do it. They were looking for a ladder, and I was praying that when it arrived it would be too tall to use, for fear they should see, or even break, the window-sill. If they had leaned a ladder against the wall for six inches below the window, it would have collapsed in a cloud of dust. We waited anxiously. Then they decided not to wait for the ladder but to get on with the work by tying the brush to the end of a stick. We put on a show of interest and watched them. As they scrubbed up and down the wall below the window I was in an agony of suspense; but it held. Then one stood on the shoulders of two others to do the roof, and I stood by with some of our concealed money handy, ready to slip it to them if they should see anything. I knew the prison staff did not speak Arabic, and I had already started chatting with the Arabs, just in case. The suspense was frightful. But by the evening the work was finished and our secret undiscovered. The window was nearly ready.

But poor Frank was having trouble with his eyes. They became red and horribly swollen. With a matchstick I removed several pieces of iron filings from them, but there was much I could not get out. They wanted to take him off to the doctor, but I was afraid that they would spot the trouble for what it was; iron filings in a prisoner's eyes are sure to arouse instant suspicion and we could not risk it. Frank said, "It's nothing, nothing at all, just a cold, I often get it." The sergeant-major was worried, but did not insist on calling the M.O. I felt sorry for Frank; the pain must have been diabolical.

Nor was this the only fright we had. The next day, when we were almost ready for the attempt, they transferred the

59

sergeant-major and sent an *appuntato*, a senior corporal, to take over. He was an unpleasant fellow. We saw at once that he was going to keep us inside the cell all the time, but this was all to the good. And we were afraid he might check the cell when he took over. But not a bit of it. He counted the two of us carefully, looked up at the tiny iron-barred grille near the roof, and locked us in. We began to realise an important factor in the mass of knowledge that an escaper must acquire. It was this: That the average prison warder has a very dull and monotonous job. Few people attempt to escape from jail (I do not include, of course, an ordinary P.O.W. camp, where the set-up is quite different), so the natural result is a slackness caused entirely by sheer boredom. The walls and bars seem enough to keep the average prisoner safe, and there is little for the warder to do except wonder when he is going to be relieved and get back to his billet for a glass of wine. The prisoner, on the other hand, once he has made up his mind to escape, has nothing to do except to think about it. He is permanently on his mettle, and everything he does or thinks has the one final object—escape. Everything is tuned to that objective. No detail escapes his attention, and he soon becomes a sharp-witted opponent for the relatively dull-witted guard to deal with. In our case we could add the fact that we were both trained in a lot of most useful things, both by nature and by the War Office, and were considerably more intelligent than the Sicilian morons, illiterate peasants, and uncouth youths they put in charge of us. The set-up was a favourable one.

One soon develops the necessary instincts. One learns how to talk without being seen so doing, how to converse in the very fluent and sometimes expressive sign-language employed by the Recidivist; how to acquire little odds and ends that might perhaps come in useful one day: a piece of broken glass left lying about in the yard is most useful for putting a point on a pencil; a piece of string will always come in handy; a nail is handy for repairing boots; a bit of rusty wire can be made into a skeleton key. All these things can serve a purpose, and one soon learns to look out for them and hide them away quickly. It soon becomes almost second nature, and it is surprising how easily one can learn to steal.

There is, too, a complete art in conversing without moving the lips at all. It has to be done well enough to deceive a warder who may have been at his job for twenty years or more. But perhaps the most astonishing method of conversation is the sign language, which is fast, fluent and universal. It also solves the difficulty of patois, dialect, and other irregularities in the spoken tongue. It is usually used at exercise time, in the yard. The guards stroll up and down, themselves taking the benefit of an hour in the fresh air, and while the guard is facing one way, the man behind his back makes his rapid signals. A moment later the warder turns round, and back comes the reply. The system is amazing in its scope. Some of the signs are obvious, others have to be learned. For instance, three fingers placed on the sleeve mean a sergeant. Three fingers held to the shoulder or head mean a Captain, four, a Major. Spreadeagled hands across the face mean the cells, as opposed to the normal freedom of the main prison buildings. A finger in the palm of the hand means a note, a hand to the rump, expressively, is the lavatory, biting the finger-nails signifies eating, an are described with the right hand means "reply, please". So that five simple signs that can be made in a split second can mean, quite clearly and with no confusion,

"When the sergeant starts eating his sandwiches, I'll put a note for you in the lavatory; let me have a reply, please."

It is as simple as all that, and by the time we had been in the Italian prisons for a few months, we could carry on a conversation with no trouble at all. It made things very much easier.

The "note in the lavatory" is one of the main means of communication. Each prisoner has his own preferred hiding-place, usually under a stone that has been loosened and removed. Some prefer the water-pipe itself, so that if the intended recipient does not get there in time, then the note will be washed away by the next user.

When, later on, we were first put behind bars and separated, we were dismayed because of the apparent impossibility of communicating with each other. But every poison has its antidote. Once we became mixed up with the regular criminals, the scum of Naples and Taranto, good fellows all of them, we were let into some of their secrets, and found it was a simple matter to send notes, cigarettes, food, papers, matches, and other little oddments and luxuries from one cell to another. The method is interesting; it is called the *cavallo*. It consists of a long piece of string, usually made from threads of a blanket, weighted at one end

61

by a small stone picked up in the yard. The sender reaches through the bars of his door (the doors are cage-type), swings his string with the weight on the end round and round to gain the necessary momentum, then lets go, hanging on to the other end of the cord. By this means, with a little practice, the weighted end, whether it be a stone or a loaf of bread, can be made to land on the floor outside the next, second, third, fourth cell along as required. The recipient then pulls it inside his cell, and there you are. If it lands too far away, then it's either tried again, or else a blanket is thrown over it through the bars, one end retained, and dragged closer, in the same way that the chimpanzees at the Zoo recover bananas. It's all very simple and the whole thing is done in a few moments. Even wine or water can be passed like this by dragging the container, a tin or mug, ever so gently along the floor from one cell to another.

Finally, there is always the stand-by—the guard who can be bribed. There is also a technique to this. One starts with a friendly gift of a loaf of bread to a hungry sentry. The next gift requires some little favour, if possible. Once the beginning is made, the rest is easy. Like the source of a river, it leads to bigger things.

But more of this in its proper place.

By now there were other details to be attended to, details that were full of interest for us because they meant that the donkey-work was finished. There was no more tearing at stones, straining against iron bars with a tiny saw; now the excitement began. We decided to make a rope from our blankets, to get from the shelf outside the window, down on to the road below, a distance which we knew to be two-and-a-half storeys. We had been saving as much bread as we could, but only had two loaves between us; but this was of little importance, the main snag being the lack of water-bottles. Again, we were lucky. Unexpectedly, an officer came to see us. He was prompted solely by curiosity, but he talked with us alone for a little while and this helped us considerably. For, as soon as he had gone I produced one of my hidden five-hundred-franc notes, and said to the sergeant-major, "Look what your officer gave us. We told him we had no money to buy food with so he gave us this." It sounded a bit thin to me, but they fell for the fiction, and agreed to buy us food with it. All the prisoners had money of their own and were allowed to spend it, though not to keep it in their cells. There was some sort of crude accounting system which kept the guards in small change. We, of course, had not been able to benefit from this; a display of money after we had been searched so carefully and so often, would have been disastrous. They bought us nuts, dates, milk and a bottle of wine. They would not buy huge quantities, but only a daily ration; however, this was better than nothing.

We gave some of it to the prisoners in the cell opposite, some nice lads who were in jail for an assortment of crimes ranging from theft to anti-fascism. Theoretically, we were not allowed to talk to anyone, but we had soon made ourselves friendly and got to know them. Some of them had committed an amusing robbery. They were N.C.Os. of an Armoured Car Brigade of the ill-fated Centaur Division. They had entered the house of a wealthy merchant in Sfax while they were on a week-end pass, and searched it quite openly. When they came to a vast hoard of money in the safe, they invented a law against hoarding, and confiscated the money, just over a million francs. They told the owner to report to the station in the morning for a receipt and to make a statement, and got away with it. It seems quite incredible. They were discovered, of course, and arrested. But the money had been safely buried, sealed up in water bottles. Now they were in prison awaiting trial or the advent of the Eighth Army, whichever came first. They were sitting pretty, with a fortune waiting for them at the end of the war. They were good fellows. We shared our wine with them, keeping the bottle (which was to be our water-bottle). The next morning they sent us an Army *boracia* full of wine, and we managed to hang on to it. It was a well-timed incident, as now we had a *fiasco* and a proper metal bottle for our water-supply, a good ration for the five days we thought it would take us to reach our lines.

There was a nasty accident at the last moment. While checking the window, I slipped from the board and fell. I threw myself sideways and landed on my shoulder on the stone floor. Frank was staring at the window, white-faced. The cement crust had cracked and a piece had fallen out. The white sky showed in a horrible bright patch where the straight silhouette was broken. Just at that moment they started unlocking the door.

I ripped a piece of cardboard from our "mattress" and

whispered quickly to Frank, "Quick, leg up. Hurry, you bloody half-wit."

He hoisted me up on to his shoulder and I pushed the straight edge of the cardboard into the "box" between the sky and the cell; it gave the impression in silhouette of being part of the original wall. I dropped down and fell to the floor where my blankets were, just as they opened the door. Frank was lounging unconcernedly against the wall, the picture of innocence. From the corner of my eye I noticed that the window line didn't look too good; I breathed a prayer.

An officer appeared at the open door and informed us that we were to be flown to Italy the next morning. He told us to be ready at the crack of dawn.

I said, "I will tell my servants to pack my bags. Do I need tails?"

He stared at me and slammed the door. He didn't come into the cell. He didn't notice the window. I said to Frank, "Only just in time."

Frank said, "I am not a bloody half-wit."

"Sorry," I said. "This is getting too bloody exciting. Bound to get a bit short-tempered."

We planned to go as soon as it was really dark. We reckoned about ten minutes to get through the window, another five to reach the street, five or ten for reconnaissance, and then . . . darkness. What lay ahead after that was guess-work and the problems would have to be solved as they arose.

The minutes crept by very slowly. We packed the nuts and dates into our pockets, checked that the two bottles were filled with water, tied the blankets together. It seemed to make a very short rope. We had to tie them near the middle, corner to corner, because they were so old and worn. It made a very bulky and not too secure means of descent. I hoped we should not have to use it.

I said, "You know, this is not very original. Everybody makes ropes out of blankets."

Frank said, "Well, what would you rather have, a silk ladder?"

"I would prefer something more original. This is most unimaginative."

"I do not like imagination. It is a most useless achievement, the imagining of things. It is always something painful that one imagines."

He heaved on one of the knots. I said, "I could not agree with you less. If I had not an aptitude for imagination I should have gone mad two days after they first put us inside. As I have, I was able to imagine the most delightful things."

"Such as what, please?"

"I imagined that the piece of meat they sometimes gave us was roast lamb, all glistening and dripping with mint sauce. Sometimes I imagined it was pork braised in sour cream. Once it was a *filet mignon*, but I had difficulty in imagining the tomato on top."

"Then you must have imagined yourself getting fatter every day."

"On the contrary. Here, if you must know, is the secret of losing weight painlessly. I had magnificent meals, and I have lost at least a stone already. This is quite an achievement."

"If the achievement had succeeded, you would not be thinking of your stomach now. You are denied by your own argument."

"The word you want is 'confounded.' But I mention this only as a simple example of the powers of a properly-trained imagination."

"Is it trained, did you say? Then can you not put it to better purpose than imagining that those horrible, slimy, warm, greasy lumps of horseflesh were steaks?"

"But of course. I sometimes imagined, for example, that you were a blonde."

"If I had realised what risks I was running I would have asked to be locked up in a safer cell." We tugged at the knots. They seemed to hold. Frank looked at me dubiously. "I hope," he said, "that you will be able to get through that hole."

"Perhaps it's a good thing the food is so bad. I've lost a lot of weight round the middle that might have been a nuisance. It's an ill wind . . ."

"What is an ill wind?"

"An English proverb."

"So now I have to have an English lesson? I would rather get through that window first."

I looked at the sky. It was quite dark. I said, "Ten more minutes."

We waited in silence. The guard at the door was singing quietly,

"Perchè, Lili Marlene . . .
Perchè, Lili Marlene?"

Otherwise there was silence. I climbed upon Frank's shoulders and struck the plaster a light blow with the heel of my hand. It was something of a ceremony. Frank squinted up at it and said,

"Jesus Christ. We can get a battalion through there."

The window looked enormous; it was magnificent. I pulled away the iron bars and handed them down. Then I slithered to the ground and grinned at Frank. It was too good to be true. I boosted him up on to my shoulders, and then felt his rubber-soled boot on my head, tearing at my scalp. He was a long time, and I was listening to the singing of the guard. I thought, *Keep singing, you bastard, keep on singing.* I saw Frank force his shoulders through the window, and for a few moments his feet slithered noisily along the ceiling, making a horrible noise. The guard was still singing,

"Una volt' ancora, la voglio salutar'
E poi contento, partiro . . ."

Then Frank started sliding back, worming his hips back again, and I thought, *Oh, God, it isn't big enough.* I had a moment of panic when I realised how much bigger I was than Frank. Then his groping feet found my shoulders again and his head reappeared.

"What's wrong?" I whispered angrily.

"I can't reach the shelf, it's too far down."

It had seemed that the shelf was only a couple of feet below, that it would have been easy to reach. There was nothing for it. I whispered,

"Well, for Christ's sake, do a neck roll or something. Get on with it, blast you."

Once more he disappeared with a wriggle, and this time his legs grew shorter, hesitated, then with a final awful slither disappeared altogether in growing momentum. There was a horrible thud outside, and I wondered if he had broken his neck. A moment later I saw his arm come through and I handed him the bottles, the blankets, just as

66

we had arranged. I gripped the rough edge of the window, pulled myself up, clawing at the wall, one foot on the board, and thrust my arms through. There was a little difficulty and Frank whispered, "Try keeping your arms to your side," and I thought, *Jesus, it's too small, I'm too wide, I shan't make it.* Frank pulled savagely at my head till my muscles were torn, but it was no good. I dropped down inside again and slipped off my jacket and shirt, handing them through to Frank. When I tried again it was better. I put one arm through first, then my head, twisting sharply at right-angles, then almost all my shoulders were through. Grunting at the strain, Frank tugged at my arm; I found the ceiling with one foot and pushed, and wriggled, and swore, and finally I was through, the rough stones scratching my flesh as I fell. I fell on my shoulders, as Frank had done, with an awful wallop.

It was quite black now. There was no moon, and we could not see the road below us. We hoped there might be a stairway down and tip-toed round to have a look-see. There was a skylight above us, and I crawled slowly up to it, testing the roof carefully before I moved. Suddenly, there in the lamplight below, were the guards and the *appuntato* playing cards together. I felt that the light was on my face and drew back. I wandered round the roof for a while looking for a way down; there was none, so I rejoined Frank who was waiting anxiously.

I whispered, "No other way, we'll have to use the blankets."

We tied them to the bars of a window which was conveniently near; the knot took up an awful lot of the "rope" and we couldn't see if it reached the ground or not in the dark pit below us. Frank looked at the clumsy rope snaking down into the silence and muttered, "*Mon Dieu.*" He swung himself slowly off the shelf, gripping the blankets tight. His eyes were anxious as they slowly sunk below. There was the sound of a tear on the way down, but they held, and a moment later I heard a whisper, "*Va bene.*"

I was worried about that tear; I could not see where it was. After a moment's anxious thought I decided to leave the glass bottle behind; I did not fancy the thought of a fall in the dark with a glass *fiasco* in my hand. Frank had the metal water-bottle; it would have to suffice for us both. This was a lucky decision; the moment I put my weight on the rope it ripped in two with a long tearing noise and I fell to the earth. I landed on a flight of steps at the bottom, and rolled on to the road. I had let myself go limp as I fell, and I was unhurt, somewhat to my surprise, as it was a long drop down.

I told Frank about the bottle and he swore softly. We stood still for a moment in the angle of the wall, listening carefully. There was not a sound. Above us, the stars were bright and the sky was black. A cricket was calling; the rest of the night was silent.

The first obstacle was past. The worst was behind us. We were out.

Chapter Five

I SAID to Frank, "*Andiamo*."

We walked briskly away from our dark corner, ready to break into a run at the first sign of trouble. We were at the side of the prison, and we had to pass the main entrance to get on to the tarmac road. We rounded the corner, and there were the iron gates on our left. Dimly we could see inside the courtyard with the well in it, faintly lit by the lamp upstairs. The light at the window above was bright. There was no guard in sight.

Two hundred yards again to the left, and there was the main road ahead of us. There was a lot of noise here; we could hear the roaring of tanks and the drumming of lorries, and shouts and oaths in German and Italian. As we drew near, we saw that a column of German tanks was on the move and had got tangled up with a column of Italian trucks. They were both going the same way—north. We walked into the main street and turned south in the pitch blackness. There was a frightful babble of voices all round us. We walked fast. I collided with a little Italian who said, "*Scusate*", and climbed back into his truck. A German shouted down at us, "Hey, you! Get that benighted lorry off the road." I said something to him in Italian and walked on. The jam was nearly a mile long, and we stayed with it till the end, knowing it was our safest cover. We passed two patrols of Carabinieri, rifles slung over their shoulders, watching the confusion. It was hard to see them in the darkness and we were always on them and past before they knew it.

At last the end of the two columns came in sight, and we were on the open, deserted road, stretching straight to the south-west. The north star was behind us, over my right shoulder. I said to Frank, "A pity there's not a bit more of that traffic. Good camouflage."

He said, "Better speak Italian, all the time."

"Good idea. If we run into Germans, speak Italian. If we get stopped by Italians, let me do the talking, we'll pretend we're German. Wish we had scissors to cut our beards."

There was a lot of confusion around Sfax in those days. Most of the Italians were trying to pluck up enough courage to desert, most of the Germans trying to stop them. The confusion was all to the good. Nobody knew quite what was happening. They only knew one thing: they had to get north, as fast as they could. The Eighth Army was after them, like a pack of hounds.

They were grand, those first few minutes. For the first time in months we felt hard, smooth asphalt under our feet, and saw the clear sky above us, and breathed good clean air untainted by the smells of prison. But best of all, we felt free. And we were not afraid any more. I realised now how unpleasant it had been, watching the interpreter choking over his translation, saying, " . . . here . . . here in the breast . . . " and stammering in his embarrassment. Then I thought of the window of our cell, not a tiny iron grille any more, but a big, open window that the guards would see when they brought us our coffee, that horrible, watery, warm *ersatz* coffee in a dirty bully-beef tin. Breakfast. I wondered if he would drop his coffee in his astonishment, a sleepy, dirty, uncouth Sicilian guard suddenly faced with the reality that he had let a prisoner escape, before he shouted, "*Scapati, scapati*," and ran to fetch the *appuntato*. I thought, *What an impertinence, trying to keep me in your dirty, stinking prison*

69

like an animal. And now the open road was before us, the Plough was low in the sky, and there were eight hours of darkness before us. I thought, *My God, we're damn nearly home.*

We were walking fast, not talking. Our rubber boots were absolutely silent on the road; not even a squeak could be heard. We had walked for less than an hour when we heard a lorry approaching, coming from behind us. I said "Come on!" and started racing ahead. Frank panted along behind and said, "It's all right, it's got no lights." We ran for a hundred yards or more, then dropped into a clump of bushes and waited. I said, "As soon as he's level, start running. This is where we bum a ride, schoolboy style." We waited; in a moment he was level with us, and we dashed from cover and raced after it. It was travelling just about as fast as we could run, no faster, no slower. We ran like hell, our rubber soles gripping the smooth road and forcing it back.

I reached out and touched the tailboards, and spurted forward and gripped them, then pulled myself up and swung my legs underneath, where the spare wheel was. I hung on with one hand and stretched the other behind me for Frank; he seemed to be dropping behind slightly. Then he made an effort and I felt him grip my hand; our fingers touched, found a hold and he was up beside me. We swung aboard and dropped flat athwart the tailboard. There were no passengers, only a load of barrels. We stretched out on them uncomfortably, and got our breath back. I said, "That was a nice bit of exercise. Does one good to run a bit."

Frank said, "When you dropped out of sight, I thought you'd fallen. I wondered what the devil had happened. I wonder where he's going?"

"South, anyway. If he turns off the main road we'll have to jump off and run for it."

"We are very lucky, really. How fast are we moving?"

"Twenty miles an hour. He's picking up speed a bit, too."

"You think he might take us near the lines?"

"Well, it can't be very far. There seems to be just the one driver. Suppose we capture the lorry and drive home in comfort?"

"We should not be able to cross the lines in a lorry, surely. Not on the main road."

"I wonder. It might only mean a dash for the last few miles."

70

"The Germans are certain to be in strength on the road farther up. There must be lots of Italians trying to desert. I cannot believe that all one has to do is drive to the Eighth Army lines and say, 'May I come in, please?' "

"No. But we might wallop the driver, take the truck, and go on till we're stopped and then run for it."

Frank hesitated. "Of course," he said diffidently, "if you think so. But it will tell them where we are, and it might be very difficult to hide near the main road if we can't make it in one night. Suppose we drive on for six hours, which would bring us near the front, we hope. It will then be one hour from daylight and we shall have to find a hiding-place right in the middle of the German defences."

"The other alternative is to keep on board for about an hour or a little more. That will take us well out of the area in which they will search tomorrow. Then strike across country about west, or a little to the south of west. That should bring us more or less in the direction of Gafsa. Can you remember how the road runs here? It's due south-west at the moment, but I think it follows the curve of the bay."

Frank thought for a moment. "Yes, I think so. But I can't remember how far it swings round to the east; it bears south-west from Sfax, follows the sea more or less, swinging round south, then swings more to the eastward direction. I can't remember how tight that curve is."

"Then, to be on the safe side, once we get well clear of the main road we carry on as we decided; south-west. We shall bisect the line between Gabes and Gafsa. The artillery should give us some idea of where the fighting is. I think we might keep out of the way of the guns."

"Yes, I do not like gunfire, really. It is very unpleasant."

"You know, everything is very much in our favour. This truck is an extraordinary piece of luck. I have only just realised it, but there ought to be a soldier on the back here, guarding the stores. I didn't think of it before."

"Perhaps it is an augury."

"Then we stay on board for about an hour, then jump off?"

"I think it would be more circumspect. Of course, if you want to take the lorry . . ."

"No. It was just an idea. It would be very difficult later on if we did that. I should hate to have a puncture right in the middle of the Germans. It would be very awkward. We

71

shall be better off without any encumbrances. I am sorry about the water-bottle, but it would have made a frightful noise when I fell."

"It might also have been dangerous. But we shall have to go carefully with the water. How much will be the ration?"

I worked it out. "We ought to allow five days. That's half a pint a day between us. Quarter of a pint each. It is not very much. It means a moderate mouthful each twice a day, no more. That will give us a small margin for safety. It's not very much, I'm afraid."

"Once we get away from the road we shall not find any more water except by the greatest of luck."

"Well, we shall just have to manage, that's all. We have practically no food, so that won't make us thirsty. Never mind, it's only for about five days. We shall manage. We can drink the Naafi dry at the end of it."

We travelled for just over an hour before the driver saw us. He stopped the truck and got down to attend to something or other, and though we lay low, like Brer Rabbit, and said nothing, he saw us and we had to jump and run. It was still pitch dark, and he shouted at us in Arabic, so we knew he thought we were stray Arabs and were quite happy about it. We had covered thirty miles, a good day's march from the prison. We decided to walk along the road a little farther, then strike off to the right, away from the sea.

We had scarcely walked for more than five minutes when we heard voices ahead of us, German voices. They were too far away to hear what was being said, but it only meant one thing: we had to get back and move off the road. We went back a quarter of a mile and struck off north-west, at right-angles to the road. Once again, as we moved slowly forward, we heard Germans. I was loth to make a wide detour, as this would have taken us too far back in the direction whence we had come, and our plan was to get as far away as possible from the jail so that we should be out of the radius within which they would probably search. So we went south again; it meant walking straight towards those Germans whom we had first heard, but we thought we might get past them if we went fast and silently; the moon was not yet up, In the absolute silence we could hear every sound they made. We heard the scraping of a match before it burst into flame. and in its light we saw a group of soldiers a hundred yards or so ahead, on the road, gathered about the door of a house.

There was a small village, and the sea was close on the left, divided from the road by a strip of sticky, smelly marshland. We heard a man cough, right beside us. Then we were in the village, walking without noise, like ghosts, in absolute, unearthly silence.

Groups of German soldiers were all about us, talking quietly, smoking. We could see the red beacons of their cigarettes, but not the smokers themselves. I was conscious that the sea beside us was lighter than the land, and we were between the Germans and the sea in silhouette. Then there was a sentry standing in the centre of the road, just ahead of us. We were about to make a dash for it, to run straight past him in the blackness, when a match flared up behind him and we saw more soldiers whom we should have to pass. I touched Frank's sleeve and we turned round and walked back. Even as we turned, one of them called out something. We did not answer. He called again and I said something in Italian. He called *"Halt!"* and we walked on, our hearts pounding, determined not to run unless he should open fire. Two soldiers broke from the shadows on our left, quite close, and reached out towards us. One of the shadows said, in bad Italian, "What do you think you're doing? Come here." Frank whispered *"Andiamo!"* and we went. We ran fast and straight, straight along the road north. There were more soldiers ahead, shouting now, but with little excitement. I said, *"Di qua!"* and we dashed into the marsh by the sea. We bore round south again, trying to pass the village so that when the fuss was over we should be beyond it. But it was no good. Only the way to the north was open. We heard them splashing about in the water, and we ran on, north, and back to the road. Only two of them were left and we soon outstripped them and sat by the road, panting and swearing, but out of danger. I said, "That's that. No shooting, so they don't know who we are. We'll have to go right round."

It seemed we had walked into a bottleneck, of which the village by the sea was the cork. We did not know how long the neck of the bottle might be, but we had no intention of retracing our steps back to the jail. We left the road and went a little north of west.

We moved slowly, crouching low, and stopping every few paces to listen, lying down on the soft earth and searching the skyline, then moving on again, slowly, quietly, then down again to watch. We passed a gun-post, revetted with sand-bags, quite close, close enough to hear the gunners talking quietly among themselves. Once we saw the light of a cigarette-end that went sailing through the air, and we moved away, though we could not see the man who had thrown it. We crawled past two Germans who were lying on their backs talking loudly, moved a little to the north, then south a bit to correct the general direction. We weaved first right, then left, trying to keep our bearings, moving steadily on, very slowly, but steadily getting farther away. Within an hour we had come to the olive-groves and we stood up and walked in the friendly black shelter of the trees. The moon was rising now, but under the trees it was as black as ever. The soil was soft, recently ploughed, and incredibly difficult to walk in. We pushed on as hard as we could, but it was slow work, with the sand trickling down the tops of our boots. We stumbled into a lorry parked under the trees, an Italian lorry. We tried to make a detour, but whichever way we turned there were lorries, so we went straight ahead, relying on the darkness and keeping our course. We crossed a broad track and went straight ahead. At last the obvious thing happened. We walked straight into a sentry and woke him up.

I was bending down to try and read the inscription on a notice-board, when right beside me a voice said, "*Ma cosa fai?*" The unexpectedness of it shocked me. Then I saw that it was a sentry, raising himself up from the ground where he had been sleeping. I turned and ran as fast as I could. I heard him pull back the bolt of his machine-pistol, and spray the trees with a vicious shower of bullets that went whistling and whining and lipping through them. He was firing in quite the wrong direction, at least twenty degrees out. He was half running, half stumbling into the darkness of the olives. I dropped to the ground, and Frank came and fell beside me, silent in the shadow. The sentry changed his magazine, fired again, then ran back to his post. We crept away and moved on. But we knew that it was going to be difficult now. We were in the middle of a Headquarters of some sort, and we did not know the quickest way out. We kept our direction, hoping that this might be the best way as well. We stumbled into trenches in the darkness, over telephone wires, over guy-ropes, into lorries, slit trenches. Once I fell over a sleeping body which grunted and swore,

74

then rolled over in sleep again. We grew more and more tired with the exertion of moving in the soft, clinging sand. We zigzagged north, south, trying to get clear.

The hours passed and we were still in the middle of it all, and I began to worry about the approach of dawn. There were more groves, then open patches of sand, then strips of cultivation, but nothing that would afford adequate cover. And everywhere around us was the camp. When the first grey began to show behind us, a lighter grey slowly changing to silver, frightening with its serious implications, the camp was still on all sides of us. We looked desperately for somewhere to hide, and at last we heard the hammering and talking and shouting that signified the awakening of the people round us. The scrub at our feet was a bare eighteen inches high. I whispered to Frank, "Lie down in that." He stretched out, pale and anxious, and I covered him with handfuls of grass. I said, "Don't move, not the slightest movement. If you can keep still for fourteen hours we shall be all right." He stared up at me and nodded his head. He looked sad, near to tears. It wasn't very good cover.

It was almost daylight. I crawled away and lay down a hundred yards away, pulling bunches of weed and grass and covering myself carefully. As I pulled the last wisps over my face it was already daylight, and I saw that there was a lorry fifteen yards away, half concealed under a tree. I closed my eyes and slept, lying straight and still.

I awoke to hear footsteps nearer than they had been before. I saw through the tickling grasses on my face that an Arab was passing, too close. A soldier shouted at him and he sheered off. Two soldiers came quite near and chatted together. One of them, still talking, urinated and put the idea into my head, and I realised that my immobile muscles had been tensed for hours. I thought, *The Doctor always turns on the tap.* Then I thought, *It's a long time since I wet the bed.* The soldiers went away, and I watched the sun crossing the sky. It was burning my face through the short grass at midday and the flies were a nuisance.

I slept again, knowing that I should not move or snore while I slept, still in precisely the same position all the time, without the movement of a finger. When I woke again the sun was lower and I thought, *Thank Christ it's afternoon.* Then it went down too low for me to see it and the burning left my face. It stayed a long, long time out of sight, yet it was

75

still day. I wondered if Frank had slept at all, and realised that I had slept at least four hours, off and on.

At dusk the darkness was still a long way off and it seemed that it would never come. The morning had passed quickly, but now the minutes were dragging. I tried to detach myself from my body so that I would not feel the aches that were in my limbs. But that only made me feel them more, and I forced myself to think of other things. I tried to remember the lines of a play I had once known, and struggled with the long-forgotten memory. I tried to piece them together in their proper sequence and could not, and as I struggled with the flashes that appeared and then were forgotten again they took some shape and the minutes went by and I tried to race them in my thoughts to get the lines sorted out before we should have to move.

"And your song, that grew in the womb of generations for the use and joy of men, may perish; that the word may go that Greece drove bloodier war than Ilium. No, that's not right, may perish ere it takes its larger music, that the tale may go that Greece drove bloodier war than Ilium. That's a poor bargain. But these thoughts, that stir like ghosts out of a life that should have been, neglect my duty . . ."

And then it was dark again. There was noise all around us, but I knew that the worst was over. If we should be seen now, we should have to run, and we should get clear. When the noise died down I raised my head slowly, feeling the painful creaking of the muscles of my neck, and looked around. There were one or two fires, and the lorry beside me had a light inside it. I crawled on my belly over to Frank, signalled to him to keep silent, and he rose up out of the ground like a phantom. We took a deep breath in the silence and quietly walked away, still moving west. There was plenty of noise about, but the camp was well dispersed, and we moved to the left or right, guided by the noises ahead of us, and the glimmerings of the last embers of fires that had been lit before it was too dark to light fires in safety. We moved with infinite caution, not speaking, dropping to the ground frequently to study the area ahead. People were still chatting, and their voices were our buoys. Within three hours we were clear, and could walk upright again.

Frank said, "Thank God that's over. Did you sleep?"

"I slept well. But I also wet the bed."

Frank giggled. "So did I. Really, it was most uncom-

76

fortable. It is very difficult to keep quite still for so long. At first I did not think we had any chance at all. I was sure we would be seen. Did you not think so?"

"No. I thought our chances were good. If we kept still."

"Really?"

"Well, perhaps I thought we should have to wait and see. There was nothing else we could have done. Once the daylight came, we had to hide somewhere. And the grass was the only hiding-place there was. What else could we have done?"

"I was ready to give myself up. I thought we had no chance at all. I was really very unhappy."

"You looked it. I have never seen such an unhappy face as the one I threw weeds over. A corpse would have looked more cheerful."

"I thought I was a corpse already."

We came to a main road, a tarmac road, and there was a column of tanks halted there. Frank whispered, "They seem to have a hell of a lot of tanks."

"Sh . . . let's go round it."

We walked a long way to the right before the road curved north. I said angrily, "I will not go north." We turned and walked back, but the road curved in again, towards the main road. Frank whispered, "Can you see any soldiers?"

"No, it's curious. I wonder if they are parked there permanently? They haven't just arrived or we should have heard them long ago. Where in hell are the drivers?"

"I wonder, really. Let us watch it for a while. Perhaps we can walk right through it."

We walked back a little way, then lay down on the summit of a tiny dune that raised us sufficiently to permit us a good clear view. We watched for perhaps fifteen minutes. I said, "There's something fishy. I'm going to have a look. Wait here." I crawled forward, right to the road. There was no noise. The tanks, mediums and lights, stretched a long way in both directions under the cypress trees that flanked the road, under each tree a tank. It was quiet and there was no movement. I watched for a long time, then walked back to Frank. I said, "There's nobody there. We can cross."

We walked quickly back to the road, and I whispered "Don't stop," and we walked silently across. We reached the other side, passing under the black shadow that loomed above us, and walked on. Fifty yards away or more the

shadows moved and split and a voice said softly, "*Hans?*"
I said, "*Nein, nein,*" and we did not stop. The shadows
became one again as the sentry moved under the tree he had
left. Two minutes later we were in the wilds again.

Frank said, "I wonder what all that was?"

"No idea. Strange how reluctant the Germans are to use
their guns. If that had been an Italian, they would still be
firing at us."

"They are more excitable, the Italians. They get frightened
if they see a shadow, so they shoot at it. Then the shooting
frightens everybody, and they all start shooting. Nobody
knows what they are shooting at, but it makes them feel safe
if their guns are getting hot. I think it must be easier to
escape from the Germans for that reason."

"Well, I hope they stay that way. We have done well so
far. This is only our second night and we must have covered
at least fifty miles. We've time for another fifteen tonight."

"I hope we get better cover to hide in tomorrow."

"Yes. I think we had better stop as soon as the very first
light starts showing. And I think tomorrow night we might
turn south a bit. I wish to hell they hadn't found our maps."

We covered a lot of ground in the next few hours. We
passed more olive groves, a few lonely houses set by themselves under the trees, a garden or two surrounded with high
cactus. We looked for water with no success, and pushed on
as fast as we could. We were in desert country when the light
in the sky appeared, and we found a very convenient hole
in the ground which we almost fell into. It was a roughly
round hole, like a filled-in well, about four feet deep and four
feet across. We curled up in the bottom quite comfortably,
a little restricted, but confident that we should not be seen
unless someone walked into it as we had done. We had our
ration of water, and not very satiated with just one mouthful, slept. I slept most of the day, waking once to find
some goats staring down at me with their bright slit eyes,
and I saw Frank raise his arm and chase them away. I
looked out cautiously and saw the goat-herd sitting with his
back to us a few hundred yards away. He was alone. In the
far distance were the tents of the Bedouin. The emptiness of
the land was an encouraging sight.

We slept most of the day, cramped but tired, and set off
again at nightfall, a little earlier than before as the desert
was empty before us. Before long we began to feel the effects

of the water-shortage. We had drunk our fill before we left Sfax but we had lost a lot of moisture from our bodies and were not in a position to replace it. We became tired easily. On this third night we found we had to rest too frequently, and our pace was slowing down considerably. Of course, we still had water in the bottle, but had to stick to the ration in case we took longer over the journey than we had expected. As the night wore on, we felt it more and more. There was none of the sore lip and swollen throat of the desert novelist. Indeed, there was very little discomfort at all. But our legs would not move fast. We had to lie flat on the ground for a few minutes every mile or so, and these effects became worse very rapidly. Long before the night had passed, we were resting every half-hour for at least ten minutes. We walked through young corn shoots and pulled them up to suck out the moisture; when the corn was high and our trousers became wet with dew we tried sucking the water from the cloth, but there was very little of it. When dawn came, we were in an open space, vast and dry, and we lay down to sleep in a patch of scrub, secure from detection, but very worried about water. We drank our miserly ration, ate a few almonds, and slept.

When darkness came and we moved on, I looked up at the stars and said to Frank, "I think we ought to start bearing south a bit."

Frank thought for a while. He said, "Do you think we have come far enough away from the road?"

"I think so. Look. We went thirty miles south-west by truck. Agreed? After that we went at right-angles to the road, but slightly more to the left, that's west, for two nights —not very far on the first night, but a total of thirty miles at least. So we ought to be thirty miles off the main road now. The coastal belt is only about fifteen or twenty miles wide, so we should be well clear of any habitation."

"You want to turn round towards the gunfire?" The flashes of the guns were bright in the sky to our left.

"I think that is probably round about Gabes. We ought to make for a point well to the right of that. I wish to hell we had a map."

"What was the village we walked into on the first night?"

"Mahares. Where the road touches the sea."

"Then we went thirty miles to the west. That should bring

79

us a long way from the road. But I can't help wondering why that camp stretched so far. It was at least ten miles from the road."

"Yes, but I suppose there must have been a track of some sort there. The place seemes riddled with tracks going into the interior."

We walked on in silence. Frank said, suddenly, "My God, what's that?" There was a railway at our feet.

I said, "There's only one railway line around here, the one that goes to Gafsa. But it can't be that, it's running north."

"Are you sure we are facing west?"

"Well, look for yourself. There's the North Star. There's the Plough. Dead west. This line goes north."

"Must be some private line or other to one of the concessions."

But Frank did not seem convinced. I said, exasperated, "Well, where the hell is west then?"

"No, we seem to be facing west all right. I was wondering how this line came to be here."

"Let's push on. I wish to hell we could find some water."

We bore round to the south. We came soon to more olive-groves, more cactus-bordered gardens, more ploughed-up soil. The gunfire was still to our half-left, but fairly close now. It was hard to judge the distance, but it seemed about thirty miles. We stopped to rest often, but it was freezing cold while we did not move. We soon realised that we could not keep it up. We were now spending more time resting than walking, far more. Frank muttered, "I can't understand it. I feel fine, but I can't move."

I said, heavily, "It's the water; we've got to find water."

Frank said, "Couldn't we have an extra ration? We can't go on like this."

I shook the bottle. It was still half full. I said, "All right, we'll have a mouthful each." We drank very slowly and stumbled on. We stopped to rest again before we had gone four hundred yards. We covered about ten miles that night. When we stopped to rest, we did not speak to each other. We knew that our troubles were beginning.

The next night we struggled onwards, very unhappily. We came across a lot of cactus hedges, and I fell into one of them and damaged my legs with the long, poisonous spikes. We tried to find a way through, hoping we might find water

80

inside the enclosure, but we couldn't make it. We went on very slowly, stopping every twenty paces or so, and lying flat on our backs. When the sand was too soft, it became easier to crawl than to walk, and we covered a mile or two like this. In the early hours of the morning, when we had covered perhaps five miles, we saw a tent, a solitary Bedouin tent, and heard the dog barking fiercely. We were too weak to run. I looked at Frank and said, "Well, shall we?"

Frank nodded miserably. He said, "We can't go on like this. We've done only a few miles all night, tomorrow it will be worse."

It was a hard decision. We had already agreed that we would not approach the Arabs for help, as we knew they were against us. And it is hard to bluff an Arab. But there was nothing else we could do. We walked across to the tent and hailed the owner. After a while he came out and silenced the dog. I said, in Arabic, "We are Italian Police. We have lost a lorry and think it might have come this way. Have you seen it?"

The Arab looked at us a long time before speaking. He was tall and thin, and straight as a rod. He looked about forty. He said, "I have seen and heard nothing. I have not even heard your lorry."

I said, "Our lorry is a long way off, you would not have heard it. Have you seen any tracks today? Near here, I mean?"

He shrugged. "Only the usual ones. Have you come far?"

"A good way. You might let us have some water while we are here. It is a long way home."

"You are from the camp?"

I hesitated before replying. "That is not your business. Let us have some water and we will go."

"I have no water here."

"Do you wish me to take you to the camp?"

The Arab shrugged his shoulders. He went inside and reappeared with a jar of water, cold and clean. We drank very heavily, as much as we could hold, and filled our bottle. I said, "Thank you. But do not try to refuse water to the Police in future. It is not wise."

When we left him we walked north for a long way to make sure he should not learn our direction. We found we could walk miraculously fast again, and we bore round to the west, then to the south. We felt a lot better, but there was a strange feeling in the air. Frank identified it first. He said, "I wonder what he meant by 'the camp'."

"Yes, I was wondering that. It must mean there is a camp here somewhere. Do you think he suspected us?"

"It's very hard to tell what they are thinking. The water was good."

"Yes, a good thing. We'd better keep moving as hard as we can. Get well away from here. Thank God we've got some water inside us again."

"I was also wondering why there were so many cactus bushes about. Is there a road running from east to west somewhere north of Gabes?"

"No, I don't think there is."

"Are you sure we are not moving too far south?"

"I don't think so. The gunfire is still to our left. That must be on the road, surely."

"I have a nasty feeling that we are nearer to the road than we ought to be."

"Damn it, how can we be? We went thirty miles due west and we reached the village by the sea, what's its bloody name —Mahares. That must have taken us thirty miles away. And unless we move due south we must still be moving farther away from the road all the time."

"I wish we had a map, really."

If we had had a map we should have seen what the trouble was. The road also turns left at Mahares. The road also moves west for thirty miles, straight as a die. Ever since we left it, we had been walking parallel to it, a few miles off. If we had known that, we should have been saved a lot of trouble. But we didn't know it; we carried on, parallel and close to the road.

There was one further incident that night. Shortly after we met the Arab, we stumbled into a water-hole. We fell into it, literally. The ground seemed to open up suddenly, and there below us in the shallow *wadi* was a streak of wet mud. We jumped down on to it and began searching for the water. Frank took the left, I took the right. In a few moments I heard him whistle softly and ran to join him. He was sitting in a large pool of water which came up to his waist, and drinking at the same time, lifting up the water with his hands cupped together, and pouring it into his mouth. I jumped in beside him and scooped water over my head and between my lips. It was as cold as ice and had a bitter taste.

82

We had stayed there for ten minutes or more, absorbing as much water as we could, and at last, when the cold became too much to be pleasant, we moved off without a care in the world. Frank said there was a superstition that water was a sign of luck. I said, "Tomorrow we shall be home. The gunfire is no more than ten miles away." I went on without stopping, and the thunder was pleasantly near.

When dawn came we lay down in a small patch of wet corn, no more than a few yards long, and went to sleep, frozen stiff but happy.

Tomorrow. Tomorrow we should be home.

This part of Tunisia is sparsely populated save for the narrow strip along the coast. To the south, to the west, lies flat and sandy desert, and to the east of it there are at first patches of native corn, interspersed with salt lakes, then olive groves and finally, by the sea, the houses and the farms. I was perturbed, therefore, that we should now be sleeping in a corn-patch, and not the open desert. But we had come so far and so fast that complete freedom seemed too near to let us worry about the present peculiarities. I toyed with the idea of changing direction completely the next night and striking due west again. But it would have taken us farther from the now-close gunfire. We wished to skirt this as closely as possible. I fell asleep while wondering about this.

At about ten o'clock I heard voices, Arab voices, not far away. I stretched out my hand and woke Frank, who was asleep beside me, and we listened together. It seemed evident that they were looking at our footprints. I remembered that there was soft sand the way we had come. We heard them say, "There they are."

We sat up. Several Arabs approached, some of them on horseback. There were many others farther away. Two of them had dogs, fine Salukis, slim and savage. The horsemen dismounted, and the leader asked, "Who are you?"

I said, "Soldiers. Italian."

"From where?"

"From Gabes."

"English or German?"

"Italian."

"Why are you here alone?"

"Just resting. We have been up all night looking for a lorry."

They stared at us with no expression in their cold eyes. I said, "Those are fine dogs. What are you hunting?"

"Gazelle." He squatted on the ground before us. I noticed some of the others were moving off. "Do you like gazelle meat?" he asked.

I said, politely, "I like it. We must go now."

We had been tightening the loosened laces of our boots. I saw with annoyance that the sole of my right boot had come adrift. It was going to make things more difficult if we had to run. I said, "Where are your friends going? Will they not join us in a little conversation?"

He looked over his shoulder. "They have work to do."

"Well, we must leave you. May God take care of you."

Frank stood up. He said, "They've gone to fetch troops, we'd better beat it."

"Let's go."

We walked quickly away. It was strange to move in daylight. I looked back and the Arab was still squatting there. Then we heard an engine and saw a truck not half a mile away, its motor roaring suddenly as it breasted a rise in the ground. It was coming towards us. An Arab was standing on the running-board, pointing. We broke into a run, and my sole went flop-flop-flopping with every step. I tried to tear it right off, but the rubber was tough and the stitching held. We ran like hell. There was a *wadi* ahead, a small ravine, and as we climbed it we saw that the truck could not follow us for far. I said, "Keep going, we might make it."

Frank was muttering, "Jesus, not so near home, *Porco Dio*, not so near home."

We heard the lorry stop at the ravine behind us, and we looked round and saw some ten or twelve soldiers jump down, Italians. They started firing, but their bullets went wide. They crossed the ravine and followed us. The desert stretched unbroken ahead for miles. A few bullets spluttered angrily in the sand ahead, but there was nothing near enough to worry us. They fired as they ran, and I remembered our first capture, but this time it was morning; there was the whole day ahead of us. I couldn't see a way out.

We ran for perhaps a mile, pulling ahead of them all the time, hoping that something would turn up, some miracle that might come to our help. Then two lorries appeared on our right, another on the left, speeding ahead over the flat, smooth hardness of the sand to cut us off. There was nothing between us, no *wadi*, no river-bed, nothing but a racing surface of sand. The lorries were coming together and swinging round like ships at sea. The rest of a small convoy was lined up at the gully behind us in the distance. They had all come to take part in the chase, to enjoy a little excitement on the winning side. It was a relief for them and they enjoyed it.

There was nothing for us to do. We sat down and waited. One of the lorries stopped with a flurry of dust, and a German officer stepped off the running-board. He asked, "Are you wounded, please?" very politely, and I shook my head. He was carrying a Walther automatic, and he carefully extracted a bullet from the breech, keeping the muzzle correctly turned away, then slipped it back into his holster. He asked, "Your names and numbers, please?" and we invented names and gave them to him. He said, "Are you Desert Group, please?" and I nodded; on the spur of the moment it provided the best reason for our presence there. He nodded his head and climbed into his lorry, leaving us to the Italians who had now come up. They all crowded round us shouting at each other, and the German looked down his nose at them and signalled to his driver to move off.

The soldiers searched us again, picking up the oddments that the first searches had missed, still not finding our money, the hacksaw or the compasses. They put us on the back of the lorry and we drove off. We said nothing to each other, because there was nothing we could think of that would fill the bill.

A few hundred yards back we drove into a Brigade H.Q., well concealed in a deep valley. The officers there wanted to have nothing to do with us. We were to be handed over to the Carabinieri. When we heard this, we looked at each other. They would soon find out who we were. The truck moved off again and in a very short time we turned into the main road. It was right beside us, not more than two miles away. Frank stared at it, then at me. I was astounded to see it so near.

As we turned north the clamour in the south redoubled its vigour. Across the open space of the desert, past the Germans guns which were thick by the road, past the burned-out lorries and charred tanks, beyond the camouflage netting and the brushwood, over the sand-bags and the confusion, the shouting and the silent waiting, new columns of dust were being swept on the wind like the smoke of a hundred fires.

Twenty miles away, the Eighth were moving up.

We took the road north to Sfax.

Chapter Six

THE dust-begrimed troops of the Eighth Army whom we had so closely and so slowly approached receded into the background of the battle with distressing rapidity. They were advancing, and advancing fast, but the truck that took us in the opposite direction moved faster and rolled along the main road undisturbed while the battle developed behind it. We stopped about twenty miles back and were led into a camouflaged compound by the side of the road; a board stuck in the sand depicted a flaming grenade, the badge of the Carabinieri. Several soldiers stood guard over us while we lay in the grass and slept a little.

We awoke to hear them telephoning inside an adjacent tent and learned that they had discovered our identity. They sent more troops to guard us and handcuffed us; to make doubly certain they chained our legs together and gave us a little lecture to boot on the subject of the Carabinieri's accurate shooting when the necessity arose. They advised us not to attempt to escape again. We were too tired of it all to pay much attention to what they were saying. But we heard them discussing the battle and learned that Gabes had fallen. We wondered if they would sweep right through to Sfax and collect us en route.

An hour or two later we were sandwiched into a tiny car, an armed guard between us, very uncomfortable, and an officer who kept his pistol handy beside the driver. We set off north again and reached Sfax without much incident, save one or two stoppages for mechanical trouble, just as the sun was setting. We went again to the Carabinieri H.Q. and the Colonel came and questioned us about our escape. The first thing he wanted to know, of course, was the source of the file with which we had cut the iron bars. We invented a pretty fiction.

I said, "It was not a file, it was a hack-saw blade."

"But we found the file outside the window."

"Oh, that. That's not a file, it's a rasp. We used a saw on the bars. The file you found is for wood only, not metal."

"Then where did you get these tools from?"

"We stole the file in the prison. I found it lying about and thought it would come in handy. It did, didn't it?"

"And the saw?"

"We bought it off one of the guards. I gave him three days' rations for it."

The Colonel was very angry. He said to the Adjutant, "Bring me the names of all the guards." Turning to me, he asked, "Which was the guard who sold you this saw?"

"I do not know his name. He was a Sicilian."

"Where did he get it from?"

"I don't know. It was only a piece of the blade, about a foot long. He probably picked it up in some workshop or other."

"Where is it now?"

"Why, I threw it away with the rasp. We thought we should have no further use for it."

The Colonel thought for a little while. "Tell me," he said, "how did you manage to get so far away in four days?"

"We climbed on the back of a lorry."

"And the driver?"

"We told him we were escaping and promised to help him desert. We promised him some money if he could get us through the lines."

"Then why did he not take you through the lines? He decided not to desert after all?"

"Some Germans stopped the truck and we had to run for it because we were in uniform. I don't know what happened to the driver."

The Colonel was very fair. He said, "Let us admit that you did extremely well. When they told us two Englishmen had been captured we did not suspect it might be you. We thought you were hiding in Sfax itself. It was unfortunate

87

that somebody mentioned your beards. Then we suspected that it might be you and asked for a full description. I am very sorry, believe me. I myself escaped once in the last war. It is not an easy thing to do."

His sympathy, not positively valuable, was none the less pleasant. I said, "Look, not even the Germans can save Africa for you, and our Army is on the way here even now. Why not let it go at that? Most of your men will be taken within a week; why not leave us with them? It would save us all a lot of trouble and do your chaps a lot of good."

"You are asking me to allow you to escape again?"

"That's it."

"You must realise that what you ask is impossible. As a soldier you should know that."

"I do not speak as a soldier. I am trying to speak as a psychologist."

The Colonel smiled. "Then your psychology is false. You must know that when everything else is lost, honour remains."

"It was to your honour that I was appealing. You cannot in your mind regard the Germans as your allies; that is an unfortunate fiction which no longer serves the purpose for which it was invented. I am also appealing to your common sense."

The Colonel said, in French, "If I were alone, perhaps we could continue this amusing argument. Unfortunately, I am not alone. I am part of an Army, and my first duty is to that Army." He spoke Italian again. "I am sorry. Your suggestion offends me."

I said, "Well, it was just an idea. I suppose that now you will shoot us immediately?"

The Colonel was genuinely surprised. "Shoot you? But of course not. Did you not make the *domanda*?"

"Yes, we did. But this will rather upset it, won't it?"

"I see. You do not understand the peculiarities of our laws. Did you escape because you thought your appeal would fail?"

"We were certainly not sure it would succeed."

"Then there was no need for all this trouble. Your appeal will most certainly be granted."

I said, "I wish I could believe that. I do not suggest that you are deliberately concealing the truth, but I fear your sympathy towards us may bias your reasoning."

"But not at all. An appeal is always granted, always."
Turning to the adjutant he asked, "*Non è vero?*" The
adjutant nodded. He said, "You have nothing to worry
about, nothing at all, nothing."

I said to Frank, "Anything you want to ask him?"

Frank shook his head, a little sadly. He said, "I wish one
could sometimes believe these people. If they would only
tell the truth occasionally, just occasionally, it would suffice
. . . I think they will shoot us in the morning."

"My friend," I said, "thinks that you are perhaps
optimistic of our chances of survival."

"Your friend," said the Colonel, "is always too preoccupied. I have seen it before; you must explain these
things to him. There is nothing to worry about, nothing,
nothing."

It was dark before we continued on our way. The kindli-
ness of the Colonel was offset by the behaviour of the guards.
They had heard the story of the hacksaw, and we learned
from them that the prison guards were all put under arrest.
That cheered us up considerably, but the Carabinieri were
very angry and took it out of us in many petty ways. They
tightened up the handcuffs more than was necessary, and
chained my left leg to Frank's left instead of his right, so that
we could not move comfortably in any direction. In the
back of the truck they made us sit on a piece of board instead
of the floor and the board was narrow and kept slipping
down. It was very cold on the lorry, and they would not let
us have blankets, or give us water to drink. And every time
we dozed off they woke us up. Little things, but they com-
bined to increase our mental anxiety with a physical
discomfort. Once a near-by place was bombed and the
guards went white with fear; when we were past the danger,
one of them punched me in the ribs with the pulled punch of
a man who is afraid to do real damage lest he be punished
for it.

We travelled all night and arrived in the morning at the
main streets of a big town. I looked at Frank and guessed
by the expression he wore that it was Tunis. He strained his
head to look down a side-street that we passed and I saw that
his eyes were moist. I guessed correctly that his family lived
in that street.

They took us to the prison there, which was an old
Government building. It was full of soldiers who had

mutinied and were kept locked in the big rooms with heavy guards of Carabinieri outside the doors. They gave us a room to ourselves.

The prison Commandant was a Captain, a very unpleasant fellow indeed. As soon as we arrived he called us in and told us not to try to escape. He said, "It will not be worth your while. I am pleased to be able to give you very good news." He paused, "You are to be exchanged for two Italian prisoners. The exchange will take place very shortly. The Italian officers have already arrived in Switzerland."

For a moment I was stunned by the suddenness of it. Then I realised that it was not true. I said so. The Captain called to the guard and summoned a priest, a tall, white-faced man with black hair and black robes. He said, "These unfortunate fellows do not believe that I am telling them the truth when I say that they are to be exchanged with Italian officers. They think I am lying to them."

The priest nodded his head and said, "It is true. An exchange has been arranged." I began to believe it. Frank said savagely, "Before you say any more, Father, you should know that I am a Catholic."

"It is true, my son," the priest insisted. Frank was livid.

"It is a lie!" he shouted. "It takes months to arrange an exchange. Why do you lie to us?"

"That is true," the priest said. "It takes a long time. But we are exchanging you for two Italian officers who have been waiting a long time for an exchange. You are very fortunate."

Frank was silent. When we got back to the cell, I asked, "You don't think it's true? They do arrange exchanges you know. If Mohamed did escape and he reached Cairo, it is at least possible."

Frank said shortly, "It is all balls. When will you learn not to believe these people?"

"I suppose you're right. It does seem a little early. I suppose he's afraid we shall escape again while he is responsible for us. But I thought priests are supposed to be models of righteousness?"

"They are worse than the others. I know. Because you are not a Catholic you think that Catholic priests are virtuous."

"I do not think any priests are virtuous."

"Well, I tell you he was lying. Exchange! Pah!"

"Then it is a very dishonourable trick. But perhaps I

90

would do the same thing; I suppose any methods are fair in the circumstances. A story like that would be worth fifty locked doors if we believed it."

"The priest should not have supported such a wicked lie."

"Now I suppose we have to start all over again."

"They will fly us to Italy in the morning."

"They might not find it so easy. Since we escaped from Sfax there has not been one hour when we have not heard bombing. The airfield here must be in the hell of a state."

"That is true. And this is the only field they have left. It would be nice if the Eighth Army got here first."

"There is also the First Army coming in from the west."

"I would prefer the Eighth Army. The First do not move fast enough."

"We shall see. I wish they'd give us some food."

"There are some very good restaurants in Tunis."

"I'll settle for a mess of beans. Even rice. I am very hungry."

We banged on the door and shouted for food. Surprisingly enough, they brought us some. It was rice.

They flew us across the next day in a Savoia Marchetta, with a guard of one warrant officer and nine Carabinieri. The N.C.O. was a thick-set stolid policeman of about fifty years. He looked disagreeable and wore a stern expression like a mask that slipped off when no one was looking and exposed instead a bovine heaviness. He was going to treat us Firmly, but Justly, in capitals. Everything he did was in Capitals. He said, "You will Talk to No one. If you want something, ask Me." He was going home to Sicily, and was precisely like a child looking after an infant at the seaside and pretending he wasn't really enjoying it but just Doing his Duty.

We made two attempts to get off. The first time we went aboard, the strong cross-wind blew another aircraft into us as we taxied across to the runway. There was a sudden ripping, tearing, screeching sound, and I saw with alarm that a knife of fabric was ripping its way down the fuselage towards us, cutting into the body of the plane from the tail end, and bits of brown plywood and white aluminium were opening before it like the sliced water at the bow of a ship. I thought at first that it was a burst of machine-gun fire and we threw ourselves on the floor, all tangled up with our arms and legs. When we looked up the Carabinieri were nowhere in sight. Then one of them reappeared at the doorway, white as a ghost, shouted "Air-raid" and dropped out of sight again. I thought, *This is a fine thing, now we shall blow up with the aircraft.* Then the pilot appeared, and said quite calmly, "It's all right, nothing to be afraid of."

I said wrathfully, "How would you like to be chained up on top of a thousand gallons of petrol in an air raid?"

He said, "It's not an air-raid. Now I don't have to go to Italy after all."

The warrant officer appeared, looking sterner than ever, and said, "There has been an unfortunate accident. We shall have to find another aircraft."

They helped us down the steps of the plane, while the pilot inspected the damage cheerfully, and we went back to the airfield buildings. There were more than a hundred assorted aircraft on the field. Frank growled, "What the hell are the Spitfires doing?"

I said, "Well, maybe we shan't go after all. If they raid the place tonight with this lot here, we shall never find another aircraft."

The office buildings were full of senior officers, all very angry and most of them frightened. They all had priorities. There must have been twenty priorities for every available seat. I began to be certain that we should not get away.

Three hours later, they found us another plane.

I said to the warrant officer, "Now that we're safely aboard you might at least take our handcuffs off in case there's a raid."

He replied, "If there is a raid, you will be released in time."

I said, "Yes, like hell we will, I saw how you tried to save your miserable skin last time."

He said, "You will please not dispute my authority." He was very angry with us.

We took off without incident; the plane was hopelessly over-loaded and I thought we should never make it. I was afraid, too, that we should meet trouble on the way. But we arrived in Sicily safely, and circled over the pretty little grey houses among the green fields and the splashes of red earth. We landed at a place called Castelvetrano. The aerodrome was small, and the buildings, that had seemed so neat from the air, were bomb-damaged and badly scarred. Neither were the little houses so pretty as they had first appeared, but the air was clean and fresh and cool, with none of the African heaviness about it. It was very pleasant.

They took us to the local lock-up for the night. It was one of the foulest places I have ever seen. The Carabinieri on guard wore the big airplane hats; they were all fat, and they all looked like Napoleon, but very dirty. The cell they put us in was wet-floored; it was urine, for the bucket in the corner had no bottom to it. The stench caught in the throat. I started to protest, but they pushed us inside and slammed the double doors, locking them both. We heard them place a guard outside in the corridor. It was quite dark in the tiny room, and the only light came from the peep-hole. There was a short plank let into the wall, and two wet and ragged blankets, blankets in the technical sense in that at a stock-taking they could have been ticked off as "blankets, two", were on the floor. We passed a wretched night there, choking on the poisonous air, and in the morning they came and took us away.

I said to the N.C.O. in charge of the prison, calling him *apparechio*, which always offended the Carabinieri, "When my people come here, I will personally see to it that you yourself wash your cells out. Then I shall have you discharged." He stared at me in silence. As the *Sergente*, the most important man in the village, it was highly probable that nobody had insulted him for twenty years or more.

They took us to the station for the start of our long journey north, in a buggy. A decrepit old horse, a decrepit old driver, and brightly-painted wheels that creaked and groaned as they turned. It was delightful. The driver was white-haired, and had white stubble on his chin, and smoked a pipe that was even closer to final ruin than the cart itself. The village in the early morning was very lovely, and the women were drawing water at the fountains, splashing about the mud in their bare feet, and carrying the water away in jars on their heads like Arabs, moving with the easy grace of animals. The old driver looked at us out of the corner of his eye and winked. The road was a mixture of cobbles and sand, and the warrant officer rode beside us in the cart, the others plodding behind with their rifles on their unpolished slings slung across their shoulders. I thought, *If this is the Imperial Chariot, we ought to be walking beside it; these people don't know their history.* I told Frank, but he didn't think it was funny.

93

We waited an hour or two at the station, locked up in a cell there. They even had cells at the station. The *capo-treno* in his gold cap came and stared at us and checked our handcuffs in order to assert his authority as commander of all that went on about the station, and at last the train slipped quickly in and we went aboard. There was a crowd of schoolgirls in the big compartment, and one by one they came and stared at us and giggled, sucking oranges and whispering to each other and staring wide-eyed. But before the train started the *capo* came along and ordered us into the guard's van. It was an order at last that he could insist upon being obeyed. He was the *capo*, the man in charge, an important person who sometimes went down the line as far as Messina.

The train journey was a nightmare, but only of agonising boredom. At first, there was plenty to see, and the earth was red and green, and there were orchards, and yellow lemons, and ripe peaches in baskets, and little bruised apricots, and strings of dried figs, and fresh figs, green and black, and boys shouting "*Mandorle, mandorle!*" holding up their almonds in little cups; then more oranges, and white-lined peel, lying in the sun, and a few big-shaded walnut trees. But we stopped so often that the zest was lost. The petty officials at every halt came to inspect us in their red hats, black hats, gold hats, the gold hats always more important than the others, demanding information from the guards and staring at us unsmiling. The guards stole fruit from the sellers, snatching it from their baskets and leaving the boys in tears, and shouting "*Arabo!*" at them. Not once did they remove our handcuffs.

We stopped the night at another tiny village, and the next night after that, and the third. We were creeping round the coast to Messina, stopping for hours at every tiny station, stopping sometimes where there was no station, just stopping for the sake of stopping, it seemed. At each tiny halt there was a cell or a locked room where we spent a few restless hours, always handcuffed and restless. We lived on fruit and an occasional piece of bread. None of us, neither the guards nor ourselves, had any rations. Sometimes the warrant officer procured a loaf or two at one of the stations, and shared it out carefully, a large piece for himself, and smaller pieces, all equally and scrupulously divided, for the rest of us. Once or twice we were bombed, from aircraft high up in the pale bright sky, just an occasional flash showing when the sunlight struck their slender bodies, and we were rushed off the train into the dubious cover of the nearest rocks. Sometimes we were held up for half a day while the line was cleared ahead of us, and when we arrived at Messina we had to wait two days for the ferry.

On the mainland of the Continent the line was in better condition. It took us three more days to get to Naples. Our guards were stopping there and we thought we might stop there too. They put us in the usual station cell while they went to find transport, but the *capo-treno* had some objection; or would it be the *capo-stazione*? It was one of the hundreds of *capi*. They left us at last on the main platform, and we watched the people go by. It was our first sight of wartime Europe, and was very interesting. There were a lot of women about, well-dressed, with silk stockings and make-up and smart clothes, all hurrying to and fro, catching trains, missing them, shopping and gossiping. The war seemed as remote here as it had seemed in the green fields of Sicily. There were a few troops hanging about in their dull grey-green uniforms and dull grey leather, with enormous kit-bags, quite dwarfing their owners, slung athwart their shoulders. Few people seemed to notice us. Those who did, stopped and stared for a moment, then hurried on with their own affairs. Everyone was hurrying. The warrant officer came back and took us out to a waiting taxi, closed in like a Black Maria. We were able to see very little of the town. Then the car started climbing steeply, and I thought, *Ah, we're going to the Fortress; at least we shall have a decent view.* It didn't occur to me at once that we were not likely to be given a room with a view.

It was the Fortress all right. We got down from the taxi inside the gates, and had a quick look at the bay and Vesuvius in the near distance, with vineyards like a travelling-rug over its feet. Everything was green and lovely; only the walls of the Fort were harsh and grey. Then the doors were pushed heavily to behind us, and we were shepherded down length after length of cold bare corridor, where the white light came slanting in from recessed windows set high in the massive walls. It was cold here, monastic in severity, and the boots of the soldiers rang loud and uncouthly on the worn stone floor. It was made to be trodden by sandals or to ring to the echo of armour; hobnails seemed to be a depressing anachronism. We were officially handed over and the Commandant came to see us. He was a fat little Colonel, a frightened little man of fifty. He stared at us and said to the Adjutant, "Have you ever seen anything so filthy? They look like beasts."

I said, "Your compatriots have not allowed us a wash since we were captured. They do not regard washing as a necessity among civilised people."

I used the term *la gente civilisata* which the slogan-boys were so fond of. It was painted all over the walls: *"Civilised people do not spit on the ground . . ."*

The Colonel stared. He said, "You look like an animal."

I gave up.

They searched us once again—this was quite a customary routine by now—and took us to two cells on the other side of the building. They were dark and the double doors were locked, but there was a clean smell of disinfectant about them. The heavy wooden door, outside the long iron-barred inner door, kept out all the light except for what penetrated the peep-hole. We discovered later that this system was in general use; the wooden door was an added precaution and closed at night-time, the iron bars sufficing during the day. Furthermore, it was a very simple form of punishment; if the warder lost his temper with a prisoner, he just slammed the outer door and left him in the dark. The effect of being blacked out in this way, knowing that everyone else was enjoying the daylight, was a very severe punishment, and a very unpleasant one; it seemed to tear one away from the companionship of the others in the adjacent cells.

In a little while a corporal came and let us out for food. We were very hungry. He told us we could have our meals "out here", which was a very small yard, the roof, perhaps, of a small room below. It was no more than a few yards square, but it was indeed a cheerful change from the cells, being open to the sky. The walls, which were of reddish brick intermingled with the original stone, towered up very high and straight, so that one felt one was standing inside an open hearth and looking up the chimney; at the top of the red walls were green creepers hanging down, yellow green and clinging as though to avoid falling into the depths of the prison.

The corporal asked, "Are you hungry?"

"We haven't had a proper meal for ten days."

96

"Ah, that's bad. But we have plenty here. You like *pasta*?"

"Is it *al napolitano*?"

"It's not bad. But there's plenty of it. They sent a large party away just before the meal was served. They do that sometimes if they want to annoy them. Wait here."

He left us in the tiny yard and returned with two steaming *gavette*. He said, "When you've finished this, I'll get you some more. It isn't always you can get a good meal in prison."

He watched us curiously while we ate. Then he said, "How does the war go in Africa? Is it nearly over?"

I raised my eyebrows and nodded my head in that gesture the Italians have which means *"Poveri noi!"* He said, "Ah, I thought so; we have lost the war already, now we shall begin to pay for it. We have a very good Army, perhaps the best in the world, and yet we always lose our battles. I cannot understand it. Do you think they will bomb Naples more now?"

"Won't you get into trouble if you talk like that?"

"You won't say anything, will you? It's what everyone wants to say, but they are afraid. I am afraid too. Only, I would like to know what is the true position. They told us we had sunk the American and British Navies; then thousands of ships came out of the sea and chased us all over Africa. Were there really three thousand of them?"

"Perhaps more."

The corporal was thoughtful. He said, "How can we make war against the Americans? They are too rich. The English are too rich also. That is why they have so many mercenaries. It is good to be rich. Then it is possible to pay others to fight instead."

I reminded him, "We also fight, you know. It is not only the 'mercenaries' as you call them."

"Yes, I suppose so. Do you think the British troops will come here, to Italy?"

"Of course."

"I do not think so. I think they will stay in Africa and make peace. They will not dare to attack Europe. We have defences everywhere. We are very strong here."

"We shall see. Why are we put in separate cells?"

"The Colonel said so. He said you are very dangerous. The Carabinieri told him about the men you killed."

I didn't get that. Frank said, "Ask him what the hell he's talking about. He says we killed some men."

"What men?" I asked.

The corporal grinned. "The two Carabinieri. Don't worry about me; we don't like them either. They are all bastards. *Siciliani.*"

Frank said, "For Christ's sake find out what it's all about. He's saying we killed a couple of their police. They'll make it very difficult for us if they think that."

I said to the corporal, "We haven't killed anybody at all. What goes on?"

The little man was still grinning. He said, "All right. So you didn't kill them." He winked enormously. "I wish I could kill two Carabinieri. I do not like them; they are very brutal. Is it true that they send a hundred bombers at a time now?"

"More, sometimes."

"*Porco Dio!* What would a hundred bombers do to Naples? This is a big city. Many people."

"Have they bombed here much?"

"They come sometimes and bomb the port. It is very dangerous when they come. Too much noise. I do not like being bombed."

"It will be worse now. Africa is nearly finished, and then they will start on Europe."

The corporal nodded. "You will be lucky, up in Gaeta. There is nothing there to bomb."

Frank said, "What's that? Ask him what he said, didn't you hear what he said?"

"I heard what he said," I answered, "but I don't know the place he mentioned." I said to the corporal, "Where did you say?"

"Gaeta. You're being sent to Gaeta, on the road to Rome. It is a very good prison. All the prisoners want to go there."

"Get that Frank?" I asked. "Know anything about this place, Gaeta?"

"Yes, I do. It is supposed to be very good there. Ask him how he knows this?"

"How the hell can one prison be better than another? All you ever see is iron bars."

"I don't know, really," said Frank. "All I know is that it has a very good reputation. Find out what he knows."

I said, "How do you know we are going to Gaeta?"

The corporal tugged at a broken bootlace. "I heard them say so. I heard them telephone the railway."

"Do you know anything else about us?"

"Please don't say I told you. I should get into serious trouble. I heard them say you were going to Gaeta. They said you were condemned to death and were waiting for *la grazia.*"

"Does that mean our appeal has succeeded?"

"An appeal is never refused. They never refuse it."

"Are you sure about that?"

He replied, "Look, two years now I have been in the prison service. Every month, they want to shoot somebody. Every month they make an appeal. Every month they change their minds. Nobody has been shot here for five years or more."

I said, "Hear that, Frank? I am beginning to believe that they are perhaps more slap-dash about the imposition of their sentences than we are. Looks cheerful to me."

Frank turned away. "I don't know. I don't know what to believe. I wish they would tell us, one way or the other."

I asked the little corporal, "Do they shoot people at Gaeta?"

"No. no. That's in Rome. Gaeta is for *ergastolo.*"

"Frank," I said, "what the hell does that last word mean?"

Frank was excited again. He said, "My God, I believe that's right. I heard somewhere once that Gaeta was for life imprisonment. That's what that word means, life imprisonment. I believe it's true."

"Well, that would be very pleasant. A life sentence is just up my street. Gives us plenty of time to think ways of escaping."

"If that is so, it is good news. They are very—how do you say—slap-dash in their legal methods, and it is possible that they would keep us there for years without telling us the result of our appeal. If only they don't shoot us I will be quite happy." He added wistfully, "I would much rather have a life sentence than be shot; then we can escape and keep on escaping. We are bound to succeed at last if we try often enough."

"In any case, a few years in jail won't hurt us. Quite an experience. No responsibilities, no worries . . ."

". . . no women," said Frank.

99

". . . no bills to pay. Yes, no women too." I said to the corporal, "Why is Gaeta such a good place? Isn't one prison the same as another?"

"I don't know. But they all like Gaeta. You see, a prison is like a woman. What is a woman? A face, two legs, two breasts—nothing else. But although all women are just the same, some are better than others. *Non è vero?* Some have big breasts, and then it is good. Others, well, *non c'e niente,* and then it is not so good. It is like that with a prison. It is always cells and bad food and no wine. But in some places the courtyard is a little bigger or there are vines on the wall, and that is good. It is like the woman with the big breasts. Others have small courtyards, or no salt in the bread, or a bad sergeant-major, and then it is very bad. It is the small things that count. And there is always the difference. That is why, perhaps, Gaeta is a good place to be in."

"So Gaeta has big breasts."

The corporal giggled. "Very big. You will see."

"When do we move?"

"I don't know. I heard them telephoning, so it might be soon. Perhaps tomorrow morning."

"Do we have to stay in separate cells?"

"The Commandant says so. It is usual, anyway. Prisoners only share cells in the very small stations, in the villages. But I will leave the wooden doors open till the Orderly Officer comes round, and when he has gone I will open them again. Please don't say I told you about Gaeta."

"No, of course not."

We chatted a little more, and then he put us back in the cells. They left the wooden doors open, and we stood close to the bars in the corner, talking over our chances. We came to call that corner "loungers' corner" because it was the habitual lounging-place for all prisoners in solitary; from the angle made by the stone wall and the iron door one could talk quietly with one's neighbour; a "friendly" prisoner was one who more or less lived in this corner, as opposed to the more comfortable but less conversationally suitable seat on the bed. It was strange at first, talking to an unseen listener, but we soon got used to it. They closed the doors when the Duty Officer came, and forgot to open them again. I banged on the door later and told the guard there was no bucket in my cell. It was not the one we had spoken to before. He said gruffly, "Well, use the floor."

It was the next day that they took us away. The same taxi took us to the station. The same crowds of people were there, ignoring us or eyeing us curiously as before. We could hardly blame them for staring; we must have looked a frightful sight. We had had no bath for two months or more, and no shave or haircut for nearly four. My hair was hanging down to my shoulders, and when I caught the startled sight of my face in a mirror I was astonished to note that my ears had almost disappeared under a tangle of uncombed multi-coloured hair. We did indeed look like animals.

The train journey was uneventful for the first day. We were in the guard's van again, and for food we had the tin of corned beef and two small loaves each that were meant to last the whole journey; we ate it all in the first few hours, as we had left the prison before meal-time. The train crept forward, oh so slowly, all day and night, creeping forward a few miles, then halting, then snailing onwards again. We slept fitfully, as best we could, no matter whether day or night. Early the following morning, a priest in a grease-spotted gown of dusty black came along to look at us. He was eating a piece of bread and a sardine. He watched us for a while, standing on the running-board of the slow train, and said to the warrant officer, "Why are they in chains?"

The guard said, shortly, "Spies."

The priest said, "Are they going to be shot?"

"I don't know. Perhaps."

The priest nodded his head. "Well," he said, "see they make a good job of it."

I said to the priest, *"Va fa'n cullu!"* and to Frank, "One of your holy men."

Frank was silent. The anger was visible in his eyes. At last he said, morosely, "They're not all like that." He was trying to convince himself.

"I know. Don't let it get you down."

It was easy to be unnecessarily upset by incidents like these. We found that we became quickly depressed by any unpleasant occurrence. Frank cheered up at last. He said, "Each of these people knows just as much as all the others: Sweet Fanny Adams. I hope we get to Gaeta soon."

The warrant officer heard the place name and looked at us queerly.

I said, quickly, "This is the line to Gaeta, isn't it? Is that

101

where we're going?" He refused to answer, so we dropped the subject.

Frank said, "That was a mistake, mentioning that name. I'm getting careless."

I said, just to make conversation, "This trip would have cost us a lot of money in peace time. Look how lovely the chestnuts are."

"I wouldn't mind all this if only they'd take these handcuffs off. I shall be very glad when we get there."

"I wonder if it's as good as the corporal said?"

"He was a nice little fellow, really. He came from Milan. They are very good people there. This sergeant fellow knows we are talking about where we are going. Look at him watching us. Well, let him look, the ignorant bastard. I don't see how one prison can be much different from another. But I'll tell you one thing. We shall never escape from there. It's the principal prison of Italy. It'll be like a fortress."

"We'll escape. Nothing else to do all day except think out how to do it. I've got plenty of patience. I'm sore that we didn't try in Tunis. We could have got out of there like a dose of salts."

"Yes, I agree with you, really. I think we were very foolish not to try the first night. But I was so preoccupied when they caught us that for a few days I didn't care what happened. If they had opened the doors and let us out, I believe I would have stayed there."

"I felt like that myself. Too bad, we could have got away with it easily. Only two guards to get past into the main street. And only one fragile door that we could have kicked open with our bare feet."

"And I could easily have found friends to hide us. Now it's too late."

"Well, we got a trip to sunny Italy in compensation. And we'll get out somehow. You don't think these people speak English?"

"I don't think so. They are just ignorant southern peasants; all the Carabinieri come from the south. The regular wages, about fourpence a day, attract them and they like to assert their authority over the northerners. That is why they are so hated."

"I wonder how that fiction got about: the story that we killed two of them? I suppose one lot told it to another to

102

make sure that we should be well looked after, and so it has been passed on. I see what you mean about their aptitude for lying. I think they prefer to lie, like the Arabs, unless there is good reason for telling the truth. And the duller the man, the more easily he lies because it is harder for him to find a good reason with his limited intelligence. What a race!"

At the end of the next slow day, we changed trains and, in a short while, while the sun was still low in the sky, we stopped at a small station at the foot of a rocky hill. We bundled out and stood stretching our legs and staring at the pink bricks of the waiting-room. The name-plate said, "Gaeta".

"Well," Frank said, "here we are, and now we'll see."

A big farm-cart came along and took us to the top of the hill, creaking painfully on its iron wheels over the cobbled stones. The air was cool and crisp in the damp of the evening, and there was the smell of the sea on the breeze. There were grape vines growing over the walls of the gardens, and flowers and shrubs everywhere, and big chestnut trees branching high above us. There were no pavements, and the stone houses seemed to crowd each other off the street. The men and women were poor, and dressed in sombre clothes, the women in black. A man was carrying a fishing-net and smoking a black cheroot. Another was pushing a hand-cart up the hill, filled with green vegetables. He called out a greeting to the driver of our cart as we passed.

The cart pulled up at a pair of enormous iron gates, fully twelve feet high. A soldier inside peered at us through the bars, then swung the gates open and let us in. The gates creaked shut behind us and we were in a broad grey court-yard. There were one or two convicts working there, or pretending to work, and they downed tools and crowded round us. Someone said, "*Inglesi*", and there was immediately a bustle of grinning prisoners round us. There seemed to be no discipline at all. The guards pushed their way through, shouldering the others aside angrily, but seeming to be conscious that they were in somebody else's territory. Somebody patted me on the back, and I had a glimpse of a toothless, grinning face, peering into mine. Everyone was excited and they all seemed to be friendly. We went up some broad stairs into the building, up three flights to the office. The walls were plastered and painted grey, with coloured friezes, and the corridors were light and airy. We reached the office and were handed over. The formalities completed, they removed our handcuffs and we rubbed our chafed and tender wrists.

This was to be our new home. We had arrived at Gaeta. But the future hung about us like a shadow.

Chapter Seven

WE SOON began to understand what there was about Gaeta that made it the Mecca of all habitual criminals. There was an air of indiscipline, a sort of nonchalance about the place that was a welcome change after the exaggerated sternness of the other, smaller prisons we had seen. Moreover, it was a fine old building and was kept much better than the others; the dirt was there, but there was not so much of it, and efforts were obviously made to clean the place up a bit. It housed a good many lifers, and most of the prisoners were in for ten years or more. A lot of those old-timers had more or less the run of the place; they were all "tradesmen" of some sort. Some were masons, and pottered about repairing cracks in the walls, broken steps, and so on; some were painters, and spent the day mixing colour-wash, designing friezes, painting them on, rubbing them off, trying again. Hence, no doubt, the air of freshness in the main corridors. And as it was so far removed from the fighting, there was not the enmity against us personally which we had felt farther south.

We were the first Englishmen ever seen in this jail, and were consequently a bit of a novelty. Our uniforms, especially the rubber-soled boots, were a source of great admiration. They had rarely seen proper woollen clothing

104

and could not understand that this precious, luxurious material should be used by the Army, which in their own country always got the worst of everything. The prison uniform was a bit of a mixture. Technically it was supposed to be the Army fatigue dress, a grey drab uniform made of flax. But in actual fact even this was in very short supply, and most of the prisoners were clothed in cast-off clothes of almost every category, from naval drill to civilian serge, with only one thing in common—their almost incredible raggedness. As for footwear, practically anything went. Some had the military *"scarpe di riposo"*, a sort of crude slipper made of treated cloth which did not stand up very well even to the smooth floors of the jail; others had old Army boots, not necessarily matched in size or colour or shape, and a few wore their own worn-out shoes. A good many were in the most fantastic rags, clothes made up of old blankets, bits of sacking, stiff canvas, patched-up sheeting. And everywhere was the feeling that nobody really minded what went on.

We sat around the office for a while waiting for someone to come and look at us and decide what to do. Several prisoners wandered in and out and made attempts at conversation with us. In reply to my question, one of them said, "Yes, it's good here; one eats well."

We were just beginning to understand now the importance of food. Unless one has actually known what hunger is, unless one has actually seen or faced starvation, plain lack of food, then it is hard to appreciate the supreme importance in life of a little rice boiled in water. Quality of food is of no importance any more, it is merely the bulk that matters, anything that will fill the stomach and take away the ache inside it. Life became a matter of eating and wondering if the next day's meal might be bigger.

The Duty Officer arrived at last, with the Commandant, a white-haired old gentleman with a red-veined face, kindly eyes and a weak chin. He was very surprised to see us. It seemed that our papers had been sent by air ahead of us and had not arrived; I was thankful that the papers and not our bodies had met the roaming Spitfires; there weren't many aircraft getting across the Mediterranean in those days. He told us that we should have to be kept away from the other prisoners and we should therefore go into solitary confinement. He said, "It's not too bad in the cells. There is

105

plenty of air and the rations are a little better than in the main yards where you have to fight to get them at all. You will be allowed out for one hour a day in the courtyard for a wash and for exercise."

I said, "There seems to be a story around that we killed two of the Carabinieri. I would like to state that it is not true. We are British officers, and not the dangerous thugs your people seem to think."

He replied, "I am not concerned with what you have done. My interest in you lies solely in the fact that you are prisoners in Gaeta. You will be treated exactly the same as any other convict, no better, but no worse."

I said, "We expect to be treated considerably better than all your thieves and murderers. I demand that we be treated as British officers. There's a Convention about it."

"This is a prison," said the Colonel, "not a prisoner-of-war camp. As far as I am concerned, you are two more convicts. You may keep your uniforms, however, if that will make you feel better."

We argued a bit, but it was no use. They searched us again, with the usual result. At this stage I still had my hacksaw, a little French money, my gold pieces, several compasses, the blade of a small knife, a piece of thick wire about eight inches long which I picked up somewhere and felt might come in useful, and a tiny piece of soap. For the rest—nothing. No handkerchief, no toothbrush, no comb, no razor, no towel; my pockets were empty. But I still had my wedding-ring. There was a bit of a fuss when they tried to take it from me. I had managed to keep it so far in the teeth of very considerable opposition from looters and "confiscators" alike. I told them it was too tight and would not come off, so the Colonel said he would send for a locksmith and have it sawn off.

"It is against the rules," he said, "to have gold in the prison. It will be returned to you at the end of your sentence."

I said, "Now look. There's been no trouble so far over this, and I am not going to hand it over. If you want to start a battle on our first day here, then try and get it. I warn you it will be quite a job."

This was the first time I had put my foot down, but the initial acquiescence to being kicked around was beginning to pass, and one felt the need to assert oneself to a ridiculous degree, just in order to recover part of one's own self-esteem. To my surprise, the Colonel took no offence. He told the Duty Officer to let me keep it, but to make sure every day that I still had it. I said, "Don't worry, that's the only thing they haven't succeeded in stealing from me; I don't intend to sell it." The Commandant shrugged his shoulders. He said, "You cannot stop soldiers from looting. I do not doubt that the English do the same." Well, that was true enough.

They took us down the stairs to another part of the building and put us in a huge room marked "*Nuovi Arrivati*" over the door. It had a long sloping bench down one side where twenty men could have slept, and a big window, covered with heavy bars, at the far end. The door was an iron grille, and outside it in the corridor, facing it, was a smaller window so that the wind went straight through and it was pleasantly cool. The guard asked us if we had eaten recently, and I promptly told him we had had no food at all for three days. I learned afterwards that this was more or less the stock reply. He brought two mess-tins filled with rice and water; it was pretty tasteless stuff, but we ate it with gusto. There was also a loaf of bread made from maize flour which was very tasty. The bread was good here except when they ran out of salt and then it was quite inedible.

We stayed in that room while they sorted out a cell for us. Every ten minutes or so a pair of hands gripped the bars of the window from outside and a grinning face was laboriously pulled up to the bars. They all thought us rather a museum-piece. One prisoner appeared at the smaller window across the corridor and stood talking to us across the guard. He said, "I'm your friend. Talk to me when you come out for exercise. Tell them you haven't eaten for three days." I showed him the mess-tin. He grinned and said, "That's right, don't let them starve you. Don't stand any nonsense." The warder threw something at him and he dropped down hurriedly as there was the clink of metal against the window-bars; the warder sauntered over and recovered the missile; it was his bunch of keys.

We leaned against the big window and chatted with one of the others.

He said, "English?"

"Uh-huh."

"You're going into the two end cells. I used to be in the

107

end one. You'll see my writing on the wall. Now I'm up in the *cortile*. It's better in solitary, nobody can steal your rations."

I asked, "What sort of a place is this?"

"It's all right. I've been here for three years. Only eight more to do. The war will be over by then, I expect. Keep out of the way of Garofalo, he's a bastard. They all are."

"Who's Garofalo?"

"The sergeant-major. He's in charge of the cells. He's a bastard. Used to be a Carabinieri. He's a bastard."

"You said that."

"Sure, he's a bastard."

I said, "Are they going to keep us here long?"

"What, in there? No, that's for new arrivals. They'll put you in the cells. You get sheets there. Plenty to eat too. Only sometimes there's no salt in the bread. Trombo sells it."

"Who's Trombo?"

"Trombo? Why, the trumpeter. He blows meal-times. He knows all the cooks. He can get you extra food. I must go now."

He dropped down out of sight and we heard one of the guards below swearing at him. I said to Frank, "Well, what do you think? Doesn't seem too bad here."

"I don't know, really. I would rather be here than in Naples. But I would like to know why they brought us all this way."

"It looks as though they are going to leave us here."

"Why? What makes you think so?"

"I don't know. I don't think they would have brought us all this way up here if they were going to . . . if they weren't going to leave us here."

"I hope you're right. I only hope it is not to make sure that we don't escape before this shooting business."

I could make no reply. The same thought was at the back of my own mind. Frank said anxiously, "Do you think it might be that?"

"I don't know. I hope not. I don't think so."

"We might ask the warder if he knows anything. You know, like the chap at Naples."

Conscious that I was searching for comfort, I asked the guard, who was leaning against the door, "Ho, what sort of place is this?"

"Not bad," he said. "Better than most, I suppose."

"Been here long?"

"Two years." He grinned. "It's better than being in the Infantry."

I tried to make it sound casual. "Do they execute people here?"

He looked at me strangely, "Then it's true?"

"What's that? What have you heard?"

"They say you killed two Carabinieri."

I said, "My God, Frank, see how that damn story's got around?"

The warder said, "It's true, isn't it? Or else why are you not in a prisoner-of-war camp?"

"It is not true at all. They sent us here because of some technical misunderstanding when we were captured. We expected to go to a camp."

The guard was silent for a moment, fingering his keys. He said, "They say upstairs that you've been sentenced to death and were waiting to hear about an appeal."

"That's right. Do you know anything about this appeal business? It's all strange to us. What usually happens?"

"It goes to the King. He either signs it or not."

"The King or the Duce?"

"Both, I suppose."

"Does he usually sign it?"

"How the hell should I know? Depends on the circurrstances. If you only killed a couple of Carabinieri he's sure to. People kill off the Carabinieri all the time. They'll probably give you two years instead."

I said, "Have they ever shot anybody here, in Gaeta?"

"No. They never execute people here."

"Well, that's a good thing, anyway."

"They send them off to Rome. There's a special squad there. It's a few hours away by truck from here. A special squad. Carabinieri."

Frank said, in a quiet, strained voice, "So that's why they brought us here. I think they might at least have told us."

I said, "I'm going to see the Colonel. Find out once and for all. This is doing us no bloody good at all. *Yes* one minute, *No* the next. I'm going to ask him what it's all about. Ask him to let us know one way or the other." I told the warder I wanted to see the Commandant. He called to a passing orderly, "*Ho, tu!* Call the Orderly Sergeant."

The interview with the Colonel was not as easy as that. First the Orderly Sergeant came and demanded to know what we wanted. Then the Duty Officer. Then the Adjutant. And before we saw the Colonel himself, it was already morning. We passed a sleepless, uncomfortable night, and soon after the arrival of early-morning coffee, the Commandant appeared. He said, "They tell me you want to see me?"

I felt very foolish discussing our problem with all the guards standing about and taking a very keen interest in what went on. I explained our case to him. I told him about the trial and about the appeal. I told him we did not like being so near Rome without knowing why. The Colonel was very courteous. He explained,

"If things are as you say, then there is nothing to do but wait. I myself know absolutely nothing. I did not even know till now what your offence was. No papers have arrived here about you, and it is probable that they have been lost. You have your own people to blame for that, no doubt. I have already written to Rome to find out why you are here. As for your appeal, well, I can say nothing. I do not want to raise your hopes without reason, and I do not want to depress you unduly. If I tell you it is bound to succeed, and it does not, I shall feel that I have been unjust to you. There is nothing to do but wait."

I said, "We felt that perhaps you considered it, well, kinder . . . not to tell us. I can assure you that we would prefer to know, one way or the other."

The old man smiled. "I am hiding nothing from you. As soon as I get information I will let you know. In any case, what you have done is very noble. If you are shot, it will be a very noble death." He puffed out his chest. "The death of a Patriot."

I said, "My God, don't talk like that. I do not like waving flags and I certainly don't want to die for one."

He stared. "That," he said, "is a very curious sentiment."

"All I want to know," I said, "is, are we going to be shot, or are we not going to be shot?"

"I will tell you as soon as I know." He looked at me in a pitying, patronising fashion. I was conscious that he was sorry for us. But only because of my "curious sentiments". I said angrily, "It's very easy to die in battle. You never know what's coming till it's come, and that's all there is to it. But it is most unpleasant to be cooped up in a cell waiting for a firing squad." I could not think of a stronger word than "*spiacevole*".

The Commandant said, "Yes, I suppose it is. But there is nothing I can do about that. I will let you know, however, the moment I get news."

I was conscious that I had been making excuses to myself. I made the last effort. I said, "Can you conceive of a successful appeal in a case such as ours?"

He thought it over, then said carefully, "It depends on whether you have told me the truth. If you were not fully disguised, yes. But the offence is espionage, and that is a very serious matter. If, as you say, there was insufficient evidence, then the sentence will be changed. In any case, the papers will go before a board of competent lawyers before they go to the King. If the trial was unjust, they will demand a retrial. Or perhaps just quash the sentence, in which case you would be sent to a prisoner-of-war camp. You must understand, there is little I can tell you. Even if I knew all the relevant facts, I am a soldier, not a barrister."

I liked the old Colonel. He was a kind man. When he had gone, Frank said, "Why did you say that about flag-waving?"

"About what? Oh, that. Well, I do not like that sort of nonsense."

"You should not have said it. Now he thinks we are afraid to die for *la Patria*."

"Oh, Jesus, don't you start. I warn you, if you ever feel like that, sing Land of Hope and Glory till it gets out of your system. Because I do not like sentiment in any form whatever." Frank was hurt. I said, "I am not afraid to die. I just think it bloody unpleasant and unnecessary. And I do not like heroics. Chins up, chests out. Balls. If they do decide to shoot us, they'll have to fight like hell to get us there, and you know it. Dignity is a very good thing to have. But only when it serves a purpose. And if it will facilitate my own execution, then I prefer to have none of it. So much for your realism. Now cheer up, for Christ's sake."

Frank was very miserable. I asked him what he thought about it all.

"I don't know. It is hard to know what to believe. If he had orders to shoot us tomorrow, he would have behaved just as he did."

"Christ!" I said. "Is that more realism?"

"Let us not quarrel, please. There are just the two of us."

"You're right. Let us not quarrel. I think it's best not to think about it at all. It's no good trying to weigh our chance like this. Try to forget it all."

Frank looked at me hard. He said, "You know, I believe that you really can do that. Just forget it."

"But of course; why not? It's the only thing to do."

"I cannot. I cannot forget going through Tunis in chains."

"I should have thought you would have been used to handcuffs by now."

"You do not understand. I have not been home for eight years or more. We passed the road where my house is. If my mother had been standing at the gate, I would have seen her. And you want me to forget it. How can I forget it?"

"I wish to hell we'd broken out in Tunis. We could have done it easily."

"I shall never forgive myself for that. You were right when you said nothing is impossible, we should have tried it. I think you are right, sometimes."

I was surprised into heavy sarcasm. "That's good of you. As I am your Commanding Officer or something, I am grateful for the compliment."

"No, please do not be angry. What I mean to say is that we sometimes do not pay sufficient attention to what each other says."

"You got a bit mixed up there, didn't you?"

Frank laughed and the spell was broken. "Well, you know what I mean. What do you make of the Colonel?"

"I am glad we spoke to him."

"Yes? Why is that?"

"I don't know. Comforting, I suppose. If he had said bluntly, *No, you will not be shot*, I would not have believed him. But somehow, it has given me hope. Only I do not like the realisation that we are looking for these little bits of comfort all the time."

"Why not?" Slyly, "Is it this dignity again?"

"I suppose we all talk a lot of rubbish most of the time."

"I suppose so. A pity we are going into separate cells. We are getting more like animals every day, really."

"Apparently it's not too bad. They leave the wooden doors open during the day."

"We shall get used to it."

"That's the spirit. I'm hungry."
"Me too."

They moved us into the cells during the morning. We left the big room and turned into a short corridor immediately beside the iron door. There were three cells in a row, in sight of the guard at the gate, then sharp left down another corridor there were six more. They put us in the two end ones. The cells were six feet wide, about seven feet deep, and ten or so high. Parallel to the door, on the opposite wall, a wood bench was cemented in about four feet off the ground. This was the bed. It left a space between its edge and the door just wide enough for the iron door to swing inwards. This door was made of long bars from top to bottom, with a horizontal flat bar a third of the way down; this construction was important because I saw at once that if a single bar were cut near the bottom, there would be sufficient leverage to bend it up without making another cut, and then bend it back into place again. This meant that a single cut would allow us free egress into the corridor; these cells were out of sight of the warder round the corner.

The heavy wooden night-door was swung back against the passage wall. The other cells were occupied, and the prisoners were standing close to the bars, gripping them with white hands as they watched us go by. One of them winked at me. They locked the doors on us and left, but reappeared again almost at once, with an orderly who carried our issue of kit; a pair of sheets, coarse but clean, three blankets, an enormous straw mattress, a tin wash-bowl which leaked, a mess-tin and mug of aluminium, and a piece of greasy soap. We started making up the beds at once, and there was another interruption. Food arrived, a bucket of the same, hot, sticky rice. It was better today, and had some cabbage in it. At last they left us alone. As soon as the sound of the closing door at the end of the passage announced the withdrawal of the guards, a babble of noise broke out. All the other prisoners wanted to know who we were, where we had come from, what was the news. They called out in mildly subdued voices. I let them call without answering; I was busy with the rice.

This was to be our home for the next six months or so. Well, it could have been a lot worse. I heard Frank giggle, and called out to know what was the joke.

113

"I don't know why," he said, "but I have the feeling we shall be here a long time."

"Funny, I was thinking the same thing. I suppose it's a relief that we've arrived somewhere at last. I was getting tired of that bloody train."

"What's your cell like?"

"Precisely the same as yours."

"No, it's not. Read what's on the walls."

"Eh?"

"Somebody has written here, 'I got five years for raping the wife of my officer. It was worth it!'"

I looked about me carefully for this new source of interest. The once-white walls were covered with tiny script, most of it illegible. But some of the more recent additions made good reading. They were mostly little bits of nonsense, some barely decipherable with age. I soon found remarks of a similar nature. *"The Adjutant's wife is a whore"* was one; there were four amusing lines on the virtues of a girl named Lola. I said to Frank, "I see sexual repression sets the standard here. There seem to have been a good many prisoners in here at one time or another. There is a recommendation here for a brothel in Rome."

"Oh yes? What does it say?"

"It says, '*If you go to Rome there is a good place at something-or-other street*'; it looks like '*Head of something*', do you know it? Then it says, '*Ask for Luana, she has long hair.*' I can't read the name of the street."

Frank giggled again. He said, "Does it say number ten?"

"My God, so it is."

"I know the place. It is quite a famous one. Nice women, really nice. I used to go there a lot in the old days." He sighed. "When we get out I will take you there. It is really a very nice place."

I did not miss the implied confidence in our getting out, and it cheered me considerably. Moods were very contagious in the cells.

I said, "You know, this isn't a bad place at all. There's plenty of light, and it's cool down here."

There was a window in the passage almost opposite our cells. It was big and low down, but unfortunately there was a stone wall close to it, so there was nothing to see. But it let in a good deal of light and air. The other prisoners started calling to us as soon as they heard us talking. The man on

114

the other side of Frank's cell told us his name was Pezzimento. He said he was a very good fellow, and had been unjustly convicted. We soon learned that this was quite normal. It was a form of righteousness invented to compensate for the indignities of prison, and was entirely spasmodic; they all said the same thing one minute, then discussed their criminal exploits the next. He asked what my name was.

I said, "Alan."

"That is not a name," Pezzimento said.

"All right, then. So it's Pietro." I mentioned the first name that occurred to me.

"Pietro. That is a nice name. I have a brother named Pietro."

"Glad you like it. Are there any other Englishmen here in the prison?"

"No, Pietro." Pezzimento had a slow, deep voice, solemn as a musical-comedy parson. He said, "I am your friend, Pietro," and Frank said, "Watch out, he wants something off you." Pezzimento went on, "If there's anything you want, let me know and I will get it for you. I want to be your friend. I have a newspaper here, would you like to see it?"

"A newspaper? How old is it?"

"It is very old, Pietro. But it has pictures in it. Can you read?"

"A little. I learned once."

"Ah, you went to school, Pietro?"

"That's right. How do I get the paper?"

"Put your hand through the bars, stretch into the corridor. Do you understand?"

I was mystified, but put my hand out. "What happens now, does the guard come along?"

"He cannot see, Pietro. He is round the corner. Is your hand out?"

"Yes."

There was a swishing noise. Nothing else happened. He said, "Have you got it?"

"Hell, no. I haven't got anything."

Frank said, "This is clever. It's on a piece of string, but it's fallen short, outside my door. He's hauling it back now."

Pezzimento said, "All right, we will try again. Are you ready?"

I put my arm through the bars again. This time the swish

was accompanied by a parcel that landed across my arm. I saw then what had taken place. It was a tightly-rolled bundle of papers on the end of a cord which he had swung along to my cell. He said, "Untie the knot and let me pull the string back, Pietro. And you must not let the guards see the papers."

Frank said cheerfully, "This is splendid. We can keep in touch after all."

Pezzimento said, "That's the *cavallo*, we call it the *cavallo*. You must have a piece of string, that is all. I will get you a piece. Then if you want to send me anything, you can do so. Matches, or a cigarette, or a note. Anything."

Frank said, "Watch out, here it comes."

I said, "What is it you want me to give you, Pezzimento?"

He wasn't long in replying. He wanted my wedding-ring.

Frank said, "You see what I mean?"

It was natural, of course, that we should become very friendly with the other occupants of the cells. We shared a common denomination—the battle that goes on in every prison between prisoners and warders. Whoever the prisoner, he is always automatically on the side of those who are confined with him and against those who hold the keys. Nationality no longer mattered; to our companions the salient fact was that two more new arrivals were there to share their secrets and to assist in the daily petty outwitting of the guards simply for the sake of outwitting them. The possession of a newspaper, or a piece of pencil, or a cigarette end, or some other little comfort was desirable not only for the pleasure it gave, but also because it was forbidden; and the knowledge that the guards would confiscate it if it were found gave the prisoner a compensating superiority over the warder who, poor fellow, was so stupid that he didn't know what was going on in his own cells. And so, as one of them, I found it very simple to get the others on our side; I felt that one day we might need their help.

There were normally about six prisoners in solitary besides ourselves. Some of them had been there a long time and were regarded, as we came to be regarded, as "regulars". The others were the transient petty offenders who were sent down for a few days at a time.

First of all, there was Pezzimento. He became mixed up

in everything we did because he was next-door to Frank and everything went past him *en route* to the others. If we passed a loaf of bread on the *cavallo* he knew about it; one could imagine his hungry eyes watching as it was hauled along the floor. If we asked Bruno for paper to write on, it was Pezzimento who passed the message along for us. He was a thief, among other things, a thief in the prison. He stole anything he could lay his hands on, and seldom came back from the office or hospital without having sneaked something or other on the way. He also stole from the other prisoners, and this made him very unpopular. He was tall, unusually tall for an Italian, with the yellow complexion that T.B. often causes, added to the normal pallor that was natural in the cells. His black, dirty hair was lank over his eyes. His voice was deep, heavy, slow and beautifully modulated. He was a consistent and cunning liar.

The cell next to him was normally empty, and beyond this was the comic of the solitaries. His name was Paglia, but he was known as the Worm. He had a tape-worm; and it was so persistent that the doctors had given up hope of ridding him of it, and had prescribed instead double rations. He had solemnly been issued with two mess-tins, two mugs, and two spoons, and if his double ration was not a generous double, then the rest of the day was given up to his howls of indignation. He ate most incredibly quickly, and was particularly adept at scoffing down his two bowlfuls while the others were being served so that he might get the scrapings of the bucket on the return journey. He invariably started the "*I'm hungry*" complaining, within ten minutes of the end of his meal. But he was never unhappy. He used to sing out, in a lusty shout of more volume than tune, "*Cosi . . . è la vita,*" and then wait for the reply, bellowed by the rest of the cells, "*Fin che dura!*" which never ceased to amuse him immensely. He liked it in prison. I believe he would have stayed there from preference. He was the thinnest man I have ever seen, and his white face shone like a billiard ball with an incredibly highly polished surface. He frequently sang loudly and with great enjoyment. If anyone mentioned his worm, he nearly collapsed with convulsions of laughter; it was his greatest pride. He was not very intelligent, and was a bag-snatcher by profession.

Then came Bruno. Bruno was the brain of the party. He could read and write properly, and add up figures, so he was employed as a clerk in the offices, and was in solitary because this was the only way his kit—his wash-bowl, his mess-tin—could be protected from theft while he was at work. Normally, all the prisoners, up in the main yards, carried everything they owned with them permanently; it was the only possible way to keep anything for more than five minutes. So poor Bruno, not being permitted to have his possessions in the office, was locked up at night in a cell so that the cell would serve to protect his belongings. I never quite understood the logic of this, but Bruno did not seem to mind. His work in the office gave him a certain status among the others and he resented our presence as taking some of the limelight away; until we came, he had been regarded as the sole authority, and he did not like to have this authority disputed. But every night, when he came down to be shut away till required again in the morning, he brought some tit-bit or other of news which was always welcome. He had access, moreover, to writing paper, so was always useful to know. He was a superior sort of person, and not very pleasant.

The next habitual lived on the corner, in one of the undesirable cells which were in view of the warder at the gate, a fact which precluded the use of the *cavallo*. He was known as the Were-wolf and was believed to be one. He was quite mad, perhaps dangerously so. The fact that he was born on Christmas Day, an essential part of the make-up of a were-wolf in Italian legend, rather scared them. He used to stand at his bars staring in front of him, and spitting at anyone who passed; from time to time he burst into a kind of wailing which I believe was really an attempt at singing, but not a successful one as he had neither voice nor ear, and his mental capacity was insufficient to keep the noises he made under any sort of control. There was always silence from the others while this wailing went on.

And one day, later in the evening, his wails reached a pitch not heard before. The warders came anxiously to the gate, but were afraid to come inside. At last the Were-wolf collapsed on the ground, and a little later his shrieking stopped. A large crowd of guards came in and carried him off, and we heard no more of him. His name was Madera. On occasion he seemed to regain a certain debased sanity, and at these times he was most offensive. He knew what his nickname was, and he knew how superstitious all the others

118

were. So sometimes he set up a sudden howl in the middle of the night in what was intended, no doubt, as an imitation of a wolf. Actually, in the silence, in the heart-beating blackness of the sleepless early-morning hours, these howls sounded like a visitation from all the banshees in Ireland, and were very frightening. We were not sorry to see him go.

Then there was Rosso. Rosso was a thoroughly unpleasant little man who spent hours every morning combing each black wave of his hair into immaculate perfection. He powdered his face, presumably with flour. He seemed to have some hold over one of the officers, because he sent for him from time to time in a most peremptory manner; and the officer always came. He was small, dapper, pasty-faced, and when Gaeta was once bombed—only one bomb dropped, some miles away, and the whole thing was presumably an accident—he fainted, and had to be brought round by the doctor. He was unbelievably conceited, and we did not like him a bit. We had as little to do with him as possible. His one saving grace was a vicious sense of humour; it was malicious and extremely vulgar, but we got an occasional laugh out of him.

These were the regulars. These were our intimate circle. These were the men whose lives we shared and who shared ours. Most of them had been in the cells for a good many years, off and on, and there was not much they didn't know about the acquisition of the little comforts that made things so much easier down there. Some of them, indeed, preferred the solitaries to the main yards, where one had to fight for rations, for water, and where there was no peace to be had. The others were all the occasional offenders. A pederast caught selling his wares; a convict who had insulted a guard; one who had refused to be silent when shouted at by the corporal; another who had stolen a sheet of paper from the office; petty offenders of petty crimes, who were there simply because they got on somebody's nerves elsewhere. They regarded these trips to solitary as by no means a punishment. They liked the privacy the cells afforded, and it was a treat to sleep between the hygienic sheets, de-loused once a week.

Besides, the people in the cells were the elite of the prison; it was an honour to join their company.

On the whole, they were a good crowd. They were not very brilliant as conversationalists, but they were interesting

119

people to talk to, solely because in one's normal life one does not have much chance of mixing with the professional cut-throat in his own environment; here, there were so many of them that the two of us were absorbed unnoticed in the general atmosphere of crime and illegality. We soon found ourselves as adept as the rest of them at thieving, lying and deceiving. It was a holiday from the strain, very seldom recognised as a strain before, of leading a moral and virtuous life. Comparatively.

Chapter Eight

I AWOKE early one morning with the feeling that I was being watched. It was an uncomfortable feeling, and I turned over to see who it was. There was an officer standing at the door of the cell. He was dressed in khaki instead of the *grigio-verdi*, and was smoking a pipe, an English-made pipe; the tobacco smelled good. He seemed not to be unpleasant, but I sensed that he had been watching me for a long time; I did not like this feeling.

I said "Good morning" politely. He did not answer, so I repeated it in Italian. He still made no reply, so I turned my back on him and lay down again. After a few minutes I heard him go. When the door at the passage-end had clanged shut, Frank called out, "What did he want?"

I said, "Came to sign the book, I suppose, or leave his card."

"He'd been there a long time before you woke up."

"I wonder what's on. Did you sleep well?"

"Mosquitoes."

"I know. I wonder what he wanted."

"Probably wanted to see the animals," Frank said. "We're a bit of a freak show, you know. I heard them dis-

120

cussing us last night. They called out first to see if you were asleep or not."

"What did they say? Any of them seem to know what was going to happen?"

"They know less than nothing. Except Bruno. He's got a lot of sense. And he works in the Colonel's office. He said that a man was once sentenced to death for shooting his Commanding Officer, and got away with it. They gave him three years instead. They seemed to think that we might go to a prisoner-of-war camp."

"That would be very pleasant. Do you know that they get Red Cross parcels in the camps?"

"Really? What sort of parcels?"

"Chocolate, soap, extra food, tooth-brushes . . ."

Frank interrupted. "Chocolate? Really? I would very much like to have a piece of chocolate."

"They get parcels every month, I believe. English food. I could do with a tin of M. and V. right now."

"I want most of all to clean my teeth. It must be very easy to escape from a camp, with so many people to help."

"Must be. They have a lot of freedom in the camps, some of them. They have their own theatre, concerts. Imagine having a piano."

"And books?"

"Books. And chess. There's always plenty to do there. I think they've forgotten about us here. Lost our papers. It might easily have happened as the Colonel suggested. There was *molta confusione* in Africa at the end."

"Bruno said they are not allowed to shoot a man more than seventy days after he is sentenced. Capellaro said that was all balls."

"I don't think any of them know very much."

"Do you think what Bruno says is true?"

"I don't know."

"He works in the Colonel's office."

"I know."

"He ought to know better than Capellaro and those other ignorant bastards."

"Well, it's nice to believe, anyway. I wish to Christ I had something to smoke. How much bread have you got?"

"Six rolls. Three whole days' ration."

"But you only had four yesterday. Didn't you eat any last night?"

"No, none at all. Actually it's five and about three-quarters. I tried very hard to keep them all, but I woke up in the night and took a piece of one; but a very small piece. I shall soak it all in the *brodo* tonight and have a good meal."

"What, all of it?"

"Most of it, anyway. Then I shall start building up again. Do you really think that they've forgotten about us?"

"Looks like it."

"If they've lost our papers," Frank said, an anxious note ill-disguised in his voice, "will they be able to shoot us?"

"I don't think so. I don't think they would dare, with the war nearly over."

"You are not just trying to encourage me?"

"Oh, shut up for Christ's sake! You make me sick."

Frank was silent. I knew it was because of the bread; I only had three loaves saved up. I thought, *This is a pretty bad state of affairs.* I said, "I'm sorry, Frank. Everything's going to be all right. It's just my nerves. I get fed up sometimes, with everything. With you, with myself, with everything. I suppose I need a woman. Cheer up."

Frank said, quietly, "It's all right, really. It's nothing."

A little while later, the khaki officer reappeared. His face and hair were precisely the same colour as his uniform. I wondered if we were forgetting what khaki looked like. He was still smoking his pipe, and this time I ignored him, I stared at him as rudely as I could, but it did not make me feel any better. He stood there for a long time, smoking and watching me. At last he said, with the air of having stood outside in the passage and rehearsed his lines, in slow and careful English,

"This is an English pipe."

"Yes?"

"I bought it from a prisoner."

"Isn't 'bought' a euphemism?"

He was silent for a long time again. Then he went on to verse two.

"I was at England."

"Really? Where?"

"At London. It is very dirty town."

"Have you ever been to Naples?"

122

"At Naples? That is our country."

"Your English is not exactly faultless, is it?"

"Yes, I learn at London. Thank you."

"Thank *you*. You wouldn't like to sell me some tobacco? I can give you three loaves of bread."

"It is also English tobacco. I bought it from a prisoner."

"Oh, God, here we go again."

"Go? Where do you go, please?"

"Naples."

"Yes, it is a very pretty town. Many English go there."

"And many Germans."

"You bomb Naples too much. It is not good to bomb civilians."

"Ever heard of Coventry? No, I thought not. What about London then?"

"London is very dirty town. I was at London once."

"Why did you come down here to see us?"

"I am new officer. I make inspection."

"So that's it." I called out, "He is a new officer, Frank. He make inspection one-time. Him velly big fella."

"We treat you good here."

"Is that a statement or a question?"

"You have food, you have blankets, you have wine."

"Wine? Since when have we had wine?"

"Today we give you wine. You like?"

"Can we have a woman as well?"

"I am sorry. No women. But we give you wine instead."

"Hear that, Frank? We get wine today."

The officer said, "Goodbye, please."

I said, "But don't go. Tell me about the wine."

"Goodbye."

The day ended peacefully. But the wine did not come. They said the cooks had drunk it all. They brought four of them, incapably drunk, down to the cells as a punishment. One of them was violently sick and the stench was intolerable. It was the last we saw of the little khaki officer and his English pipe.

One of the minor inconveniences of the cells was their proximity to a place called the "fifties". This was a sort of super punishment cell, down in the depths immediately under our own. A door to it, seldom used, led from the corridor into a small sunken yard one floor down, and thence into a tiny, wet, and dark dungeon which we never

123

saw but heard a great deal about. It was reserved for a rather unpleasant kind of punishment; the offender was handcuffed with his hands behind his back, and then a long chain was attached to his wrists, passed over a creaking pulley in the roof, and he was hauled up to hang there in mid-air. This left-over of the Inquisition was attended by the doctor who decided on the spot how long the prisoner could hang; and then, after perhaps five or ten minutes off the ground, he was left there with his toes touching the floor for the rest of his punishment period, with a varying number of subsequent visits when he was hung up again. We never saw the cell, fortunately, but the horror with which the others who had seen it described it was even more impressive than their description of the method itself; they had a very profound respect for it, and a threat of *la cinquanta* was enough to silence even the most recalcitrant convict.

They brought a recaptured escapee there one day. He had escaped from one of the minor jails in Sicily, and was having a pretty raw time at the hands of the Carabinieri. He was stark naked, for some reason or other, and his body was white and skinny. The popular story was that he had been caught while swimming a river, but others said that he had been stripped by the police, and it is possible that the latter story was correct; this stripping was sometimes employed, I had heard, as a psychological weapon which denuded the offender of his will to resist questioning. A man feels pretty low without his trousers.

By straining to get my face close enough to the bars of the door, I watched him being taken down the stairs to the "fifties", followed by the Commandant, the Adjutant, the Duty Officer, the Orderly Sergeant, the Doctor, the Doctor's clerk, and a few interested spectators; it was quite a procession, and seemed a very important occasion. We heard him being thumped a bit, and the noises he made in protest. We heard the creak and chink of the *catena*. Then he suddenly screamed most horribly, and set our nerves on edge. We heard him calling, "*Ai, Madonna, ai, Madonna!*" two or three times, and "*Mamma mia!*" and again "*Ai, Madonna, ai, Madonna!*" He went on calling in a throaty voice as though he were in acute agony, and at last they let him down and we heard him moaning softly. Then he was hauled up again and the screams sounded once more. They let him down again, and left him moaning there, and every half-hour

124

the Doctor came to examine him. I noticed that as soon as the gates at the end of the passage could be heard being unlocked, his groans grew louder. I mentioned this quietly to the others, but they thought I was being unkind, which I probably was.

This was the first time that the "fifties" had been used since our arrival, and we hoped it was to be the last. It gave us a wretched feeling, not so much on account of the victim, but on our own; altruism was lost in the fear of what might happen to us; it showed us what they were capable of. It made everybody in the cells very miserable and bad-tempered, and talking, our only pastime (an illegal one at that), was reduced to a very depressing minimum.

It was probably worse for Frank than it was for me; I, at least, missed half of what was going on through ignorance of the dialects in which these things were discussed. I sometimes wondered how Frank managed to keep up the pretence of not understanding, which must have been very difficult indeed. On occasion, he had to help me out with translations, and this was also very dangerous. I had to interrupt my conversation when I got into difficulty and say, "May I see what my friend has to say about it?" and then say to Frank, speaking as rapidly as possible, as one never knew how much English they might understand, "How the hell do you say so-and-so?" and Frank would spell out the word as fast as he could, and I would get it wrong and we would have to start all over again. In my ignorance, also, I sometimes used words that were quite normal in the debased society of the cells, but must have sometimes given offence. Frank had to endure it all and then lecture me later on about it, spelling out the words with the syllables broken up so that the others would not catch on. He would say, "You shouldn't use the word b-u-t- are you following me? a-n- and then a final a, particularly in conjunction with the Virgin Mary. It means a whore. And don't use the word for brothel when you want to say 'trouble'; say the word for confusion. The brothel word is slang, and very bad slang, really."

"Can I say 'God is a Pig' in polite society? Everybody seems to use that phrase, and it rolls very nicely off the tongue."

"Jesus, no. You can say 'My God', or 'By Bacchus', or

125

even 'Miserable Pig'. And for Heaven's sake don't say
m-e-r-d-a. You're not in the slums of Paris now."

"Unfortunately."

"Of course, they know you pick these phrases up down
here. I'm afraid they might try and stop us talking; we're
supposed to keep silence down here, you know."

"What did the Adjutant mean when he said that piece
about the laundry?"

"He said they were going to make us wash our own
clothes. And you said, 'Splendid!' "

"I thought he said we could go and collect it. Hell."

"It makes no difference. It will pass the time. But you
shouldn't be so bloody enthusiastic when you don't understand what he says, really."

"He's a Sicilian. I do not wish to learn that frightful
dialect."

"You'll catch on. Is it pasta or rice today?"

"Friday. Pasta." He knew very well it was pasta. But it
was pleasant to be reminded of the bi-weekly change. He
said, "I had my tin filled right up last night. This new mess
orderly is good."

"The thing is to have a piece of paper handy and tip some
out when he's refilling the ladle. You can get a lot more like
that. Or start eating before he finishes dishing out; it's surprising how fast you can eat the first few mouthfuls. Berto
is Orderly Sergeant today, so there should be plenty."

"How do you know?"

"I heard our neighbour P. say so."

"Huh. Fat lot he knows. Do you think we shall ever get
out of here?"

"Listen," I told him, "I'll tell you something. You know
the store in the yard, where the masons keep their kit?
There's a rope in there, a long one. There's also a ladder.
The road is immediately under the wall of the yard, because
you can hear the cars passing. Right. Now, they always keep
the key to that store under a stone on the roof of that shack
thing, I've seen them slip it there before they go in."

"That's right, I've seen them do that. Are you sure there's
a rope there?"

"I saw it last evening. I've been thinking it over. Look,
we can get from these cells into the corridor by cutting one
bar, right? I've already nearly finished cutting mine. That's
already half the battle. Then if we can only get to the yard,

126

we can open the store, climb on the roof with the ladder, drop to the road with the rope. We're out. The only obstacle is getting from the passage here into the yard. Concentrate on working that out."

"That's all? What about clothes, food, water? How do we get from Italy to Africa without a boat? Where do we sleep?"

"Don't be obstructive. We travel at night in our uniforms, hide up during daylight. Or break into a house and steal some civvies. There's plenty of fruit about, we can live on that, and plenty of water everywhere. Getting out of this corridor is all I'm worrying about; I think the easiest way is through the door of the 'fifties', then up on the roof by means of the drain-pipe there. Straight across and drop down into the yard—it's only a short drop if we get on top of the roof of the shack. The snag is, how to open that door. But it's only one barrier instead of a hell of a lot more."

"Somebody's smoking. Smell it?"

"I wish to Christ I had some tobacco."

"I have a fag-end. Shall we smoke it?"

"Have you got a match? I have one if you haven't."

"Good. Send it along. It is a very small piece, I am afraid."

I sent the match along on the *cavallo*, and in a little while the smouldering cigarette-end came back. There was not much of it. But it cheered things up a bit and served to divide the day.

I said, "How do you feel, Frank?"

"I don't know why, I feel good today."

"So do I. I think we'll be out soon."

"Do you really? Escape?"

"Yes. When we first came and I counted the seven doors we passed through to get down here, I thought it was going to be impossible. But now I can see the way out. It's not easy, but it's there. Before, I thought there just wasn't a way, but now I think we've found it. It's something to work on."

"Do you think we shall be in Cairo again one day? And Piccadilly?"

"Ah, it'll be good, won't it?"

"It seems a long way away."

"So much the better when we get there."

"Do you really think we shall? There's the bugle; lunch.

127

Apparently somebody did escape from here once. The only time it's been done."

"Who said so?"

"Bruno. He said that one of the clerks was sent to the Colonel's house to deliver a parcel two years ago and hasn't reported back yet. But he was an honour prisoner, allowed out and all that."

"They weren't talking about us, were they?"

"No, no. It was apropos sending an orderly to town for something. He mentioned it *en passant*."

But there was an escape scare after all.

I had a bit of pencil in my cell, and a piece of paper which I had picked up in the yard and was fairly clean on one side. On this, I had designed the layout of a small house, just to pass the time a little. I had been at great pains to put the showers in the proper place, to plan the kitchen properly, to have a shady verandah and so on, and it was pretty obviously the crudely-sketched plan of a bungalow and nothing else. I'd had this hidden for several weeks, and whenever I felt like it, I went on with the design till there was quite a lot of measurement there, in full detail, including a design for a garden and orchard.

Then one day, when we came back from the yard, I saw that the cell had been searched. Everything was almost as I left it, but not quite. The matchstick with which I cleaned my nails was gone from its usual place; it was very harmless, a dead match, but I suppose that from their point of view it meant also live matches and therefore cigarettes, and therefore dealings with the guards and a whole rigmarole of illicit undertakings as the logical conclusion. I saw that my sanitary bucket had been moved. I used to keep it most precisely in the centre of the corner flat-stone, and this fetish of precision was liable to grow in the boxed confinement to such a degree that on one occasion when I moved the bucket accidentally during the night, I was unable to sleep again because it was out of position, and I could not see to replace it properly. I do not know why they had been at such pains to replace my things so carefully, because my house plan was obviously gone. It was all they had found, but it upset me badly because I had grown very fond of it. However, they had missed my pencil, the piece of glass to sharpen it, and another two sheets of paper which were fastened with rice-paste to the under planks of the bed. My *cavallo* was

128

still safe; fortunately, because a good *cavallo* was hard to come by. String made from blankets broke very easily, and mine was proper cord, which I had stolen in the yard from another prisoner.

Then Frank called out, "They've been at my cell," and almost at the same moment Pezzimento started wailing; he had lost half a cigarette. Then everyone started. Some had lost matches, some papers, some soap. Most bitter of all was the Worm, who swore they had taken a loaf he had saved up. This made everyone laugh, because the idea of the Worm saving his bread was ludicrous. He complained loudly for a while, then shouted, "*Ma . . . cosi è la vita*," and we all bellowed "*Fin' che dura!*" and everyone was happy again.

But the next morning the Colonel sent for me and showed me my plan. He wanted to know if it was a plan of the prison. I said, "Of course not. One sees that it is the plan of a house."

Another officer who was standing there (it was quite a parade; there were eight of them) said, "That is how it appears. It is also the way I would disguise a plan of the prison if I were trying to escape."

The Colonel said, "Where is this house?"

"It is an imaginary house, such as I would wish to live in."

"Who gave it to you?"

"But I drew it myself. You can see that it is my writing."

"You have no pencil in your cell, we looked for one. So how did you draw it?"

"I used to have a pencil. But I sold it a few days ago in the yard for a loaf of bread."

"To whom?"

"One of the prisoners. I do not know his name."

"Who was the Orderly Sergeant on duty that day?"

"I don't remember. It was several days ago, more than a week."

"Why did you sell it?"

"I was hungry. I am still hungry."

One of the other officers, in the uniform of the Black-shirts, a young Lieutenant who we called the Horse because of his face, said, "We believe it is a plan of the prison. We wish to know who gave it to you."

I said, "Don't be a fool. I have already told you what it is. Why don't you compare it with a real plan of the prison? It

129

should be simple to settle one way or the other. Or point out what you think is my cell on the plan."

He started to argue, but the Colonel silenced him. He said, "You cannot escape from here. It has never been done yet. So do not try it."

I said, "May I have my drawing back, please?"

"No."

They took me back to the cells, and I told Frank what had happened. They searched our cells every day for a week while we were in the yard. They were most careful to leave our scanty belongings as we had left them, but they did not understand how precise was our regimentation, so that if the mattress were moved the merest fraction of an inch, we knew it at once. I do not think the warders ever realised how minutely one gets to know the world when the world is six feet square. At the end of a week I drew an indecent picture for them and stuck it on the wall over my bed, the kind of thing one sees in public conveniences, which was a device I had heard of before for the prevention of searches. Surprisingly, it worked.

Our plans for escaping were static. It seemed impossible to find a way out of the corridor. If the other cells had been empty we could have tackled the door to the "fifties", but we knew that there was no chance of trying it with the sycophant Pezzimento next door; he would have given us away at once in the hope of getting a cigarette for his trouble from one of the warders.

Then a few days later, help came from an unexpected quarter.

During the hours in the yard for exercise, we had become quite friendly with the masons there, honour prisoners, who spent most of their time out, mixing cement and colour-wash. We talked with them in sign language, and occasionally passed notes to and fro. One of these men particularly, named Buonavoglia, was very helpful and sometimes slipped us a lettuce, or a couple of tomatoes or onions which we were able to hide and then eat when we reached the cells. We were on very good terms indeed. So a few days after the episode of the plan, he signed to me as soon as I went out, saying that there was a note in the lavatory. I knew his normal hiding-place was behind the cistern, so I found it easily enough. I read, in very uncouth script,

"There is a rumour in the prison that they found plans for

130

your escape. There is a big scare about it. If you want to get away I will help you. I know how it can be done but it needs a lot of money. Don't take this note back to the cells but destroy it immediately."

I came out of the lavatory and made no sign. Buonavoglia was going on with his work. A little while later he looked up, and from the other end of the yard I signalled that the note was destroyed and that I had no money but could arrange to pay afterwards. I also asked for some paper to write notes on, and he said he would bring some to the cells; I wondered how he was going to manage this.

When we were inside again, I told Frank what was in the note, and asked what he thought about it.

He said, "We'd better be very careful. He may be an *agent provocateur*."

"I wonder how we can find that out?"

"We'll ask him something which we know already and see if he tells us the truth."

"He said he'd bring some paper down here; I wonder how he'll manage that. He must be friendly with the warder at the gates."

"He said 'send', not 'bring'. A line across the body means 'send'. He's apparently very friendly with Sergeant Berto, and Berto is Orderly Sergeant today, so he might bring it."

I said, "If we can get one of the staff to help like that, we're made."

"Why?"

"Well, if he starts accepting bribes on our behalf, a loaf of bread even, we've got him by the short hairs."

"I wonder if it is Sergeant Berto. I hope so, he's a nice fellow. Did you destroy the note?"

"They'll have a sticky job finding it after what I used it for."

"We must be careful how we reply."

"I'll ask what's behind the wall of these cells and see what he says. We know it's the church. I shall be glad when he brings the paper. Would you like some?"

"Can you give me a piece of pencil, too? I would like to draw something, really."

"I've got about two inches; that's plenty for both of us."

The food arrived a little later, accompanied by Sergeant Berto. But it was not Berto who brought the paper. Instead, when the sergeant's back was turned for a moment, the mess orderly dropped his ladle, pulled a bundle from inside his shirt, slipped it across to me, and started ladling again so quickly that it was all over in a split second and the bundle was hidden under my mattress before the sergeant turned round. My mess-tin was filled to the brim, and the hot, sticky rice dripped over the edge and I got an extra helping by catching it as it fell and stuffing it into my mouth. As soon as they had gone, I left the food to cool and get thicker, and opened the bundle. It contained a dozen sheets of old office paper, used on one side, and two old copies of *Il Tempo* There was a note. I read it aloud to Frank.

"*Do not trust any of the sergeants. They are all bastards, especially Sergeant Berto. If you want to escape, the best way is through the church which is behind your cell if you can make a hole in the wall, The church leads straight to the road. My brother is a P.O.W. in Kenya, I got a letter last month. He has plenty to eat but it is hot. If you want some spaghetti I will put some in the lavatory for you tomorrow. We have plenty. My brother brings it, he is very rich. He says the war will be over soon. We all like you. Write clear, when you reply, I can't read so good. Put it in the lavatory basin near the water-pipe.*"

When I had finished the translation, I passed the original on the *cavallo* so that Frank could inspect it. I asked what he thought of it.

He said, "It is certainly written by an illiterate, and a Southerner at that. I think it's genuine. That word he uses for 'lavatory' is pure Taranto; anyone else would have used the word beginning with c-e-s—you know the one?"

"It looks all right to me."

"You know, I've believed for some time that they had their own food supplies. You know how they all troop off downstairs to that workshop place? In the yard? I've noticed that when they come back, the Orderly Sergeant leaves a warder in charge—says he's going to inspect the workshops —and goes down himself for a good fifteen minutes. He gets his share of the meal as the price of his silence. A very nice set-up, really."

"My God, I could do with a nice bowl of spaghetti, with plenty of tomatoes and onions. I wonder where they get it all?"

"As he says, his brother smuggles it in to him; by letting

all the others in on the deal, he manages to keep it dark. These good-conduct prisoners are allowed two visits a month. And I'll tell you something else. That thin fellow they're always whispering to, the one who comes in and out every five minutes, is the Colonel's gardener. So there'll be plenty of sauce with it! I think we are going to have a good meal tomorrow."

"I hope so. Think out what to say in our reply. We'll give him a note tomorrow. I shall say we like him too. Let us not forget the little courtesies. Have you eaten your dinner?"

"Nearly finished. It's very thick today, and a lot of beans. I always save the beans till last. I've got three, four, five, one-two-three eight, ten, ten beans. No, two more, that's twelve beans today. That's the most I've ever had."

"I haven't started mine yet. It's still full, full right up. I got some while he was filling my tin, so I can still taste it. I'm going to pretend I've had it, and then eat it as a second meal when everyone else has finished. When they start talking about tomorrow's meal, I shall start mine."

But I didn't keep it long. I was too hungry. It was better than usual, and thicker. I counted twenty-three beans.

The days were long in the cells, waiting for the daily exercise routine, twenty-three hours long, and the time passed slowly. I soon got used to being locked up, once the initial claustrophobia had passed. After that, one's cell became one's home, and one took a certain pride in it, in the smallest most insignificant things. For example "getting up" was a process that involved dressing with the most meticulous care, and then making up the bed. The coarse sheets and blankets were folded most carefully, not a fraction out of true line, then placed on top of the palliasse so precisely straight that one studied it at great length to make sure that it was absolutely correct; then one would start all over again to see if perhaps it could not be done better this time. . . . This sometimes took as much as an hour off the morning. We never rose early. Coffee came round at about six, and I used to roll naked out of bed, collect, then sleepily climb in again and go on sleeping. It was quite a trick not to wake up properly so that one could easily get to sleep again. The coffee was always cold anyway. Then an hour or two later, when sleep was reluctantly admitted to have gone for that day, one stretched, rubbed the sleep out of one's eyes, and set about dressing. I always took great care over the creases in my trousers; this was simply a matter of wetting them while we were in the yard in the evening, then sleeping on them at night. The other prisoners always slept in their clothes, and never ceased admiring our trouser-creases. . . . Such things took on a great importance. Then conversation, prison style, would begin, always with the same words.

"Frank! What are you doing?"

And Frank would say, "I'm just sitting on my bed. Have you drunk your coffee yet?"

"Not yet. I'm tidying the cell. You should see the creases in my trousers this morning. What's the coffee like today?"

"It's very good. I like this barley stuff, really."

This was a sure sign that it was going to be a "good" day.

Then Pezzimento would call out, "Ho, Pietro! What are you doing?"

"Just sitting. What are you doing?"

"Guess, Pietro. Guess what I am doing now."

"Drinking your coffee?"

"No, Pietro."

"Sitting on the *cesso*?"

"No, Pietro." And the game, a children's game, would go on for half an hour or more. Finally the plan would be made clear. Pezzimento would say, "I'm drawing, Pietro, with a piece of pencil. Would you like to have a piece of pencil, Pietro?"

"How much?"

"I would like to give it to you for nothing, but I am very hungry, Pietro. How much bread have you got?"

"*Poco, poco.* How long is the pencil?"

"Very long, Pietro."

"How long?"

"I have no measure, Pietro, but it is very long indeed."

"How long?"

Reluctantly, "About five centimetres, Pietro."

"All right, I'll give you half a loaf for it."

"Can you not make it a whole loaf? I am very hungry and I owe Bruno half."

"Half a loaf."

"Very well, Pietro. Send the bread along on your *cavallo*."

Then Bruno would shout out, "Ho, Pietro, can you hear me? Make him send the pencil first or you'll never get it. You must not trust Pezzimento, he's a thief." And Pezzimento would leap off his bed, and argue and sulk for the

134

rest of the day. When the arguing was at its height, and everyone was talking at the same time, he would get back on his bed and keep silent in the general brouhaha to show that he was offended, but no one took any notice of him. This sort of talk would go on till someone lit a cigarette and puffed the smoke out into the passage so that the others could smell it and argue as to who was smoking. Sometimes an exchange would take place; one loaf of bread to a cigarette, and a crust for a *cica' cesa*, in which there was the barest puff left. Then the *addonata* would sound for the parade of warders and everyone would say "Half-past ten" and start talking about the approaching lunch. Everyone was always hungry. I drew my belt tighter and tighter as the days went by, for the complete day's ration was less in bulk than a good hearty breakfast. Sometimes a newcomer would be brought down and would provide an impetus for the day's talk; where did he come from, what was he in for, what was the news in the yards, did he know *paese mio*, how many children had he, what was his wife like? Nobody ever asked about the war; it was of insufficient interest.

They brought a pederast down one day. Pederasty was common enough in the yards, where everyone lived, slept, ate, talked together all day long, and the authorities took little notice of it. It went on in any darkened corner which would provide a minimum of privacy. But on occasion, when the instance was too flagrant, then both parties were given ten days or so in the cells. In this case, one of them had protested his innocence and the other had been sent down pending the M.O.'s inspection. He himself admitted it quite openly. The price, he told us, was two loaves of bread. In the afternoon, the Doctor came indignantly down to make his report; we heard what went on with great amusement. He refused to enter the contaminated cell. He said, "I am filled with disgust, you dirty beast. Come near the door." There was a long, probing silence. Then the Doctor shouted, "Bah! I spit upon it!" and returned in high dudgeon. I heard Frank trying to muffle his laughter in a blanket. For a long time after, the most popular ejaculation of contempt in the cells was "Bah! I spit upon it!" The Commandant himself came down to inspect the youth who was, by all reports, quite a good-looking fellow; there was a whispered conversation that even the next-door prisoner could not overhear, but the pederast himself told us what had taken place. The Colonel, he said, had arranged for his release the next day so that he could go back to the yard. And the next morning, sure enough, they came and took him away, grinning. We never saw him again.

The cells were full at this time, and we could do little about escaping, so we began to pin our hopes on Buonavoglia. We discovered that he was inside for robbing a woman in a brothel. Of an incredibly severe fourteen-year sentence he had already served eleven. The evening after the delivery of the note, he signed to me immediately we went to the yard. I went quickly to the lavatory and found a huge basin of pasta there. One of the other prisoners was "holding the fort" till I arrived, to keep out anyone who was not in the know. I sat on the seat and had an enormous meal, leaving half for Frank who followed me in. When he came out he looked for all the world like the tiger in the limerick. He said, "My God, that was good. But you missed something. There was a note."

"Yes? What did it say?"

"What do you think? Tunis has fallen. He said the batman to the Adjutant listens in to the B.B.C. and passes the word on. He said he will keep us supplied with news *and* food."

"My God, it won't be long now."

"If only they leave us here. Leave us alone. You think they will?"

"They're not likely to move us now. This is the safest prison in Italy."

"You don't think they'll put us under the earth?"

"Not now. I feel sure they've lost our papers and don't even know our names. Besides, they wouldn't touch us after all this time."

"It's very easy to believe that. I am afraid that you are really very optimistic, always. It is not realistic, not logical, to ignore anything which does not please you. That is very bad."

That made me very angry, partly because it was true. I said, "Oh, shut up, for Christ's sake."

Frank got up and walked away. I said, "You're behaving like a bloody schoolboy. If they're going to shoot us, they'll shoot us, and there's nothing we can do about it." I wanted to hurt him, to make him sorry for having found so easily the weakness in my egoism. I thought, *I'll make you squirm, you little bastard.*

136

Frank sat down again and said, "You only say that to make me angry, you don't believe it yourself."

"So cheer up, then, for Christ's sake, and don't be so bloody depressing."

"Really, we are very much, how do you say, not like each other?"

"Mutt and Jeff."

"Eh? What?"

"Bacon and eggs."

"Oh. And which of us is the pig?"

"I'll take a bet with you that we spend Christmas in Cairo."

"You really think that?" Frank was excited again.

"I do. And don't worry if I bawl at you sometimes, if I get on your nerves a bit. You get on mine too sometimes, you know. It's quite natural. Just one of those unpleasant things I like to ignore."

"But you really are an incurable optimist."

I thought, *Here we go again.* I said, "If I hadn't been an optimist, we should never have got out of Sfax; remember how you thought it was not possible?"

"That is true. But remember how certain you were afterwards that we were thirty miles from the road, and where were we? Right on top of the bloody road, walking beside it. That is what I mean when I say that you like to think that everything is all right."

I knew he was right. I knew I was sulking about it. I said, "All right, all right. Next time I'll take your advice and we won't even try. It will be impossible, impossible. I hate that bloody word."

"No, I don't mean that, really. But let us try to be realists."

I said sourly, "The only realistic thing is that we've got to get out of here whether it's possible or not."

"And that I am hungry again."

"What, after that enormous dish? Already?"

"I ate it too quickly. Now I have regurgitations."

"My God, you've got what?"

"Is that not the right word?"

"Say 'I gurk'. It is more fitting to your environment."

I was glad that the quarrel had not developed. Frank was always gentle when these embryo fights began. He never lost his temper. Only once did I see him lose that polish of

137

kind-heartedness. When we were caught on the road just after I had declared that we were so far away, I saw a flash of hatred in his face that was diabolical. It was gone in an instant and I saw it no more. It was the only time.

We went back to the cells, filled with our meal of pasta. It was pasta again that night for supper, but only flour and water.

The big event of the day, of course, was exercise time. Normally we had an hour in the open air, from five till six o'clock. The tiny yard gave little room to run around, but it was cheerful simply because there were other people there. All the cells were emptied, there was a rush for the yard gates as soon as they were opened, and the sergeant in charge usually got shouldered out of the way with little ceremony.

There was nothing much to see out there. The yard ran down one short wall of the prison, and was enclosed on the other three sides by twenty-foot walls. One of them was the side of a prison-house where the Adjutant lived, and sometimes he used to come into the yard and call up to his wife, a hulking great woman with a scar on her face, who would then appear at the window and shout down a conversation. Frank said, "Bah! A woman with a scar on her face! It looks like the mark of a broken bottle." The Adjutant used to call her "little treasure". We thought this was damn funny. She used to lean out of the window and abuse us from time to time, and ask the sergeant why he didn't keep us in the cell where we belonged. This was a good thing because it put the sergeants, who hated her, on our side. We often heard her taking her bath with much noise of rushing water, and she would call out coyly to the batman, "Don't come in, I'm naked." She never said "undressed", always "*nuda*". One could hear quite clearly. I said to the sergeant one day, "That must be a horrible sight." And she heard me. She leaned out of the window with a towel over her shoulders and her lank, unbrushed hair hanging over her face, and screamed at us; the grinning sergeant was obliged to put us inside again. The next day the Adjutant tried to pick a quarrel with me, but failed. She kept up her abuse almost to the end.

There was a well in one corner of the yard, filled with clean, cold water. One had to draw it in a leaky bucket and throw it over one's shoulders before it all ran away. On these occasions we did not use precious soap, but reserved it for the fortnightly bath, but the water was clean and refreshing. After some weeks I procured a piece of comb, and the evening wash became quite a ceremony. We were never able to do more than refresh ourselves, then, clean and cool, stride up and down and try to keep fit. But it was incredible how tired one became after a few hundred paces' fast walking. Lack of exercise and bad food had a wicked effect on our strength. At least half the time was spent in talking to the other convicts in signs, at which we became very proficient. What they had learned in the space of years, we picked up in a few weeks.

During this hour, each of us had his favourite pastime. Frank and I used to walk hard. One of the others used to gather leaves from the over-worked vine that straggled over the walls and cut them up with a borrowed knife to make tobacco; this was subsequently rolled into a kind of cigarette with newspaper. These weeds gave out a rich and horrible blue smoke. But for the most part, the solitaries spent their hour's daylight slouching around with their hands in their pockets, if they had any pockets, some of them not even bothering to wash. It always seemed to me that they were happier inside; but they raised hell if the sergeant forgot to let us out.

At about five-thirty or six, Trombo sounded the dinner-call, and we trooped back inside and waited for the rations to come. I soon found out why solitary confinement was not as bad as it might have been; why some of them preferred it. In the main part of the prison, the convicts were divided into two companies, housed in big, barrack-like rooms, each with its own yard; they had the run of the place all day, and at night the yards were sealed off and the prisoners locked inside. But when the rations came, they all got more or less the proper amount, or perhaps a little less to make sure that there was enough for everyone. In the cells, however, the orderly simply drew a bucketful from the kitchen, not bothering to check each day how many rations were required; it was simpler to fill the bucket, in case the cells were full, than to find the Duty Officer and check the number of prisoners down there. So, unless the cells happened to be full up, which was rare, we had a fair amount over the proper ration; this was known as the *gavetta piena*, and was

139

well worth the loss of the doubtful companionship of the *cortile*. Theoretically, what was left in the bucket was supposed to be handed back to the kitchen, but in practice, unless the orderly was hungry, we always got a better ration. It was quite a business to devise means of getting the mess-tin filled or more than filled, especially on Mondays and Fridays when it was pasta instead of rice. It was only plain flour and water, with a few rare beans for thickening, and no salt either. But it was a lot better than the rice in cabbage-water that was the other stand-by.

One had to wait for some time after the bugle for the meal, and one could feel the tension in the cells. The longer we waited, the less there would be, because delay always meant that others were being served first from the same bucket. The red-letter days were when we found the orderly with the food-pail waiting for us as we trooped in from the yard; everyone would shout *"Rancio!"* and rush for the cells, and the whole block was permeated with pleasure, the orderlies and sergeants themselves beaming with reflected excitement, so that the tins were always filled to overflowing and everyone was happy. And then came always the inevitable yelling for water. One had to shout *"Acqua!"* at the top of one's lungs, so loudly and so often that the warder at the gate tired of the noise and condescended to shout for the water-bearer to come and fill up our mugs for the night. This gave us the opportunity to swill out our mess-tins quickly and fill them too, so that we had plenty of water for the night and could sip it all evening, pretending it was wine.

The evenings always dragged a little, mainly because the next meal was not until the following midday, and it was a long time to wait with an empty stomach. Breakfast was a little black coffee only, and it was hard to resist the temptation to make a *zuppa* of it with the bread which we were saving for emergency. On the other hand, one felt clean and refreshed after the evening wash and everyone was in a good temper. On most nights we sang. Pezzimento would start the singing. He was the only man in the cells who was physically incapable of singing a note, and he would say, sombrely: *"Ho, Pietro! Canta qualchecosa."*

Then I would sing a Negro spiritual or "There Lived a King", or the Catalogue Song, and Frank would sing for his turn, "Taboo", which pleased them immensely because he used to accompany himself on the drums by

140

beating on the floor with his feet and the bed-boards with his hands. Sometimes we all joined in by beating on the bars with tin mugs, wooden spoons, anything we could lay hands on that would sound louder than the rest; this would upset the warder and make him call for silence. Then, after a token silence, one of the others would sing one of the songs of Naples in a high-pitched, choking tenor. And so the time would pass.

One evening, a fine voice was singing one of the arias which I knew, but momentarily could not place. The notes hung true in the still air of the cells and everyone was listening. Then Frank said, in a forced whisper, "For Christ's sake stop him singing."

Surprised, I asked, "But why? He has a wonderful voice."

Frank said furiously, "I said stop him, for God's sake, I can't stand it." His voice rose to a shout.

I was puzzled, but I called out and said, "My friend has a bad headache; tomorrow, perhaps?"

The voice stopped and there was a long silence. Then I heard Bruno say to his neighbour, "Ah, yes. For them it is not a good song."

Pezzimento said, "*Coraggio, Pietro.*"

I was getting angry because I could not understand what it was all about. Then I remembered. It was Cavaradossi's Aria from *Tosca*.

The rest of the evening was heavy, disturbed. We spent a restless night, tossing and turning on the hard beds, staring through the peep-hole at the harsh light of the bare bulb outside, listening to the changing of the warders; stifling in the heat, waiting for the morning. It was an unpleasant night. The words of the song lingered in the oppressive, lonely silence:

> "... *Un passo sfiorava la rena*
> *Entrav' ella, fragrante,*
> *Mi cadea fra le braccia* . . .
> *O dolci baci, languide carezze,*
> *Mentr'io fremente,*
> *Le belle forme disciogliea dai veli.* . . ."

141

Chapter Nine

I AWOKE one day with an unpleasant itch along my right arm. When the guard came and opened the wooden doors and let in the light, I examined it carefully and found a long strip of sore red rash. It seemed to have spread in the last few hours and scratching made it worse. Frank was awake, moving about in his cell, so I told him about it.

I said, "How many kinds of parasites have you on your body?"

Frank came over to the corner of his cell and thought it over. Finally, he said, "I think three. Lice, and fleas, and crabs."

"There are fairies at the bottom of my garden."

He said, "Yes, three. I do not like the lice."

"Well, I have five."

"Five? Wait a minute. Do you count ordinary bugs?"

"But of course."

"Then I have four. Wait a minute." There was a long silence while Frank examined himself. "No," he said at last, "I am sorry, but I have only four."

"I have five. I have a new one."

"A new one? Is it a special kind?"

" I will give you three guesses."

"That is unfair. All the kinds of parasites I know by name, I already have. If I knew any other names, I should certainly be able to find them too. I believe all the lice of Italy live right here. They like the warmth."

"Yes, lice are a nuisance. But I prefer them to fleas. Fleas make me very angry. They bite harder, and they hop too fast to catch. At least lice can be killed in large numbers with great satisfaction, but it takes all day to catch just one flea."

"No, I do not like lice, they are dirty beasts. Pah! I spit upon them."

"But you can at least get some of your own back. They are very easy to find. All except the last half-dozen and then, after a really good blitz, the last half-dozen get down to an orgy of procreation to make up for their casualties."

"Like Brighton beach on a Sunday."

"Please do not be vulgar, or I shall not tell you about my new one."

"What is it really?"

"Scabies. My Fifth Column."

"Isn't that very painful?"

"Itches. I wonder if I can see the doctor?"

"Ask these people here how to get the doctor."

I called out to Pezzimento. He said, "Yes, Pietro, there is a doctor in the prison. But he is very wicked. If you are ill he gives you castor oil, and then the bucket gets too full and overflows and so nobody goes to see him any more. Are you ill?"

I said, "Yes. I've got . . . " I did not know the word for scabies, so I said, "little animals that go under the skin."

"Ah, you mean lice. We all have lice, Pietro. They don't hurt you."

I said, patiently, "No Pezzimento, you misunderstand me. I have lice also. But now there is another one." I guessed at the name and got it more or less right. "I want to see the doctor about it."

Pezzimento said, "He will give you castor oil."

"Never mind, I want to see him."

"All right. I will call him for you. I am your friend, Pietro."

I thought, *He hasn't given up hope of getting my ring yet.* He called to the guard, "Ho! Guardia!" The guard took no notice and we learned later that they never did take any notice of Pezzimento. But someone farther up butted in with, "What's wrong, Pietro?" shouted along the passage.

I said, "I want to see the doctor. Who's that, Bruno?"

The voice said, "No, this is Paglia. I will call the guard for you."

He called out a string of invective to the warder concerning his amatory experiences with the Virgin Mary. The warder unlocked the door to the cells and wanted to know what was the matter. He said to Paglia, "If you swear at me like that, you bastard, I'll stop your rations."

Paglia said, "The Englishman is ill. I think he's dying. He has consumption."

The guard came down to my cell and said, "What's the matter with you? You don't look sick to me."

I said, "That's because of my beard. Underneath all that my face is very pale. I think I'm dying."

He could not decide whether or not I was serious. He grumbled, "All right, I'll get the sergeant."

143

He came back in a little while with the Orderly Sergeant, who also wanted to know what was the matter, but at last I convinced them that I had all the diseases in the pharmacopoeia and they unlocked the door and let me out. As I passed Frank, leaning against his bars, white-faced and bearded, with a tiny cell behind him and grinning because something to break the monotony was happening today, I said, "You look like an animal."

The sergeant took me along the passage, round a few corners, up a few flights of stairs, and finally we arrived at the hospital, smelling strongly of hospital as all hospitals do. There were several prisoners in a small room waiting to see the M.O., prisoners from the main yards who had heard of our presence in the cells but had never seen us, so I was well received. There was a warder, technically in charge, asleep by the window where the sun streamed in. The sergeant woke him up and handed me over, and the guard sleepily nodded his head and went back to sleep again. All the convicts started talking to me at once. One of them said, "Don't go inside till the doctor calls you personally. You can stay here a long time if you draw it out. Only the newcomers go in as soon as he says 'next'."

There was a big heavily-barred window low in the wall, with a fine view of fields and trees and gentle downs, with white clouds hanging silent above. It was unbelievably green and fresh. Then one of the prisoners produced a litre bottle of wine and offered it to me. I took a polite sip and handed it back. It was very good. He said, "No, no, it's all for you. We have plenty more."

The drowsing warder took no notice, and I presumed that hospital guard was counted a good spell of duty; there was wine on the ration, and no one seemed to worry if the patients got any or not. It probably accounted for his sleepiness. When I had drunk it all, someone gave me three apricots which I stuffed into my pockets for later. Then the doctor poked his face round the door, saw me, and called me in.

He was a fat little man with dirty hands. He said, "Ah, the Englishman."

I said, "I have seabies."

He looked at my arms and said, "That is scabies." He spoke a kind of English, and the clerk and assistants were visibly impressed. I asked if he could cure it and he asked if

144

I had any other parasites. I told him plenty. He said, "You should have come to me before. I will tell them to disinfest your clothes. Everyone here has lice, but we roast them all from time to time. I will give you some ointment. It will kill any other parasites as well."

He didn't give me castor oil, but a blue grease instead. But as I went out, someone pushed a rustling piece of paper into my hand and said, "Hide it, quick." They all grinned and winked at me. The sergeant came and escorted me back to the cells.

Coming down the stairs I realised that the wine had gone to my head and I was very nearly drunk. It was only one bottle, but my stomach had been empty, its now permanent state, and it was the first drink I had taken for some time. And the effect of climbing so many stairs after close confinement was considerable. I started singing "*La Donna e Mobile*", which is not my best song; I am no tenor. As I passed Frank I saw that his eyes were wide with astonishment, and he was laughing with delight. When they had locked me away, and the sergeant had gone, he called out,

"So that's the hospital. I didn't know that castor oil was alcoholic."

I said, "I have been given some medicine."

"Not castor oil?"

"Not castor oil. It comes in a tall, slim bottle, and is sweet and red."

"Not wine? They didn't give you wine?"

"Marsala. I had a whole bottle. At least fourteen grade. It is now cheerfully chasing grains of last night's rice along my intestines. I can feel them jumping about. It is very difficult not to gurk. It has made me feel considerably better, and I am not even sorry that I could not save some for you. But I brought you some apricots. And some sugar." The paper parcel contained nearly a pound of good white sugar.

"For Christ's sake, what is all this? Is that how they treat scabies?"

"I will tell you about the hospital. First, there is a window you can see out of. You can see trees, and grass, and hills, and a village. Proper trees, I mean, not those horrible stunted things we used to call trees in North Africa, but tall, graceful trees that sway in the wind. I had forgotten that such things exist. It is a magnificent sight. The grass is green

145

everywhere, not just a few dull patches. The sky is just as blue as in Africa, and it has white clouds in it. And it is real sky, not just the roof of a cell; and there is the hell of a lot of it. And trees all over the damn place. It is a magnificent sight."

"You said that already. I want to hear about the wine."

"Marsala. A very nice wine indeed. I had to wait in the waiting-room which is full of malingerers earning their castor oil. They go there to look at the view. There are also a lot of orderlies and you cannot tell which are which. The orderlies slink about and give you wine, they give you sugar, they give you apricots. We are very popular in the prison."

"Do you mean that you drank a whole bottle? Not just a little drop?"

"A whole bottle. I took just a little at first, and they insisted that I drink it all. It was really very good. If you put your arm through the bars I will send you half the sugar and two apricots. Or would you like all the apricots to make up for the wine?"

"No, really, one will be plenty."

"You shall have them all." But I only sent two. I thought, *Well, I'll have one just to see what they taste like*, and anyway, Frank insisted. I divided the sugar most scrupulously into two and sent his share along on the *cavallo* wrapped in a piece of paper. I meant to keep mine for sweetening the coffee, but after tasting it I found it too good to waste on bad coffee, so I ate it all there and then by dipping my tongue into it and lapping it up slowly. I asked Frank, "Are you keeping the sugar for your coffee?" I felt guilty about the wine.

He said, briefly, "It's gone."

"Gone?" I was alarmed; I thought perhaps the paper had burst and it had been lost.

"I've eaten it."

"What, already?"

"Yes, three good mouthfuls. Are you keeping yours?"

"I was going to, but I'm eating it slowly, lapping it like a cat. I still have a little left. It's like a drug, you can't stop eating it."

Frank said, brightly, "Tomorrow, I shall go to the doctor myself. I shall show him my lice. I want to see some of that wine. You know, there is supposed to be a ration here. I heard them talking about it. It seems they haven't had the

146

ration for a long time except in the hospital. What did the doctor say about the scabies?"

"He gave me some blue butter in a piece of paper. I will send you some."

"No, no, please. I must keep my lice for the M.O. tomorrow."

"They are going to let us disinfest our clothes. If we keep the bath business organised, we might be able to keep clean."

When I had first raised the question of baths with the Colonel, he had stated that the bath ration was one a month. After a bit of an argument he had agreed to let us have one every two weeks instead. More was out of the question. The water was heated, and the baths opened, every fifteen days only, and each company took its turn during the day. We could join each company in turn. When I said we would not object to cold water, he was horrified at the idea of opening up the block for just two people. He said, "In any case, you cannot possibly get dirty in the cells." And that was that.

But bath-night was good. It was each second Saturday. The solitaries took their bath alone, with a few senior N.C.Os., clerks, orderlies, and other privileged persons. We were marched to the bath-house in a very ragged crocodile, and took up our place down the two long walls of a long narrow room. Down the centre was a double row of three-sided cement cubicles, with showers in them, and two pipes running above them. The control tap was at one end of the room and manned by one of the convicts. We all undressed, and when the sergeant blew his whistle, we moved into the cubicles. The naked sergeant, whistle between his teeth, moved under also. The second whistle was the signal for the water to be turned on. It was also the signal for the general hullaballoo to start. There were no taps in the cubicles and the tap-man at the end had us all by the short hairs. He invariably started off with boiling water only. The water in the wide pipes would be pleasantly warm, until suddenly the scalding water would come through, hissing hot, and everyone would leap to safety. Then he would turn off the hot till we were all under the water again, cautiously feeling it first, then turn the ice-cold tap on full, and we all had to yell and leap for safety again. There was always plenty of pressure, and another scheme was to turn the taps off slowly so that less and less water came through, till only the slightest trickle remained and the controller would be fairly sure that everyone was staring up at the roses, mouths hanging open, wondering what had happened. Then he would turn it all on fast, at full strength. This sort of horse-play would go on until the sergeant had had enough, when he would stalk up in naked dignity and flick the offending tap-man all round the room with the end of a wet towel. The narrowness of the room made him run the gauntlet of all the cubicles, whence sudden feet would stick out to trip him up. It was great fun.

Finally, the bath proper would begin. The water would be just right, and turned on for several minutes, then off at the sound of the whistle, when we were supposed to soap ourselves. The next whistle brought the water on again for the final rinsing. The soap, which was issued in tiny pieces on bath-night, was crude green stuff made of flour, olive oil, soda and sand. It was made in the prison and when the convicts employed on this job managed to steal the oil, then the soap was very poor stuff indeed. None the less, it was hard to come by and very valuable. It had to be watched most carefully in the shower. The natural place to put it was on the ledge of the wall over one's head, but this was exposed to prying hands from three sides, and the soap soon got lost if left for more than a moment. In fact, the way we managed to keep enough soap for all our baths was by this simple method of stealing. Normally, stealing from one's fellow-convicts was frowned upon; but soap-stealing was allowed, and final possession was the only arbitration.

While the water was off, we would soap away cheerfully, keeping our eyes open for an unwary move of a hand on the wall dividing the cubicles which would mean another piece of soap to steal, everyone surreptitiously or blatantly examining everyone else's body all along the line. And when the whistle came for the last rinse, everyone would shout, *Too hot, Too cold, No, no, too hot*, according to his own fancy. There was bedlam in the place and the idea was to make it last as long as possible. Then the whistle, from the now clean and highly polished sergeant, caused the water to be turned off and we started drying ourselves on the ragged towels. I once asked the sergeant why he took his bath with us instead of at home. He answered quite simply and honestly. He had a well for water in his garden, but could not afford to buy fuel for heating. I said, "What about your wife?" He shrugged. "There is plenty of water in the well." This was the notorious Sergeant Garofalo whom the convicts hated so much; but he always treated us with relative kindness.

They allowed us plenty of time to dry our bodies. And during this time the control man, who had been at the taps, was allowed to take his own shower. During the last few noisy minutes he had been carefully regulating the heat to the temperature he liked best. There were two things to do during the period. One, you could nip back under the shower and have another bath, or two, with a wink at the sergeant you could slip up to the taps and turn one off, so that the water ran hot or cold and scalded or froze the control-man. The first was more pleasant, the second more fun, particularly as someone was sure to swipe him across the bare behind with a wet towel as he bent down to re-control the taps, and someone else was equally certain to steal his soap while he was doing this. It was an unenviable job. With enough horseplay one could make the bath last well over an hour. Then back to the cells, clean, wet hair smarmed down, smelling of soap and feeling good.

The day after the hospital episode they took our uniforms away for disinfesting, and gave us Italian Army clothes. We looked ridiculous in them, but they gave us also two sets of underwear made of stiff flax. It was comic stuff, with long-legged pants that tied under the knee with tapes. We tore the legs off them and made them into bags for keeping bread in, with a borrowed needle and some cotton pulled from the sheets. They were very useful as we could now hang our bread on the wall away from the rats. We used to keep it on the bed at first—there was nowhere else—till one night I felt a rat run across my face. After that we stuffed it hard between the bars of the door, as high as possible. All night long we could hear the hungry, angry rats leaping for it; and sometimes the guards stole it if we were asleep when they brought the morning coffee. But the bags hung well on the wall over our heads, and put a stop to all that. We always had a few loaves in reserve. We saved the daily ration for five or six days or more till we were desperately hungry; then we ate the lot at once and had a real good meal. By this means our stomachs were full at least once a week. I told the others in the cells about it, but they weren't interested. They couldn't be bothered.

The Commandant came down to see us very rarely, and

this was just as well because we knew that sooner or later he would have to inform us of the result of our appeal. We wanted to put this fearsome moment off as long as possible; even the unpleasant *status quo* was preferable to the chance that the verdict would not be in our favour. In our clearer moments we thought that our chances were not very good, and on these days we spent many unpleasant hours thinking about it. It was easy to become acutely superstitious; if the numbers of the day, week, month, year, added up to what we thought might be an unlucky number . . . Or if the same orderly brought the food three times running . . . Or if it were cloudy when we went to the yard . . . This sort of thing was very easy to fall into. It was not so much the physical fact of death, but rather the acute distaste of not living any more. The fear was a purely negative one. It was being unable to go on living any more that was distasteful, just plain living as one had always lived. Not even the awful cold-bloodedness of it all, or the indignity, seemed so hateful as the simple fact that so many pleasant things would never be experienced again: eating good food, drinking with friends, riding in cars, sailing a boat, standing in a Tube, looking at shop windows, sleeping in a good bed, making love, buying a suit of clothes, going to the theatre, listening to music, making jokes, playing poker, having a shampoo, reading poetry, chatting with lovely women, sitting in restaurants, running for trains, gossiping in pubs, talking, arguing, laughing, swimming, walking, writing, smoking, riding; a thousand little things that were important because in the aggregate they were just normal living. It didn't really matter being shot at by a dozen dirty rifles, only deadly at such close range, slowly aimed and deliberate; but it mattered a lot that there would afterwards be no more of all this. There seemed a lot of things left undone. It mattered a lot, even, that I had an expensive sweater in Cairo that I had forgotten to put away in moth-balls for the summer. Such was the state of mind one got into.

On other occasions we deduced that they wouldn't dare to touch us. Then we wondered which was the more logical view: whether one was undue optimism or the other undue pessimism. And having finally worried it all out and decided where the logic lay, we began to wonder if, after all, they would take the logical course, and we would spend hours proving to ourselves their logic or their lack of it. Then it would start all over again. These spasms of introspection came more often in the early days, but more violently later on. At first, once the initial shock was over, and there was no hope at all, everything seemed all right; we were really resigned to it. But as the time passed and our hopes rose, then the fear became more passionate. We caught this fear, each from the other, and an unduly long silence from the cell next door would set each of us thinking unhappily again; it became necessary for us to force each other not to start the depression rolling. Whenever a senior officer came down to the cells it seemed to have a personal significance for us. We knew it to be the worst possible form of fear, but there was nothing much we could do about it.

It was a hot, sultry day, when we heard the Colonel coming. It was just such a day as we had decided was unlucky. We knew it was the Commandant because the warder at the end of the passage clicked his heels to attention, and they did that for no one else. I heard Frank jump off his bed and say softly, "It's the Colonel". I stood by the door and waited; the heat was oppressive and I could feel my heart pounding with mounting fear. There was a long delay while they fumbled with the keys. Then we heard his footsteps approaching, and suddenly he was in front of my cell. He was holding a bundle of papers that looked very important and sinister, and I felt, waiting for him to speak, that the blood had left my face.

I tried to appear casual and started to say, "*Buon' giorno, Signor Colonello*", but the words stuck in my throat and sounded strange, so I stopped. Then he looked up suddenly and I saw he was smiling. The moment of acute, complete, petrifying fear passed completely with ludicrous suddenness. It had lasted a long time, but it was gone completely. It was not only the momentary fear which had gone; it was the fear that had grown drop by drop through the past long months with insidious slowness till one only realised its extent when one was at last free of it. It was a drug that killed itself as it grew. I was suddenly surprised that we had ever worried about it.

The Colonel said, smiling, "I have good news for you. Your appeal has been accepted, and your sentence commuted to thirty years in prison."

I suppose I stared. The anti-climax was intolerable, and the idea of thirty years in jail, with the war fast coming to an end, was ludicrous. He mistook my stare for a sign of displeasure, and added, "But you will not have to serve so long. There is sure to be an amnesty at the end of the war. You will probably not serve much more than five."

I wanted desperately to laugh. I covered up by saying, "Thank you for coming yourself to inform us. It was a kind thought. I will just tell my friend." I called out to Frank, "I really cannot resist saying I told you so. Now you can bawl me out as much as you like."

Frank didn't quite know what to say. He said, "Now I am really very happy indeed. I would like to stay here for ten years, it is really a very nice place. I also like the Colonel. Please tell him I like him very much."

I said, "I like even the Duty Sergeant. Now nothing can stop us. We shall be in Cairo for Christmas. Do you want to bet on it?"

When the Colonel had gone I sat on the edge of the bed feeling considerably better, but suddenly very tired. It was four months since we had heard sentence passed, and I was slowly realising how frightened we had been all that time, and now, in retrospect, it seemed a little shameful. There had passed a hundred and twenty-two very unpleasant days.

I could hear Frank doing exercises on the bars of the door. He said, "We shall be out in 1972. Really, it is not long to wait for a good meal."

I said, "It was hard not to laugh at the idea of the amnesty, I really think he believes that."

"I was afraid you were going to laugh. He is a nice man, but very ignorant. I forgot to tell you, he told the adjutant out in the yard one day that you didn't believe in God because you weren't a Catholic. The adjutant was filled with contempt."

"The bastard. But today, I think I like even the adjutant."

"Really, it would have been an indignity to have been shot by such ignorant people. Do you remember the time Pezzimento asked how long it would take to drive a lorry from London to New York?"

Pezzimento heard his name and wanted to know what we had said.

"Pezzimento," I shouted, "our sentence has been commuted to thirty years' imprisonment. This is good news. I told my friend here, 'We must tell our good friend Pezzimento, he will be very happy for us'."

152

"I am very happy for you," Pezzimento said. His solemn voice came from the depth of the sepulchre. "But you will not have to serve so long. In a few years you will be released. Maybe five years only. That is not very long, Pietro, I have been here longer than that already."

Paglia, the Worm, burst into laughter. He shouted, "Pezzimento, you are a fool. In a few weeks their people will be here and will let them out. In a month's time they will be presenting your wife with silk stockings and taking her up to bed. They will be sure that her husband will not be able to walk in unexpectedly and disturb them." He thought this was a huge joke. Everybody was bellowing with laughter. "Ho! Pietro!" he called. "Will you write and tell me what Pezzimento's wife is like? They say she is very fat—you don't need any blankets with her."

Bruno said, "You are right. They chased us out of Africa, and now they will chase us out of Italy. We shall all have to go to Russia."

"Ho! Bruno!" I shouted. "We are going to stay here for ten years. I like it in prison."

"Ai, ai. He likes it in prison," Paglia said. "It is all right in the cells, but it is bad in the yard. But you will not be here for long. Don't forget your friends when you get out, will you? When your soldiers come, will you take me along with you? I can cook good."

I said, to everybody, "I'll take the Worm along as a cook. Then I shall be sure of getting big helpings. *La gavetta piena.*"

Paglia roared with laughter. He shouted, "If you take me, Pietro, you'll have to feed another regiment. But I will come with you. I want to rape Pezzimento's wife. She lives in Taranto. Bah, dirty people in Taranto."

I said, "*Ci sputo!*"

Everyone was happy, roaring with delight and shouting at poor Pezzimento. Only he was silent, sulking.

Frank said, "They are right. We shall be out of here very soon. But," he went on wistfully, "they will say in Cairo, 'Well, why didn't you escape?' That is what they will say, 'Why didn't you escape?' No, I think now we must hurry up and escape before they come and release us. It would not be dignified to be released."

He was doing exercises on the door again. I heard him fall to the floor with a thump. As he picked himself up he said,

153

"Yes, it is a pity. I am beginning to like it here, really."

It was *brodo* for supper that night, weak and cold. I thought, *Now why couldn't it have been pasta tonight to end the day nicely?* But there was a pleasant surprise after all. The orderly had heard the news and slipped us two raw onions each, stolen from the Colonel's garden, We ate them with our bread reserve and had a splendid meal. They were hot and strong.

That night, we had no worries in the world. Life could not have been better. I thought, *Now the road is open.*

But I was wrong. I had forgotten about the Germans.

Chapter Ten

CONSCIOUSLY or subconsciously, the thought of escape was never far from our minds. In the long, weary hours locked in our cells, staring heavily at the grey wall, with nothing to do but think, it was this that kept us from madness. The knowledge, the certainty that somehow or other, given time, we would escape, was the only thought that consistently gnawed at our minds. We knew that there *must* be a way out, *somewhere*. It did not seem easy, but as the time passed and we learned the lie of the land, the difficulties became less severe. As we learned the routine of the prison, so we learned also which of the many potential ways out was likely to be the surest. We had discovered that the rear wall of our cell (which must have been six feet or more thick) was also the wall of a church which gave almost direct access to the main road. This was at least encouraging, because although there were seven locked iron doors to pass through to get down to the cells, here was a way we might use which contained only one solid barrier. The snag here was that we could not possibly have made the necessary hole in the solid stone wall during one night, and the cells were, if not exactly examined, at least looked at daily, and any tampering with the stonework would have been seen at once. We tried hard to think up a way to overcome this snag, without much success; we applied the diverting theory that if a way were to be found of breaking down the wall quickly and in silence, as we had done in Sfax, then intelligence, rather than physical force, would have to find the answer, and in intelligence we were much superior to our warders though our physical capabilities were limited, Therefore, we argued, we have a leg start if only we can think the problem out. If . . .

We did not find the answer, but the promise gave us something to argue about and there was always something or other we could learn from such discussions. Another route, and the one we finally decided on, was through the door leading down to the "fifties". Step by step we could trace the projected route, and the only serious barrier was the door itself; the rest was well within our capabilities. We had already cut the centre bar of each of the cell doors, low down where the camouflage was at its best, and by bending the bar in and up, a space large enough to squeeze through could be made, and the bar could be re-bent into its original position. So that on the rare occasion when the rest of the cells were empty, we could nip out into the corridor and, working most quietly (as the guard was just round the corner), tackle the cement round the door, into which the hasp was fitted. During three days when we happened to be the only occupants of the cell block, we advanced so fast with this work that by removing an entire slice of cement and a stone brick under it, using a nail to scrape with, we could almost release the bolt from its fastening and throw open the door. The work was brought to a halt only by the refilling of the cells, and we waited anxiously but in vain for another occasion. They never discovered this tampering with the solid masonry.

But our discussions by means of notes to Buonavoglia were bearing fruit. We became on very good terms with him, and it was most useful to have such a friend among the honour prisoners. Through him we learned that a friend of his, an ex-convict and a professional thief, living in Taranto, was very pro-British. By promise of heavy repayment when the time came, and by smuggling out notes through Buona-

155

voglia's brother who came to visit him frequently, we arranged that this man would come up to Gaeta, hire a cottage on the outskirts of the town where we could hide till the fuss died down, and then find us a small sailing dinghy—there were plenty lying idle in the little harbour—so that we could slip off one night and sail to Africa. We would make straight for the innocent rented cottage and hide there as long as necessary, living on vegetables and fruit while our aide looked round for a stealable boat. This solved the problem of finding civilian clothes, which in solitary confinement is almost impossible, and we could be sure enough of finding some part of the African coast-line with the most rule-of-thumb navigation.

We thought the trip would take about seven days, and we knew that we could manage this without any food if necessary. We arranged that he was to hold the cottage for us indefinitely, living there himself, and the actual breakout was to be on the first night when the opportunity arose for forcing the door to the "fifties". It was always possible, at a pinch, to bribe the Duty Sergeant to leave the wooden night-door of the cells open, with the plea that we were frightened to be so darkly locked up, though this could not be done very often. We knew where the key was to the store that held ropes and ladders, and careful reconnaissance had shown us that the yard was out of sight of the guards and that the road below it was far enough away from the main gate to permit of a certain amount of careful activity there. The ex-convict agreed to help and left Taranto for Gaeta. Buonavoglia sent us a note saying he was on his way and the tension rose. Escape was near. All this work was accomplished by these smuggled notes and took the very devil of a time.

At this stage, I produced one of my sovereigns. It was needed to bribe the man who acted as go-between for us outside the prison. We sold it inside the jail for four hundred lire, very much less than its proper value. This was a risky business, because we knew that if the news leaked out, our plans would be jeopardised; but it had to be done. We sent some of the money out to our go-between and spent some of it on sugar, wine and fruit, which were smuggled in to us from the hospital, and by judiciously sharing these luxuries with the others in the cells we managed to keep the whole thing secret. They decided, by discussion amongst themselves one night when they thought I was asleep, that the money for all this had been smuggled in to us from British agents in the town who were even then working on our behalf! When we learned of this harmless fiction we neither denied nor admitted it, and our attitude caused them to respect us considerably more as they didn't quite know who or what we or our friends were. One amusing corollary of this was that we heard the idea put forward in all seriousness that Gaeta was not bombed by the Anglo-Americans because the Air Forces knew we were there. This, of course, did us a lot of good, though in truth, the War Office did not find out where we were until after we had escaped. We were simply posted as missing.

Our surreptitious meals in the lavatory continued, and we slowly built up our strength; even at this time I was down forty-two pounds on my normal weight.

It was a week later that Buonavoglia signalled to me in the yard to the effect that a note was waiting for me in my cell. On my return from exercise I made a search and found it stuck with rice paste to the underside of the lowest flat cross-bar of the iron gate. This was a cunning hiding-place, and had I not known definitely that this piece of paper was somewhere in the cell, it might have remained there till this day. The note said briefly, "He has been arrested."

This was the explanation of a certain air of despondency; I had noticed in the yard that Buonavoglia had been unwilling to talk to me and it seemed that having passed his brief message, he had wanted to have nothing more to do with us. Three days later we discovered what had really happened, by a series of notes, when the scare had passed. The ex-convict had certainly come up from Taranto to Gaeta. He had agreed "in principle" to the plan he had learned from Buonavoglia's brother, and was leaving to our post-war generosity the question of any payment, other than the amount sufficient to cover the rental of a cottage for a month or two and enough to keep us in food.

But he was a Southerner. No Southerner can move from A to B without attempting to make a little money to pay the fare. Our friend simply carried four tins of olive oil hidden under rags in the bottom of the lorry that carried him. The difference in price of oil between Taranto and the near-north was high and a little smuggling was indicated. But, as a professional criminal—always the most careless of all who break the law—he was not smart enough and got caught. The last we heard was that he was sitting in jail in Naples awaiting trial, and that was the bitter end of our careful scheming. We could not at first believe that his arrest and our own plans were not connected; but Buonavoglia's change back to friendliness in a few days showed that this was not the case. It was hard, bitterly hard, to throw the plan completely aside and start from scratch again.

Then, with startling suddenness, more startling because we were out of touch with the fast moving events outside, our chance came, There was a commotion in the cells. We felt it first as a tension in the air which nobody could place. It may have been started in a hundred different ways: the unusual sound of running feet, a scared look on the face of an orderly, a shout within the walls of the office compound, a shot fired in the town, or simply the fact that no coffee came that morning. All the solitaries knew that something was in the wind; *something*, good or bad, was happening. We all shouted for water, so that we could find out from the water-boy what it was all about, but he didn't come, and that increased our excitement. There were shouts in the distance. I said to Frank, "Something's going on. What is it?"

Frank said, "Shush! I'm trying to listen. It's something big."

"Can you hear what they're saying outside?"

"Yes, a bit." He said slowly, "I can't make it out. It sounds as if the number one had resigned."

This did not sound possible. I said,

"Resigned? That's nonsense. Either they shoot him or he stays: he can't resign."

"That's what I thought. Listen, they're whispering up by the gate."

There was a long silence, so tense that I could hear Paglia's asthmatic breathing. I heard Pezzimento fidgeting in his cell. I knew that everyone was gripping his bars, trying to catch a word or two that would solve the mystery. Frank was straining to hear what was going on. Then Pezzimento called out solemnly,

"Pietro!" He sounded strangely cool.

"Ho, Pezzimento!" I called quickly. "What goes on?"

"We don't know exactly, Pietro, but they say that Il Duce has resigned."

158

I said, "That means the end of the war."

"Yes, I hope so. Shall we all be released now?"

There was always humour in the incredible outlook of our friend. I did not tell him that the war had nothing to do with professional jail-birds. I said,

"Wait a minute, Pezzimento. Let's first find out if it is true."

I called to Bruno, more intelligent than the others.

"What's happened, Bruno? Can a man in his position resign?"

"That's what we all want to know. They say Marshal Badoglio has taken over."

Then one of the warders came to the passage door and talked in great excitement to a favoured prisoner. It was Bruno. He told us what was happening. The Lieutenant on the staff, who was a Blackshirt and rather threw his Party weight about, had been seen in civilian clothes creeping out of the prison with a suitcase. That told us all we wanted to know. They said that two other officers had sneaked out, leaving their uniforms behind. I called Bruno,

"It isn't Mussolini. It's Fascism. It's Fascism that has fallen, the whole damn issue." It seemed like sacrilege even to say so, but Bruno agreed.

There was a burst of shouting and arguing. There were two or three warders hanging about in the corridors, and they all joined in. We heard them professing their life-long antagonism to Fascism. It was obvious that the news was true. Everyone was friendly to us. They said, "You're lucky. You'll be out of here in no time at all."

I asked to see the Colonel and he told us that the war was *not* over. He said cautiously, "There seems to be a change in Government."

The day passed terribly slowly, but with great suppressed excitement, and as the time went by and we heard of Badoglio's "Fight on" speech, a heavy depression spread over the whole jail; it was as though we had been deprived of our rights. We had no patience to see what was going to happen. Our plans seemed to have been completely cascaded. But behind it all was the conviction that one way or another it would not be long now. That's what we thought.

Then came the Armistice.

I saw the Colonel and demanded our release. As senior Allied Officer in the area, I demanded the surrender of the garrison. The Commandant heard me coldly, then just as coldly informed me that we were not prisoners-of-war, but common criminals and would still be held. We were forced back to the cells in silent fury. Then came the worst news of all. There was sporadic shooting outside and we heard that a German anti-aircraft detachment (fifteen men under a *feldwebel*) had attacked the Gaeta garrison (four thousand strong) because they would not surrender their arms. The Germans had won, by threatening to call for reinforcements. The garrison Commander, a Colonel, had handed his force over to the German corporal. Worse, the Germans were taking over the prison.

The prisoners rose against this new indignity. Rioting in Italian prisons is a pretty popular pastime, and as soon as it started we saw our only chance to get out before the Germans took control. We shouted advice to them, encouraged them with our new authority as officers of a victorious army. They threw the warders out and barricaded themselves in. Shots were fired, frightened shots before the Commandant saw that their own men were deserting rather than fight a battle which looked too easy to lose. There was *molta confusione*.

Only a few of the guards remained. Garofalo was one. Bleeding from a cut on the head, he came and took us from the cells. The Colonel had told him to take us down to the dungeons "to protect us from the rioters". I felt it was time for a little straight talking. I told him that he could either help us or hinder us; that if he did the latter he would be treated as a partisan and shot by the Occupying Forces. On the other hand . . . I produced a sovereign. He was very thoughtful, and I explained the position carefully.

I said, "Look. The officers have deserted. The guards have deserted. This is not a prison any more. Legally, you have to obey my orders now. Your Army has surrendered to mine and that means that you yourself are a prisoner-of-war. All I want is an Italian uniform for each of us and the keys to the main gates."

He said nothing for a while. We had passed into the corridor, but the double gates dividing us from the compound we wished to reach, where the rioters were, were locked. The stairs led down to the underground cells. As we moved towards them, I said, "Your own country has been overrun in a few days and we'll do the same in Italy. I don't want the Germans to get us before our troops arrive. Be smart, you can't be a sergeant all your life."

He pushed us down the stairs to the cells below. He said, "The Colonel's orders are that you stay in the cells." He pushed us inside. The new cells were dark and dismal, and we started quarrelling at once. We were worse off than we were before. We didn't like the idea, but there was only one thing to do; we decided to fight our way out with our bare hands the moment the doors were opened.

But it wasn't necessary after all. Garofalo came back in a very short while, another man with him. He was very bitter. He said, "The Colonel, almost all the officers, have deserted. I am the only sergeant here. What can I do, I have a family? This is the barber. Hurry up, there's not much time."

I could scarcely believe what was happening. The barber snipped off my beard and gave me a haircut, then did the same for Frank. Garofalo was on our side now, and we decided what to do. He told us the Germans were already in the offices, looking over the records. I thought, *My God, if they see our names, we're done for*. Frank looked as frightened as I felt; he also looked damn funny without his beard. Garofalo seemed to be nursing a grievance against us. He said reproachfully, "You started this riot. We heard you shouting to them. If you had not done so we could have controlled it." Frank grinned and said, "We were bored." I said, "Hurry up, for Christ's sake! We haven't got all day."

As soon as we had finished, Garofalo led us to the stores, forcing a way through crowds of prisoners half rioting, half escaping. There was still a certain amount of shooting, but the prison was now firmly in the hands of the convicts. They were looting the place pretty thoroughly.

Garofalo looked a little worried as he pushed through the mob, but they ignored him in their anxiety to get away. They crowded about the stores, trying, as we were, to find better clothing. As we were at the tail-end there was very little left, but we found ragged trousers each, a torn shirt, and broken boots. I picked up a good Army jacket and Frank found a greatcoat with the lining torn out. It took him sometime to find a pair of boots that would fit and I got very angry with him. We kept hearing shouts from frightened prisoners that the Germans were coming, in the corridor, down the stairs, along the passage. I cursed Frank with everything that

161

was foul in every language I could think of, anything that was blasphemous and spiteful. Garofalo suddenly disappeared and there were no more convicts either, save those scrambling fast out of the door into the yard.

There was the ring of disciplined feet in the passage, a shot was fired. I waited no more and ran for it. Frank was behind me, still struggling with odd boots and cursing most horribly. We followed the other running convicts into the yard, across the square, and when they turned to the main gates, we stopped. There was a German officer there, fingering a Schmeisser. He was letting them all pass him, out into the street, but we were still in British uniform. We stopped and pulled back frantically, looking round for a way of escape. Garofalo was suddenly beside us, dragging us through a small gate in the wall. He slammed it shut behind us and locked it. He leaned on the door and said, heavily, "This is the prison garden, they won't come in here. If they do, you can hide in the barn."

We went to the barn and sat down on the floor. Frank was still cursing. He said, "Look at this boot. Look at it!" He thrust his hand through the sole and waggled his fingers. "This is the one that fits; the other is too small. Couldn't you have waited another five minutes?" Then he suddenly burst out laughing. We felt safe suddenly, and very pleased with ourselves. We changed into our Italian rags as quickly as we could, and buried our uniforms. My boots were quite hopeless too, so Garofalo gave me his, standing about in grey, dirty socks with holes in the toes. They were three sizes too long and a size too narrow. We had no socks, so we wrapped rags around our feet. Frank found an abandoned shoe and tied it to his foot with a bit of string, forcing his foot into the other boot most painfully. I saw that we were going to have foot trouble, but the first thing was to get away. The rest would follow after. We wore knee breeches which, without stockings, looked comic, ragged shirts and jackets, and side caps on the tops of our heads, Italian style. It was very hard not to giggle.

We raided the garden and had a good meal of lettuce and tomato, with raw turnips for good measure. One or two other prisoners found their way into the garden and did the same. They did not recognise us without our long beards. They told us the Germans were letting everyone get clear of Gaeta, then picking them up at Formia, on the main road, and sending them north in trucks, It didn't sound so good. We learned that Buonavoglia had been picked up, had tried to get away and had been shot. Some of the others had got clear and had come back into the village to think it over. But, they said, there was a way out, if we could climb. They told us of a way that led to the mainland but by-passed the road. They explained it most carefully till we were certain that we could find it by ourselves.

We decided to spend the night among the cabbages—it was not worth risking the curfew, because if the Italian prisoners who had not seen us before had not recognised us as English, we were sure that we would get past the Germans as normal Italian refugees. We discussed the ways and means, ate some green stuff, and lay down in the barn to sleep.

During the night one of the cows beside us complained. It gave me an idea, and I inexpertly drew off two tins of milk. It was warm, and the cow was friendly. We slept like logs.

Chapter Eleven

A YELLOW, cheerful sun was splashing the walls of the garden in the early morning when we awoke. Everything was bright green, cool, and friendly. It was the first time for many months that we had slept in the open and there was dew on our clothes and straw in our hair. The air was fresh, cold and clean. It was like an iced draught to the lungs.

"Well," I said, "this is our first day of liberty. If we take it easy and make no mistakes, we are as good as home. If the Germans find us in Italian clothes and we can't prove we are escaping prisoners, we shall have the whole thing all over again. So watch out."

163

Frank said, "It's in the bag. This time we will make no mistakes. This time we shall do it. Only, we must keep away from the Germans. I do not like Germans, really."

"That goes for the Italians. We must trust nobody. If they offer us help, run for it. We must keep absolutely on our own. You do the talking when necessary."

We strapped our boots to our feet—there is no other phrase for it—and washed briefly at the well. My sovereigns were still in their secure hiding-place and I extracted one for Garofalo. He came along as he heard us moving and brought milk and a bottle of red wine. We pulled a few swedes and ate them before we started. Then, out of the blue, the Colonel appeared. He was ten years older, tired and disillusioned. He wore grey trousers and shirt, and no collar or tie. He watched us in silence for a while. I thought he was trying to feel the atmosphere, and I felt sorry for him, so I wished him good morning. Garofalo eyed him curiously.

I said, "You realise that you are to blame for all this? By refusing to free us at once you have placed us, and yourself, in a very awkward position. If you tell your German friends that we are here, there will be trouble." He did not answer. I went on,

"If you had released us at once, as you should have done, you could not have been held responsible should we subsequently be captured again. Now, I do not know what will happen. Technically it is aid to the enemy by a defeated and surrendered army. You know what that means."

He said, painfully, "The Germans are not my friends. They have thrown me out of my prison. Thrown me out by force. We have been much deceived."

"Your stupidity is your own affair. I am concerned only with our position."

He said, awkwardly, "There was much confusion. We were out of contact. Perhaps . . . I do not know, perhaps I was wrong. I did not understand, *figliolo*."

I was surprised at the "my son". It was rather pathetic. He said, "Now . . . if there is anything I can do to help . . . perhaps . . . I do not think the Germans will catch you."

"They are on the main road."

"Why don't you hide here, in the village?"

"Don't be bloody silly. You would be the first to betray us if there was any danger to yourself."

164

"I am sorry," he said. "It is all very confused."

"To me it is clear enough. We shall escape. But if we are caught we shall say that you released us. We shall tell them that you helped us. I do not like to take this attitude but I cannot afford to run the risk of trusting, not your good will, but your intelligence. I do not doubt that you would like to help us now; but your attitude in the past gives me no reason to trust your discretion."

We went on with our preparations. The Colonel went to one side and called Garofalo over. Frank sauntered over to pull a lettuce and heard the Colonel warn him that if he helped us the Germans would punish him. I was very angry and called Garofalo away.

I said, "Look here, you've done well so far. Don't let your officer spoil it all for you."

I gave him the sovereign. He said, "The Colonel is an old man. I have said I will help you and I will do so." He gave us the loose change from his pockets, a few one- and five-lire notes. On an impulse he went away and came back with his wife and child. The wife was a blowsy woman of thirty, the child a sick and wretched infant of four.

He said, "This is my family, I want them to know that you are my friends." He embraced me and kissed me on both cheeks. It was the first time I had been kissed by a sergeant-major. His three-day-old beard was like barbed wire, and I felt very sorry for his wife.

The Colonel, a tired old man, watched us go.

We left the prison grounds through a side-door on to the street. We carried a bottle each, one of milk and one of wine, a couple of baked potatoes in our pockets. Lippi, one of the honour-prisoners, had explained the road well. We kept straight on till we came to a hut standing on the left, then turned left for a hundred paces. Then to a tiny side-street, no more than a path between two houses. Then straight on till we came to the stairway on the right. We turned down the broad stone steps. Frank said, "Oh, my God," and stopped short. A German sentry was leaning on his rifle at the bottom. I whispered furiously, "Come on, for God's sake, he's seen us." We carried on down the stairway, our hearts beating furiously.

I said, in Italian, "Pretend you own the bloody place. Whatever happens, don't run. Try and appear to be friendly; we were allies a few days ago." The sentry watched us as we approached. There were few people about. I remembered to hunch my shoulders and shuffle like an Italian soldier. We came very close to him. He stared hard at us and I wondered whether we should salute him or say something. I kept my eyes on the ground. As we drew near I raised the wine bottle to my lips and drank, then offered it to him with a gesture. He ignored us completely. We walked past him and I felt his eyes boring into the back of my head. I felt the contempt there.

I said to Frank, "For Christ's sake, don't look round."

We walked on, resisting the temptation to run. I thought, *He knows we can't get past. He knows we'll be picked up on the main road.* We walked on, slowly. When we were out of hearing, Frank said, "My God, I didn't like that. I wonder why he didn't stop us?"

"He must know we're prisoners, the town must be lousy with them. He thinks we'll be picked up on the main road."

"I suppose that's it. But it shows at least that we can fool the Germans who we are. I only hope the Carabinieri are not working with them."

I said, "That's your worry. From now on you do all the talking. If we are questioned, say you met me on the road and don't know who I am. I'll say I come from Tunisia; that will account for my accent."

"No, no, don't say that. Say you come from Milano. We are only likely to meet Southerners down here and you'll get away with it. If you say Tunisia they'll ask a lot of questions because none of them will know where that is. We have to turn off soon. Keep your eyes open for a red tree-stump on the side of the road."

We found the tree-stump with difficulty; there were too many of them. But at last we turned off across a stretch of open ground and into a vineyard on the slope of the hill. We lay among the vines for an hour or more, eating the early-morning grapes, still wet with dew. We were already tired out after walking for a mere hour or two, but the physical fact of being in the open was wonderful. We set off again, climbing the hill till we could feel the breeze of the sea in the distance, then across to the right and up a sharp precipitous face of sandstone where a weathered goat-track wound round the crumbling bluff. It was hard going, and we were forced to rest again at the top. But there was a cool breeze blowing and we soon came to a track where the going was

166

better. There was plenty of fruit about and we stopped often to fill up with grapes or apricots. We came at last to our first objective—the steep slope of the hill behind which lay the mainland. There was a narrow path among the rocks, and it was very, very steep. We pulled ourselves up the weary slope most painfully, feeling behind us the months of inactivity and bad food; several others joined us, mostly, I guessed, ex-prisoners themselves. Nobody paid us any attention; they all concentrated on keeping out of the way of the Germans.

We reached the top of the little mountain at midday, and started down the road to the mainland. It would have been easy to have turned south and to have by-passed Formia by striking inland, but an extraordinary rumour reached us and made us change our plans: we heard that the British had landed at Anzio. This was in September 1943, and the rumour was so strong that the roads were thronged with refugees trying to get there. We joined them and set off north.

For the first few days we tied up with a party of ex-convicts going the same way. It was risky, as we were determined to keep our identity secret, but Frank did all the talking and it was fairly easy to keep up the pretence. The idea was this: it seemed that we should have to spend a good time on the road and I was anxious to find out how this tramping was being done by the thousands of refugees, deserters and plain tramps amongst whom we were to lose ourselves. I felt that if we behaved exactly as the others did, then we should be less noticeable and this turned out to be a very good thing. We learned during the first night that one could break into anyone's barn to sleep, and if the irate owner protested simply bawl him out and threaten to break a stick over his head. Left to our own devices we should undoubtedly have asked most politely for leave to sleep in someone else's property and thus been conspicuous by our politeness, or, at best, just turned away. We learned in the first morning how to trample the fields and help ourselves to fruit and vegetables or any stray chicken. We learned to spot a good resting-place from a bad one, and how to hide near a prepared "back door" before we slept. Our companions were all professional criminals, and they really knew their way about.

We reached the main road on the second day and turned due north along the Via Appia towards Rome, two of a vast crowd of pedestrians thronging in all directions. Some pushed hand-carts, some carried bundles; all were hungry.

167

Peasants stood by the roadside offering food in exchange for whatever they could get, shoes, clothes and old blankets, some sentimental trinket. We had nothing to trade, so we lived on fruit. On the third day, after a night spent curled up in the cold wind, one of the party said,

"I want some bread—I'm going to pay a visit to that farm over there."

Feeling that I might learn something, I followed. I did learn something, too; I learned how to beg. It was a valuable lesson and I taught it to Frank (who was a little reserved about the idea) as soon as I could. The tale that was told was always based on the same thing—the poor Italian soldier trying to find his way home, always hungry. It usually worked, and we were able in the days to come to supplement our diet of fruit with an occasional piece of bread or a dish of beans. No one ever suspected that we were not what we pretended to be—poor Italian soldiers, hungrily hiking home. But our begging failed us once: an irate peasant woman threw a broken casserole at me because, she said, it was men like me who had lost the war. I felt this was very unfair of her.

We plodded on north, passing one awkward spot where a German patrol was out looking for man-power to send north, by joining in with a party of ten or twelve others who dropped down to the sea and hired a fishing-boat to row us along the coast for a day. We all lay in the bottom of the boat, out of sight of the land and when the danger was over, drew in to the shore and walked on again; this cost us some of our precious lire.

We reached Taracina before we discovered that the rumour was false, and that our own troops were miles away to the south. It was hard to turn round and plod all the way back again, by the same road we had already spent five days on, but those five days were not entirely wasted. We were able to stand on our own now, and the hard walking had already given us strength. Our fruit diet was having an unfortunate effect on our stomachs, but this was no more than uncomfortable. The main problem we had to face was how to pass Formia, but it turned out to be no longer necessary as the Germans there had been bombed out by the Air Force, and three days later we reached the town; it was desolate and almost entirely destroyed. We stopped in a vineyard to take some wine and were told that the Germans

168

had posts at unexpected corners on the main road where they collected slave-labour, but that there was nothing else to worry about. On the whole they were leaving the Italians alone.

We picked up a lot of useful gossip in these vineyards. They were no more than wine-pressers' huts by the side of the road where new wine could be bought for next to nothing. We decided to save our small amount of money in case of emergeney, so we begged for wine too. Once we had persuaded ourselves that begging was morally permissible under the peculiar circumstances pertaining at the time, we enjoyed it immensely; we were playing at tramps, and we played at it thoroughly. We would enter the vineyard when there were others drinking there and ask for water to drink. We looked as miserable as we could while we drank it—this was not hard in our frightful rags—and it was never long before someone took pity on us and gave us a drink; we did not drink for the sake of alcohol, but simply because our weakened bodies were strengthened by the sugar and fruit in the wine. It did us good, it gave us strength and it was necessary.

It was on one of these occasions that my "cover-story" nearly fell through. As reluctantly as possible I had divulged my Milanese "origin" to a persistently inquisitive fellow, and with the best will in the world he called his friend over to meet me. He also came from Milano. I couldn't run for it, as I had taken off my boots to wash the sores on my feet, so I had rapidly to invent a secondary story. I told him that although my family was Milanese, I myself had never been there; I was born in Tunis of Italian parents. I said we spoke French at home, I said I'd never been to Italy before, what a lovely country, nice people, friendly, really I was proud to be an Italian. I said I had joined the Army when our victorious and glorious forces landed, and now had been chased out of my own home by the *Americani*. He sympathised and gave me another drink. Frank was trying hard not to laugh as my story got more and more involved. To be on the safe side he whispered to the others that I was a little, you know, not *mad* exactly, but . . . well, not very bright. I thought it was quite unnecessary. We got our boots on as soon as possible, and left.

We were eventually arrested, as refugees, on the main road just south of Formia. It was to be the last time. We walked right into a German post, having comfortably and in the most casual manner passed many Germans on the road, and were picked up with several others. They stood guard over us while we filled in bomb-holes on the road with picks and shovels. It was hard work and they drove us hard. Every time we stopped for breath, one of the soldiers lashed out with his foot, arm or the butt of his rifle, and I was soon a mass of bruises. We worked for about four hours, and then some lorries appeared. My heart sank. We thought of making a dash for it, but that had apparently been tried before. They posted sentries round us and started pushing us aboard. I thought, *Ah, there won't be room for all of us*, and said to Frank, "Try and hang back, we shan't all get on."

When the last lorry was loaded to capacity, there were four of us left. One of the soldiers called out and said to the corporal who was loading, "Four more here; can you squeeze them in?"

The officer in charge turned and said, "No. Don't overload. Let them go if there's no room. They'll be picked up again down the road. If we keep them here they'll start asking for food."

They let us go. As we went, I held out my hand and said "*Sigaretta, sigaretta.*" He gave me a cigarette and we walked away. I said to Frank, "This is where we leave the road. And if I ever say again, *let's go back on the road*, hit me over the head with a stone. They said we would be picked up again a little farther along."

"Is that what he said? I was hoping you might understand what he was saying."

"I only know three words of German; he said all of them. We'll have to get right off the road and make for the mountains. Looks about twenty miles away. Then we get to the top and walk along the summit." It sounded easy.

We climbed through the coarse fence at the roadside as soon as we were well out of sight. We stumbled over a field of cut maize, across a farm, and into an orchard where we stopped a while to eat figs. It seemed that we could never satisfy our hunger. Besides, it was a good plan to eat while we could. We knew that it might be necessary to go several days without food, as indeed it was, and we wanted to catch up on what we had missed in jail.

170

It was hard going across the fields to the mountains, but it was harder still when we came to the slopes and started climbing. We had difficulty finding water, but by the evening we were well up the heights. There were trees all round us, and when evening fell we lay down in a patch of fern and slept. It was easy enough to sleep, but when morning came we were frozen stiff. We found some potatoes in a garden, and boiled some up in a tin for breakfast, drinking the hot water as soup. It was not too tasty, and we wished we had found some salt. In the safety and quiet of the friendly forest we took stock of our position. We were pretty well off, on the whole. We had plenty to eat and drink, and there was always a soft patch of fern or leaves to sleep on at night. The main trouble was our feet: Frank's boots were much too small for him and he had the most frightful sores: my own were not much better, and the rags we used as socks were hard and did not absorb the perspiration. From now on, however, it seemed simply a question of patience. We did not realise how sorely our patience was going to be tried.

We climbed up the mountain for the rest of the day. We met several other parties, but they usually left us alone. We were once asked by some passing peasants why we didn't use the road, and Frank invented a likely story that I had hit a German officer who had called us dirty Italians and we were anxious to keep out of their way. And once, passing through a tiny mountain village, we slipped on to the road to draw water at the fountain and were surrounded at once by some twenty or thirty women who wanted to know where we had come from. They took us for refugees, however, and explained that a patrol was just around the corner looking for men for labour; all their men had been taken a week before, but the patrol had already picked up one or two stragglers. Just then one of them, who had gone to "keep cave", came running back and said the patrol was returning. They pushed us inside one of the houses till they had passed. They gave us wine to drink and bread to take with us. As soon as the coast was clear, they showed us the quickest way to the mountain-tops; they seemed sorry to see us go.

We climbed and climbed, and stopped for the night near the rise of the summit. We had passed a field of maize with the husks turned back to dry out the corn, and though it seemed a bit hard, we were hungry and decided to try and cook some. So we lit a small fire and put the pot on to boil.

We lay down to rest while we were waiting and soon fell asleep.

I woke suddenly to find a man standing over me. It was barely dusk and I wondered where he had come from. He pointed to the bubbling mess-tin and asked what it was; I thought perhaps he was the owner of the corn we had stolen, and looked round to see if he was alone. I said, "Corn; we've had no food for three days."

He put out a foot and kicked it off the fire. The water sizzled and the golden-red corn, still hard, scattered over the green-brown earth. It did not look particularly appetising, but it was all we had and I was very angry. I jumped up and said, "What the hell's the idea?" Frank woke up and got to his feet.

The man said, "You can't eat that rubbish. Come over here, I'll give you a good meal." I looked at Frank; he raised his eyebrows. We followed the man to a spot no more than a few hundred yards away, and there, concealed from sight by vegetation and clever camouflage, was a tiny cave, built up with timber and earth-clods. It was made of no more than a dozen logs wedged into the side of the hill and covered over with earth and shrub. A smokeless fire was burning by it; in a pot was a thick red sauce and *pasta*, and beans were stewing in another. The rich smell of food was on the air. Grinning at us he explained:

"I know how to live," he said. "I'm going to wait for the Allies to get here before I go back to my village. The Germans have carried off all the men of my village to work in Bolzano." He winked. "All except one. I'm staying here till the *Americani* come. I have everything here; beans, pasta, wine, fruit, everything. I have the woman, too." He called out and a young girl came out of the shelter. He said, "Make food. We are three."

The woman, a heavy, unwashed peasant girl of fifteen or so, with straggling black hair and a loose-fitting black dress that dropped slackly about her shoulders, said nothing, but produced spoons and bowls for all of us. She sat on one side and watched us eat. Our friend saw me watching her and said, "*Bella, eh?*" I thought for a moment he was going to offer her to me. She was too old for her age, with the heavy breasts of a plump woman of thirty. She looked sullen, almost savage, bad-tempered. I said, "*Bella, molta bella.*"

172

He said, "Tonight you will sleep here. In the morning I will give you milk."

We sat up most of the night talking. He was a good-hearted fellow, but there was something about him I did not like. Maybe he grinned too easily. However, we accepted his invitation to stay the night. He wanted us to sleep inside, all of us together, but I insisted that we stay outside in the lee of the shelter. He refused to listen to my arguments till I indicated the woman and made a vulgar gesture. He laughed and said, "Ah, never mind about that, we're all men, aren't we? You don't have to watch." But I won, and we lay down outside the door. He covered us with a blanket. I noticed that it was a prison blanket, but said nothing.

We waited for him to get to sleep. We heard him making violent love to the woman, groaning and straining and breathing heavily. We heard the fast breathing of the girl, like an animal. At last it was all over and we heard him snoring. I tapped Frank on the shoulder and we got up quietly and stole away. As we reached the next hill Frank said, "I was going to wake you up. I didn't like the look of that, but I don't know why."

I said "It's easy to believe that the Germans have people on the hills here looking for refugees. They seem to be determined to pick up all they can. There are plenty of Italians about trying to keep out of their way."

"That's what I was thinking. But perhaps we are being unkind."

"Better be unkind than back in jail."

Frank demanded, "Did you hear what was going on? Really, I wanted to get up and cheer him on. Really, I never heard a man make so much noise; it is not decent."

"I hope she enjoyed it. But what a face, she must be a bitch."

"I thought she was rather pretty. I like a woman to be fat, really."

"Do you want to go back?"

Frank giggled. He said, "First, I want to go to Cairo."

Chapter Twelve

WE DID a lot of walking in the next few days. Every tiny village had its quota of rumour-mongers. The Allies were moving up from Calabria, so much we knew, but we could not get any information as to where they were. No one knew about the Salerno landings, except one fellow who said they had been repulsed and, remembering Anzio, we treated that as a complete falsehood. But the Americans, they said, were in Avellino; so we went to Avellino and it took us three days to get there, only to learn on arrival that they were not there. But, they said, the English are in Benevento, so we walked to Benevento, and they weren't there either. But in Benevento they knew that the Americans were in Avellino . . . We explained patiently that we had just come from Avellino and it was full of Germans. Ah, they said, then the Allies are not in Avellino at all. But it is certain that the parachutists have taken Frozione, that much we *know*. How did they know? Well, so they had *heard*.

We walked from near Naples on the west coast to Foggia on the east. We walked and walked back till at last we came to a huge plain, high, high above Avellino, which could be gained only by a rough and narrow track leading up to the sky. There were sheep there and cows and water and fruit. It was a tiny Paradise, and there could be no Germans there because no wheeled vehicle could go there. It was safe, perfectly safe, the ideal hide-out. But alas, it was too safe. It was crowded with wealthy refugees from Naples, hiding from the Germans, knowing that they were safe up there, and the peasants had taken over. Meat was for sale, firewood was for sale; two hefty farmers sat on the water-supply filling their hats with ten lire notes. We were not even able to get a drink of water. "*No, signori,*" they said, "*si paga, si paga.*"

Most wearily we moved on. As we started down the weary track again, shots rang out behind us and we threw ourselves to the ground. A peasant stood near-by and stared at us in amazement. There were more shots, very close. Frank said, "But they're firing, can't you hear them?" The

174

peasant spat and moved on. There were more shots. We stood up to look and saw that it was charcoal exploding in the pits. We felt a little foolish.

"All right," Frank said the next day, "let's keep walking in the same direction, south. We must get somewhere if we do that. I'm tired of all these rumours. Really, it is too much. There are two foreign armies overrunning their country and they don't know where they are. It is preposterous. What do you say?"

"I couldn't disagree with you less. We'll go to Salerno."

"All right, Salerno. Keep moving and listen to no rumours."

"Good, Salerno."

So we walked on south, but we still heard the rumours. At last, one cool and pleasant evening, we walked into a German gun position in the woods. It was medium artillery. We had not been seen and we drew back cautiously. I whispered to Frank, "One thing is certain. We're in range of something worth shooting at."

Frank said, "If this is their front line, our own troops can't be far away."

"We'll have to pass this lot, and go very carefully from now on."

We spent the rest of the daylight most cautiously picking our way silently forward. We moved to the side for a few hundred yards and tried again. There were more guns. Each time we tried, we failed to penetrate the screen. Once we were seen and had to run for it. Once they fired at us as we drew back. Once we were chased and nearly caught. It seemed as if there was no way through. We made our way back a few miles and slept, lying hidden in the fine cover of heavy scrub.

We played hide and seek again in the morning with no better results, and at midday we started climbing to the high mountains once more. We met two peasants, incredibly old and wiry little men, looking for some lost cattle. They told us that the Monastery was full of refugees.

Frank said, "What Monastery?"

"There on the top. The priests are feeding the homeless."

Frank said, happily, "What do you say, aren't we homeless? Let's go and find this wonderful place."

I said to the old man, "What's everyone doing up there?"

175

"Oh, I don't know. Waiting for the Americans, I suppose."

"They've got a long time to wait."

"Oh, I don't know; they're in Salerno now. That's not far."

"I've heard that story before," I said, "you don't want to believe all those yarns."

The old man puffed his pipe complacently. He said, "I've seen them."

We both shouted together, "What!"

"Well, I've seen the boats they came in. That's the same thing, isn't it?"

"But where? What have you seen?"

"You can see too, if you walk a bit beyond the Monastery. Harbour's full of them. Over a thousand, I shouldn't be surprised."

I said to Frank, "You know, I think we are technically homeless. We will go and have a meal at the soup-kitchen."

We told the peasants they were walking straight into the Germans. They knew already. They said they were going to get their cows back. I wouldn't be surprised to hear that they did, too.

We reached the Monastery late that night. It was perched very high on the edge of a steep bluff and the air was magnificent. It was dark and we were able to talk to the people wandering about the gardens without being seen very much. The grounds were full of men, women and children Someone told us to sleep outside as the building was reserved for women; there were hundreds of them sleeping inside. But we had no blankets and it was freezing cold, so we stole quietly into the Monastery through a side door which led behind the altar and lay down on the floor.

Beyond the curtain the women slept, or dozed, or talked. The strong smell of them was stifling, but it was a warm and friendly smell. Their conversation was highly entertaining, and it was sometimes hard to control our laughter. It is not often one overhears, willy-nilly, the conversation of a hundred women who think they are alone; the sanctity of their surroundings did not seem to restrain them, and we spent a hilarious night, stifling our laughter in the folds of our jackets.

I slept for an hour or two and went outside when dawn

was fresh in the east across the valley. I woke Frank and we went to look for food. There was no fruit about, but we found the body of a freshly-killed cow with the butcher lying asleep beside it. We had no knife to help ourselves with so we woke the butcher and asked him to sell us meat for twelve lire, all we had left. He grumbled and told us the meat would be sold at ten o'clock, not before. We told him the tale, laying on the pathos heavily, and he sold us a small piece of meat off the neck. We lit a fire of twigs and roasted it on the end of a stick.

There were many people about, huddled in blankets, even at this early hour, ex-soldiers, civilians, men, women, all driven from their homes and waiting for the line to pass them. A pretty child of eight or nine, thin as a stick but very sweet and smiling, came and watched us roasting. She said, "No, not like that. Let me do it for you." She ran and fetched a frying-pan and cooked the meat for us. She said, "Cooking is a woman's job." She was very sweet and we shared it with her. Her mother suddenly appeared and greeted us. She brought us some potatoes and told us the priests would give them free to the poor.

We spent all morning there. There was a lot of movement, but everyone was minding his own business. Most of the time was spent leaning on the low wall of the grounds, watching the splendid panorama of the valley below, rippling with gun-flashes. There was a road far below us, with a tiny sentry on a toy bridge. It was like a mock battle on a sand-table.

I had one nasty moment. I turned away from the wall to find a priest standing beside me. Frank had gone off somewhere.

He said, "My son, are you a Catholic?"

I wasn't sure how to address a priest, so I said, "*Si, Padre.*"

"Then why," he asked, "did you not attend Mass this morning?"

I tried to look uncomfortable, which was not very difficult. I was trying to choose the words of my answer carefully, to make no mistakes. I wondered where the hell Frank was.

I said, "I do not go to Church."

"But why not, my son?"

"I don't know," I spoke shortly. I wanted to end the conversation before it began. I hoped that rudeness might get rid of him, but the ruder I became the more gently he answered. I suppose he was a good man. I was afraid of running out of phrases which I could speak with precise correctness. I promised to go to Mass that evening. It was the easiest way out.

When I found Frank, I said to him, "For Christ's sake don't leave me alone here; I've just been buttonholed by a priest."

Frank said, "My God, did he suspect anything?"

"I don't think so. But I've got to go to Mass this evening or he'll be after me again. What do I have to do?"

"That's easy. We'll go together and you just do as I do. If I can remember. Mumble anything you can think of all the time, it sounds holy. I used to recite nursery rhymes."

"But don't I have to talk to him? Confess or something?"

"Don't be ridiculous, please. You just have to pray. Really, it is very easy. He will sprinkle water on you."

"Does it smell nice?"

"It's straight from the well."

"Oh. Do we get wine?"

"No wine. Just well-water."

I went to Mass that evening, with Frank taking the lead. It was all very difficult and one of the things they left out when they taught me how to escape. But the priest never found out. He thought I was an irreligious soldier saved from the jaws of hell.

There was an incident that night. Three German soldiers appeared from nowhere. They were at the gate in the semi-darkness before we saw them and there was an immediate panic. A crowd milled about them when it was seen that they were alone, and it looked as if they were in for a rough time, which might have given rise to complications affecting us. They said they were deserters. They wanted to hand over their rifles, get some plain clothes, and walk to the Vatican. They said they were Austrian Catholics and the only survivors of a bombardment which had wiped out their unit. I hung about on the edge of the crowd listening. The priest spoke to them in German and translated into Italian for the benefit of the crowd. Then he took them inside to feed them.

I walked slowly back to where Frank was and told him what had happened.

"What do you think?" he asked.

"I don't know. I would feel happier if there were two of them, or four; not three. There are three entrances to this place if the doors on the other side were forced. If a few trucks came up the track in the early morning, we should have at least an hour's notice—it would take them as long as that to climb the track up here and they'd be in sight the whole way. There'd be plenty of time for everyone to get out; unless we found three pseudo-deserters with sub-machine-guns at the entrances."

Frank was thoughtful. He said, "They handed over their arms. I wonder if they would bother with that sort of thing so near the front line?"

"They might have hidden other weapons in the shrubbery outside; you know the length they go to, to get labourers."

Frank said, "I'm going to see what I can find out. Hang about till I get back—I'll go and talk to the priest."

He came back in ten minutes or so. He said, "The priests think it's all right. They say they are Austrians, not Germans. They are certainly Catholics. But I'll tell you something more important than that."

"Oh, yes?"

"There are several people here who have just the same idea as you; and they are talking of moving off to Salerno during the night, as soon as it's really dark. There's one man who says he has seen the ships in the harbour, and that the English and Americans are holding a thin strip of coast, so what the peasants told us is true."

"Well, let's try and join them. Do they know a way through?"

"I don't know. I only overheard them discussing it in whispers. I heard them say that there is a way to get across the top of the mountain, but that there are German patrols of five men scattered about up there."

"All right. So we can make up a strong party, say twenty of us. If we are strong enough we shall probably be safe from interference. Let's go and talk to them."

We found the party sitting under a tree whispering. They stopped as we approached. Frank told them that we thought the Germans had been sent to stop any attempted escape from the Monastery and that we were going to clear off in the night. He didn't say that he had overheard them discussing the same idea. They objected at first and said it was not possible, but finally admitted that they were going

179

to do the same; when they saw we were adamant, I suppose, they feared that our plans might interfere with theirs.

I told them my idea of making up a strong party and they agreed, though one of them looked at me queerly. I said, "A pity none of us is armed." They said nothing, but I saw that the one man who seemed different from the others was carrying a small pistol in his belt, under his jacket. It was clearly visible in outline when he moved. He looked like a middle-class Government official. We made our plans and decided to leave at ten, getting well away from the Monastery before we slept, then continuing in daylight.

When we left, I told Frank about the gun. He said,

"That's the man who said he's been up to the top."

"Is he one of the guides?"

"No, the guides are the two little fellows."

"He may be an *agent provocateur*. Better keep close to him all the time. We don't want any trouble at this stage. And warn the others that he might not be all he pretends."

"I think they are a little suspicious of you."

"Really? That's bad."

"I don't think we need worry. They probably think you are an escaped prisoner. It's only because you haven't been able to talk as freely as the rest. They think you've got something up your sleeve."

"We'll stay close to them tonight. If they start off an hour earlier, we'll go too. We need those guides."

"There's one other thing. One of the party asked me earlier in the evening who you were. I said you came from Tunis, so don't be surprised if he speaks to you in French. He only knows a little. It's the man with the grey sweater."

"Do you think they suspect anything?"

"No, no. They are just desperately frightened of Germans who might try to pass as Italians. I said we'd come a long way together and that I was quite sure you were all right. They seemed satisfied."

"Good. How are your feet? This might be the last hike."

"Terrible, really. Look at my boots. I beg of you, look at my boots."

They were truly in a shocking state: two red, swollen toes were protruding through the uppers like a musical-comedy tramp. The visible flesh was discoloured and sore. My own feet were in much the same state. A piece of flesh, the size of a walnut, had gone completely away from my left heel; I was afraid of gangrene. I hoped this was to be the last stretch of the long journey home.

Our feet were torn and bleeding; our clothes were in a worse condition than when we had first found them; our complete equipment consisted of two glass bottles and a mess-tin; we had no coats, no blankets, no stockings, no soap, comb or razor. We stood out even among the wretched refugees as the worst dressed, the dirtiest, the poorest of all, We had our legs to move with and the knowledge that the worst was behind us. The end was in sight and that was all we needed. We were as contented as the next man.

We started out in silence at ten o'clock. The party was fifteen strong, including the guides. We walked hard till we were five or six miles away, then lay down and slept. As soon as everyone was fast asleep, Frank and I got up silently and sneaked deeper into the woods, covering ourselves with leaves and twigs. We were not going to take any chances. We slept lightly, waking at every sound, and in the morning, before the sun was up, went back and found the others where we had left them, just beginning to stir. They asked where we had been and we told them that, blanket-less, we had looked for warmth in the thicker shrub. They looked at us with evident suspicion, but said nothing. It was obvious that no one was going to trust anybody else, which was all to the good.

Then the long, steep climb began. I thought we had regained a certain strength, but soon found out how wrong I was. Before, we had moved in our own time, and rested when we were tired. Now, the pace was set by two young and agile mountain men and it was hard to keep up with them. They were as anxious as the rest of us to cross the line; they knew the way and would wait for no one. When they got too far ahead, I was forced to drop to my knees and crawl up the steep, grassy slopes, as my boots slipped back as fast as I went forward; the unstudded and worn-out leather was worse than useless. I tried going barefoot, but there were too many thorns, and finally was forced to crawl. I had no strength left at the end of the first two hours, so that when my bottle of water slipped from my hand and rolled back fifty yards, I was too exhausted to recover it, and too frightened to get still farther behind. I suddenly found

181

myself crying from sheer frustration. It was agony, and quite the worst part of the whole trip.

We reached the highest summit, and there beyond us towered another. We reached that and there was yet a third, and a fourth, and still another. It was hard not to weep from sheer impotent anger. Only in desperation, sure that it was the last hill of all, did we reach that and there, higher still, a mile or more away, was another. We forced ourselves forward all through the day as the sun got hotter and hotter, and we had no water to replace the lost perspiration.

Finally, one of the party compelled the guides to call a halt. We lay on the burned grass too tired to move to the shade, and by the time we caught up with the others, it was time to move on again. I lay on my back with my arms spread-eagled. Frank was taking it well, but was all-in too. One of the guides came over and gave me his stick, then cut another for Frank. I think my physical condition finally proved to them that I wasn't a German after all. We struggled on and on, until at last we saw it.

We breasted a short rise, and there beyond us was the sea. There also, in the blue and wispy distance, was the port of Salerno, a long way off in the haze, but undeniably Salerno. And best of all, beyond in the grey sea were ships and tugs and boats of all classes, an imposing array of ships, packed close together, scorning dispersal, magnificent in power and beauty. One moment there was nothing to see but burnt grass and spindly hazel, and then, without warning, the wonderful panorama of the sea and all that it meant to us.

We sat down the better to watch. The guides grinned. Everyone was staring, silent. It was not a proper time to speak.

I said, "*Eh, è tornato Cristoforo Colombo.*"

One of the guides said, "*Eh, gia.* And in the family way, too." Everyone roared with laughter. The spell was broken. We moved off again, walking downhill now. The guides told us to look out for the odd German; there might still be one or two about up here, but it wasn't likely. It was technically no-man's-land.

We took it easy now and dropped behind the others. Had we wanted, we could have caught up, running downhill, easily enough. We rested when we felt like it, and gradually we lost them.

We reached the valley below at about two in the afternoon. There was an old man there, cutting hazel sticks. We asked him if there was any news.

"News?" he asked. "What kind of news?"

"Where are all the Germans?"

"Germans? They've gone. Went last night. Took all my pigs with them. Nobody here now."

"What about the English?"

"English? I haven't seen any English."

My heart sank. I thought, *Here we go again, next village . . .*

"They say," the old fellow said, "they say the English are in the village. I don't know. Don't care. All the same to me, English, German. I don't like any of them. They took my pigs."

I said, "Are there any Germans in the village?"

"Didn't I tell you? No Germans here. They went last night. Woke up this morning, all gone. They took my pigs. Didn't I tell you? Went last night . . ."

I said, "Took all your pigs?"

"That's right, took all my pigs."

I said to Frank, "Let's go to the village and see if there are any pigs or Germans there. Maybe somebody will stand us a drink."

We found the village a few miles away. There was not a soul in sight, and we walked on till we came to the outskirts on the far side. There were a lot of women standing there in the middle of the road. I said to one of them, "Ho, where are all the men?"

A pretty young girl in her best frock answered, "They've gone to meet the English."

Frank said, "Where?"

The girl and I answered together, like a chorus, "In the next village."

The girl stared and I winked at her. I said, "I'll come back soon; will you be kind to me?"

She said, "I can give you some wine if you want it."

I said, "Where's your husband?"

"A long way away."

"All right, wait for me. My friend can drink the wine, he's celibate."

The women guffawed and the girl laughed. I said to Frank, "Let's try the next village. We know they're in Salerno, anyway."

Frank said, "Nice girl that. Pity we have no time."

"Just what I was thinking."

Frank said happily, "If you feel like that it means that we are nearly home."

We stopped for a drink at the fountain and walked on. It was easy walking on the tarmac road after the grass and rocks of the mountains. We walked fast, cheerfully.

The next village was about three miles down the road. We were very excited. There was no sign of life anywhere on the road. We saw the low red houses in the distance. Frank said, "What will you bet that it's not *this* village but the next one?"

I said, "My God, I believe you're right. We may have to swim for it. At least we've seen the ships. We know *those* are ours."

"First I want a really good bath. Then some food."

"You remember those things we used to buy in Tunisia, what do they call them, *maakrout*?"

"I would like to eat twenty of them, really."

"Made with nuts and dates and all dripping with raisins and honey? I will buy you a cartload of them. For myself, I want six *filets mignons* with ten pounds of mushrooms. And some of Mr Goppi's Cassata ice cream, maybe ten kilos of it."

"This village is empty also. I win my bet."

The village *was* empty. The main street stretched down the centre of it, with low red houses on either side. The bomb-scarred Town Hall loomed high in the square, empty and desolate. We turned with the road from the square, and I pulled up short round the sharp corner. The shock of surprise was a blow on the heart. A tank stood a few feet ahead of me. A Colonel was sitting on it, drinking a mug of tea. He looked incredibly spruce and trim. He was tall and thin, with a fair moustache, and the enamel of his mug was chipped. Beside him, on the ground, a soldier was throwing a handful of tea leaves into a boiling billy. The small fire was perilously near the petrol tins on the side of the tank.

Frank was suddenly beside me, gaping. I said, in Italian, "Shall we watch this for a little while? Let's prolong the pleasure." There were several Italians standing about, staring at the tanks, which snuggled under the trees for a long way into the distance. Soldiers were standing by, smoking, chatting, trying a few words of Italian here and

184

there, buying eggs, drinking tea, lighting fires, oiling the tanks, refuelling, passing plates, joking or just hanging about. I waited till the Colonel had finished his tea and walked over to him. He stared at me for a moment, quite dispassionately. I felt that he was wondering how people could get quite so filthy, and whether I was going to ask for a cigarette.

I said, "In spite of my somewhat uncouth appearance, I am a British officer."

He raised his eyebrows very slightly, "Well," he said, "in that case I expect you'd like to have some tea. Come along and I'll take you to the Mess. We haven't got much of a Mess, you know, but we'll be able to fix you up with a meal or something. You'd like that, wouldn't you?"

He did not betray the slightest surprise. One might have thought that scruffy, bearded, lice-infested louts proclaimed themselves to him as British officers every five minutes of the day. I felt hurt. I thought he might have shown a little *surprise*. We walked along the road together. The troops who were sitting on the wall of an orchard guffawed as we passed. One of them said, "Sign them up, sir, before they get off the leash again." They were all smiling. Frank was beaming so broadly that when I introduced him he could do nothing but giggle. I thought he was going to burst.

The Colonel said, "Get you fixed up with a bath, you know. We have a very good river here, nice clean water. Cold too, you know. Have you got soap and towels? No, I suppose not. Are you hungry? Yes, I expect you are. Well, we'll give you a meal and then try and fix you up with some kit, What size shoes do you take?" He glanced at my feet, then at Frank's. "I say," he remarked, "they *are* in a shocking state. Would you like to see the M.O. or something?"

Frank said, "I'd rather have a piece of *maakrout*." The Colonel stared.

I thanked him and said we'd settle for a bath and a meal. We entered the orchard and went to the Mess. The Colonel took us to his tent and gave us soap, towels and a new toothbrush. He handed me his hairbrush, then took it back and said, "No, wait a minute." He dived into his trunk and brought forth a fine old silver brush. He handled it lovingly and said, "You may use this one. It used to belong to my

185

grandfather." He couldn't do enough for us. I remembered Garofalo's last gesture and wondered what would happen if I kissed him. He said, pointing to the river, "There's the bath. Under the bridge is best. By the time you're ready I'll have some clothes for you. See what the Quarter-master's got. Probably not very much. Then come across to the Mess and there'll be some food."

We tore off our clothes and hurled them into the river, then jumped in after them and lay in the shallows and relaxed. Frank examined the red, swollen monstrosities at the end of his legs and we compared sores. He said, "This is what I really want, just to lie here and relax. Really, these are very nice people. I like the Colonel."

I said, "I think I have discovered what is the real fundamental difference between this side of the fence and the other. Everyone's happy here. Remember how serious and stern the Italians always were? Here, everything's a joke. As soon as you meet a man he starts to grin. In Gaeta it was almost forbidden to be cheerful. I think I like it here."

The Colonel's batman came and squatted by the river, showing us our new clothes. He didn't quite know what to say to us, so he sat there grinning happily.

We watched the water, cold and fresh, running past our feet. I thought of the Monastery, of Avellino, of the Germans at the road-block, of the boat to Terracina, of the yard at Gaeta, of Garofalo, Buonavoglia, Paglia the Worm, of Pezzimento, Bruno and the others, of Luzzati and the English-speaking officer, of the sergeant in Sfax, of that awful day in the grass in the middle of a camp, of the *Signor Colonello* and Saturday bath-nights.

A wet and ragged boot was caught in the twigs by the bank. It was one of Garofalo's. The current was tugging at it, pushing it, twisting it. I gave it a push with my foot and freed it. It swung round and drifted slowly into mid-stream. As the ripples caught it and turned it over before it half-sunk and went slowly, bobbing, down the river and under the bridge, a boy fishing by the bank threw a pebble at it. It disappeared under the grey-green-covered stone that hung above the water.

THE END

THE OTHER SIDE OF THE HILL
by B. H. Liddell Hart
Originally published by Cassell at 17/6

This is the German view of the war, told in statements by the leading German generals, and linked by shrewd comments from the author, who interrogated all the generals during their captivity. Liddell Hart is famed as a military writer, and this is " the best book that even he has written . . ."

3/6

THE VALLEY OF THE SHADOW
by Hugh Oloff de Wet

If you saw the TV programme "This Is Your Life" on March 8th, 1956, you will remember this remarkable story and its remarkable author. de Wet was a Secret Service agent for France, was captured by the Gestapo, and spent six years in solitary confinement, two of them in a strait-jacket. This astonishing story of courage and endurance made a great impression on those who heard it on TV, and de Wet's account of his captivity and attempts at escape will make this the most sought-after pocketbook of the year.

2/–

Ask for these books from your newsagent or bookseller. If you have any difficulty in obtaining supplies, copies can be obtained post-free from Panther Books, 30/32 Lancelot Place, Knightsbridge, London, S.W.7.

MONSARRAT

"H.M.S. Marlborough Will Enter Harbour"

Panther Books have the distinction of being the first British pocketbook publisher to issue a paper-backed edition of a Nicholas Monsarrat war book.

" H.M.S. Marlborough Will Enter Harbour " is a story in the tradition of Monsarrat's great sea novel, " The Cruel Sea ". It tells how a warship, crippled and sinking after a U-boat attack, is somehow kept afloat and manages to struggle to a safe harbour.

That is all. But written as it is by a great writer, it is a compelling, authentic story of disaster and men's bravery that will thrill every reader.

Selling at two shillings only, this Panther edition also contains two other fine war stories by Nicholas Monsarrat.

Ask for this book from your newsagent or bookseller. If you have any difficulty in obtaining supplies, copies can be obtained post-free from Panther Books, 30/32 Lancelot Place, Knightsbridge, London, S.W.7.

VERY ORDINARY SEAMAN

by J. P. W. Mallalieu

Originally published by Gollancz at 9/6

The fact that this book has had ten reprints in ten years as a bound book puts it in a class by itself. It is one of the finest accounts of war at sea ever written, and, since the author himself was a lower-deck man, is completely authentic. The story starts in the Recruiting Centre in the early days of the war, and ends with the return of a destroyer from convoy duty in Arctic waters.

No one who served in the Navy should miss this book, and others will learn more from it of life in a destroyer during the war than from any other war books.

2/6

Ask for this book from your newsagent or bookseller. If you have any difficulty in obtaining supplies, copies can be obtained post-free from Panther Books, 30/32 Lancelot Place, Knightsbridge, London, S.W.7.